SKELMERSDALE

-2 JAN 2013

D1313281

FICTION RESERVE STOCK LL60

AUTHOR	CLASS
NELSON, K.	F

TITLE

Tea and tiramisu

Lancashire County Library

30118085061368

Karen Nelson lives and works in the West Country and also for part of each year in Italy.

She is the author of *Foreign Fields*, also by Piatkus.

Also by Karen Nelson

Foreign Fields

Tea & Tiramisu

KAREN NELSON

PIATKUS

08506136

For more information on other books
published by Piatkus, visit our website at
www.piatkus.co.uk

First published in Great Britain in 2001 by
Judy Piatkus (Publishers) Ltd of
5 Windmill Street, London W1T 2JA
email: info@piatkus.co.uk

A catalogue record for this book is available from the British Library

ISBN 0 7499 3241 4

Typeset by Palimpsest Book Production Limited,
Polmont, Stirlingshire
Printed and bound in Great Britain by
Cox & Wyman Ltd, Reading, Berkshire

For my sister, Chris

Acknowledgements

A huge heartfelt thank you to Marina Baruffaldi, not only for letting me stay in her home in Venice while writing this book, but for welcoming me back time and time again even without the excuse of a book to write.

I would like to also thank all my Venetian friends who helped with their knowledge, time and hospitality, especially to Roberto Zammattio for sharing with me the Venice he grew up in.

Chapter One

'Oh Venice! At last!' Netty, jostled about at Arrivals in Marco Polo Airport, fell to her knees on the ground. An elderly Italian, thinking he had inadvertently pushed her, stooped to apologize and charmingly help her up, until he noticed that she was, like the Pope, kissing the ground. She looked rather like the Papa as well, with her long flowing white skirt and snowy loose tunic top, with ebony beads dangling like rosaries down her ample bosom.

'It's just that I'm so thrilled to be here, at last,' she twittered, without a blush of embarrassment as she clutched the arm he had rather impetuously offered her. 'City of my dreams,' she trilled on, wiping the dust from her plump knees, 'the beautiful, *bella*, Venice.' She pronounced it Vee-nee-cee.

The Italian, whose name was Silvano, was torn between gallantry and fear. He looked around surreptitiously for his wife, who might or might not be meeting him at the airport. Netty's hand was stuck to his bare arm like a fly in honey; he had to admit it was not an unpleasant situation. She was waffling on in that peculiar mouth-full-of-cotton-wool way that certain English people had, sure that he would understand her if she talked loudly enough. It was most flattering.

'You know Venezia well, then?' he asked. Though he spoke

1

in English, he pronounced the name of the city in proper Italian, to gently teach her.

'But of course. *Si, si*! I know Vee-nee-cee as I know my own heart, my own soul!'

'Ah.'

'And praise God, here I am!'

Silvano said hastily, for she looked as if she were about to fall to her knees again, 'So, it is a long time ago that you were last in our beautiful city?'

'Oh yes,' Netty breathed. 'Another lifetime. A dream ago.'

'*Scusi?*'

She sighed, and her large firm body trembled; she shook her head, and a tumble of blinding red curls fell about her shoulders. 'Actually, I speak metaphorically. This is my very first time. But I know Venice as I know my own heart, my own soul.'

Oh Madonna Madre di Dio, Silvano thought. *Another one.*

Outside the airport, hailing a water taxi, Lissabelle said, 'Thank God we're off the plane. It's scandalous how just *anyone* can fly with British Airways these days. Why don't they go on Ryanair or one of the other economy ones? All those backpacks hitting you in the face whenever you turn around.'

'The proletariat are richer these days,' Simon muttered as he heaved one of Lissabelle's many suitcases into the water taxi. The driver, a handsome Italian with more flashy white teeth than was good for him, was smoking a fag and discussing football with the captain of the public transport motorboat. Neither of them was in the least bit concerned over their passengers. A fat woman dressed in some kind of a flowing white summery dress was wobbling up the gangplank into the large public transport vessel, holding on to a small Italian man with a bald head enlivened by two puffballs of woolly white hair. The woman, busy enrapturing over the boat, the lagoon, the kindliness of strangers, nearly fell into the water, threatening to drag the man with her. This commotion snapped the captain to attention. But the taxi driver carried on smoking his MS, ignoring his own passengers. Simon thought with satisfaction that at least the toothy Italian had no chance of a tip now, for Lissabelle, waiting to board, was frowning at him.

Turning away from the irresponsible taxi driver, Lissabelle stood and watched while Simon heaved cases of clothes and books, computers and printers, into the sleek swaying motorboat. It did not occur to her to help, and anyway, why should she? She was paying for this trip. April and Simon, though dear, dear friends, knew their place.

April, with pen and notebook in hand, was ticking off the various items, to make sure British Airways had not chewed, swallowed and digested their vital luggage to be excreted in obscurity and never to be seen again. Both Simon and April were sweating profusely; it was early June; hot. Lissabelle, in sheer stockings, soft Italian shoes and a casual Armani summer suit with a skirt that showed her knickers, was cool and poised. Posed, too; she stood this way and that, until finally the taxi driver took notice of her and escorted her, with a gorgeous leer, into the waiting boat.

'I told you he'd get a tip,' April muttered. 'They all do, in the end.'

'Shut up,' Simon said, 'and help me load these last cases in.'

Lissabelle, staring passionately across the lagoon, said, 'Venezia, at last! Darlings, it's been far, far too long. But never mind, we're home at last.'

The driver of the water taxi said, 'You know Venezia well, Signorina?' He could see that Lissabelle was really a *signora*, that is, over a certain age, pushing forty or even, possibly, just past that tricky milestone. But he also knew that the Englishwoman would give him a much bigger tip if he addressed her as *signorina*.

'It's my second home,' Lissabelle said, injecting just the right note of jaded boredom into her response. 'I work here often. I'm a novelist, you see.' She waited for him to be impressed.

Benedetto Gesù, the driver thought: *Another one*. He tried not to let his eyes glaze over as he smiled with what he hoped was polite interest.

Around the corner from the blue shining lagoon and the water taxis and the Number One pier where the public *motoscafi* leave every half hour for St Mark's Square, are the bus stops. Here, the less romantic, or less rich, or downright poor travellers catch a bus into the Piazzale Roma, the bus station at the edge of Venice beyond which no wheeled traffic can go. This, though perhaps not as thrilling, is quicker and cheaper than floating into the city extravagantly in a water taxi, or even in the far less expensive public transport boats.

In one of the cheapest of the buses, the ordinary yellow one that stops at every small hamlet between Marco Polo Airport and the city, sat Marco Polo himself. Actually, his name was Markian Polonski, being the product of a Polish father and an English mother, but he had taken the name Marco Polo professionally. He thought it an inspired idea.

'Quite hot here, isn't it,' Marco said conversationally in Italian to the young woman seated beside him, a Venetian whom he had noticed in the plane. He knew she was Venetian from her high cheekbones, a look about her that told of centuries of Turkish influence, of Moorish conquests and interbreeding.

The woman, Nina, was actually from Sicily, but she had lived in Venice since student days. She saw a good opportunity to practise her English, which she had perfected while visiting her sister in London this past week. 'Yes, it is very hot, but so nice after your wet and cold English May.'

Marco was cross that she did not reply in Italian. Persisting in that flowery language, which he knew perfectly well, he said,

4

'Venezia can be wet and cold in May as well. Last May was terrible.'

Nina stifled a giggle at the Englishman's dreadful accent. She looked out the window at the odd dusty field and dull square houses rolling by, deciding to ignore him if he refused to speak his own language. Marco, noticing the glow the sun made on her warm olive-gold skin, and the shine of her short dark hair, plodded on in Italian, 'Yes, the weather here can be as bad as England sometimes.' He smiled complacently, to himself for she still was not looking at him. He thought how smoothly he had let her know that not only did he speak her language impeccably, but that he was also on familiar terms with Venice.

Nina still did not reply. Thinking she had not heard, he repeated the sentence, but forgot and said it in English. He was rewarded for this with a full-face view and a to-die-for smile. He was so blown out by the smile that he did not notice what language she was speaking as he listened, enraptured, while she went on at great length about the Venetian climate. Finally, she finished with, 'But you must know all this, if you've been here before. You did say, that you were in Venice last year?'

'Oh, I come every year.' He didn't add, if he could afford it. If he could scrounge a bed at a friend's house, or find a cheap flat to share with other impecunious artists, or sell a painting so that he could afford some nasty hotel with a minus-star in one of the towns outside the city.

Nina said, with the smugness of one who had her own tiny flat and her own job in the city, 'Tourists often do. Come back year after year. It's a beautiful city.'

'Tourist?' Marco was indignant. 'I'm not a *tourist*.' He looked as if she had accused him of being a pimp, or worse.

'No?' Her tone was polite, if not overly enthusiastic.

'Definitely not. I'm a . . .' He faltered.

'A visitor, then?' she said helpfully.

5

'No.' He realized he had shouted petulantly at her. He tried a playful laugh, at which she narrowed her beautiful brown eyes and said, in an unnecessarily shirty manner, 'Well, what, then?'

He smiled, and pulled out his ace. 'I'm an artist.'

Nina said, without thinking, 'Oh *Dio*, not another one,' and turned her back to him for the rest of the short journey into the Piazzale Roma.

Chapter Two

At the Palazzo Bobolino, on the Grand Canal not far down from the Rialto Bridge, there was ferocious banging on the great weatherbeaten oak doors. Miranda, a small rucksack on her back and a large black crunchy bag on wheels, was standing helplessly in the narrow *calle*, the street entrance of the dilapidated palazzo. It was eighteenth century and looked every year of it; it was shedding plaster like a snake and everything brick-like and stone-like was crumbling fast. It smelled, too, like something damp and dead for years. Miranda hated it.

She tried, once again, every bell she could find, but either no one was home, or the bells were all out of order. Since the palazzo was divided into at least four separate apartments, it was hard to believe that the occupants were all, every one of them, out. Since everything was out of order at the Palazzo Bobolino, Miranda gave up and began banging on the door again.

'Do you want to get in?' A not-young woman with hair dyed the colour of tar and dressed in skin-tight black velveteen trousers, though the temperature was in the eighties, glared at Miranda. The woman spoke in Italian.

'Of course not,' she replied in rapid English, 'I'm just deeply bored and standing here with all my bags, banging away at the

7

door, for the hell of it.' Then she added, in Italian, that yes please, she would like to get inside the palazzo.

The woman produced a key and unlocked the outsized door. Miranda followed her into an overgrown courtyard full of scruffy plants and wild grass growing out of the stone slabs. A broken marble wellhead stood in the centre of some erratic cobblestones, and riotous vines and mould covered pitted ancient statues of ancient ancestors, not all of them becoming. An ancient fig tree loomed. On either side of the courtyard were wonky doors leading to the apartments, and on one side, opposite the street entrance, was the Grand Canal, seeping at high tide over the seaweedy marble steps and on to the cracked and mottled paving stones of the courtyard.

'Who are you looking for?' the woman asked. She had a face like a crocodile, long, with bulging eyes and a snappy jaw. She was far older than she had first appeared. Miranda did not remember seeing her the last time she was at the Palazzo Bobolino, but then it was winter, and an icy wind had kept most of the natives indoors.

'My daughter,' Miranda answered. 'She's English, young.' Well, young-ish, she thought. Not yet thirty. And me barely a child myself, not even out of my forties. Though it would not be long, a nasty brain cell reminded her. She did not want to think about being out of her forties yet; if she did that, she would have to think of Life, and Death and the Meaning of it All.

She certainly did not want to think about that. Life was difficult to figure out anyway, with post-modern novels, trendy surreal foreign films and trying to keep up with whatever it was New Labour was on about. She went hurriedly on. 'My daughter lives there, in that flat facing the canal, the one on the bottom. Apt. 1, it is. With her husband, a Venetian, Piero. They have two children. Do you know them?'

Before the woman could answer, the door of the apartment

8

flew open and two young adults, a toddler, and a crawling baby began shrieking and gurgling and making what Miranda supposed were noises of welcome. Jessica and Piero were hugging and kissing Miranda impetuously, grabbing her bags and pushing and pulling her up some steep marble steps, pitted with holes the size of gondolas, into the large drawing room looking out over the canal. A broken glass chandelier hung limply from the high ceilings, reflecting water and light from outside. Faded pink wallpaper, embossed with raised velveteen flowers which looked like a nasty armpit rash, peeled here and there in corners. An attempt had been made to patch it up in places, to no avail. But there were jolly and tasteful posters of Carnival plastered over the horrid wallpaper, and huge Paul Klee prints framed and hung, along with gaily costumed *commedia dell'arte* actors in various poses. There were colourful throws on the weary furniture, and a great bowl of daisies stood in the centre of a rickety table, jollying up the whole place immensely. The scent of lilies, sitting in a ceramic vase in the corner of the vast and unwieldy room, managed to nearly eradicate the smell of damp.

Jessica, seeing her mother looking around her, said cheerily, 'It's a tip, but we do what we can.'

Despite herself, Miranda was pleased to see her daughter. She should not be, she told herself sternly, for Jessica had dragged her away from her contented solitary home in Shropshire, to house-sit and cat-sit while she and her family swanned off down to the seaside for a month.

'The fridge is stacked with food,' Piero cried, 'and the cats are so pleased that you'll be minding them. They grew so fond of you last February, when you visited us last.'

As if on cue, two white cats stalked into the room, one fat as a round of *parmigiano*, the other skinny as celery. The toddler pulled the fat one's tail, which made it snarl. The baby gurgled. Miranda tried to pet the scrawny cat, who bit her.

Jessica pretended not to see this. She had disappeared off to the kitchen to bring back a tray of coffee and sweet Venetian biscuits, which they ate hurriedly. 'Sorry to rush off, Mum,' Jessica cried after a half-hour, 'but we must dash to Mestre and get our car and be off. We want to get there before dark.' Like many Venetians, they kept an old car on the mainland, for excursions such as this.

'We thought you'd be here this morning,' Piero added, rounding up children, cases, his wife.

'I flew Ryanair. The plane landed in Treviso; I had to wait for a coach. And then an hour in the coach . . .'

But they were no longer listening. Smothering Miranda with more hugs and kisses, telling her she was a star, brill, ace, to do this for them while at the same time gathering up bags and belongings, they fled the palazzo. 'There's a list on the table. Who's arriving when.'

'List?' Miranda had to screech down the marble steps. 'Arriving?'

'Didn't Jessica tell you?' Piero called. 'About the lodgers?'

'What lodgers?'

But they were off, with much blowing of kisses and waving of hands, and enough *ciao*s to take care of a dozen partings, and greetings too for that matter. Miranda thought sourly that it did not become her daughter, playing at being Venetian. But maybe she was just jealous, that Jessica did it so well despite being English through and through.

Well, perhaps not quite through and through. But that was something Miranda, as usual, refused to think about.

When they had gone, Miranda tossed away the vile strong coffee Jessica had made and found some China teabags in the archaic kitchen, filled with ill-fitting cupboards and a kitchen tap that had leaked the last time she was here, and seemed to still be leaking

10

now. One of the cats, the thin one, Tommasina, reached out a dainty claw and scratched her, hard, on her calf, indicating that food was required. Miranda was wearing a knee-length skirt and one bare leg now began to show traces of blood. Dashing about on her way to the bathroom, she noticed that the bedrooms, and not just her own, were clean and sparkly, with fresh flowers and clean ironed covers on the duvets, as if awaiting guests. Suddenly suspicious, she ran to all the bedrooms, and noticed that every one of them was ready and expectant, as if for . . . *lodgers.*

'Bloody hell,' Miranda swore, trying to remember where Jessica had put the list. But before she could find it, there was a shout outside the window, a kind of surprised gurgle, as if someone were drowning in the Grand Canal.

Stepping on to the balcony, which tilted precariously over the water, she looked down to see a water taxi moored at the rickety old wooden landing stage in the courtyard of the palazzo. 'Ahoy,' called a woman with shiny blonde hair of the shampoo commercial type. She kept tossing it about too, exactly like the model in the advertisement. The Dolce and Gabbana shades perched on her pale mane like crows on a field of daffodils, trembled slightly, threatening to slide right off that glistening sleek hair. 'We're English, can you help us?'

Miranda muttered from the balcony that she was English too, but nobody gave a damn about helping *her*. Her bloodied leg was sticky; she wanted to have a shower, change.

In the *motoscafo*, Lissabelle was frantic. After the idyllic ride from the airport across the lagoon and down the Grand Canal, where she loftily explained to Simon and April all they needed to know about Venice, the wretched Italian driver had taken her to *this* place, this shambolic ruin that he dared to call the Palazzo Bobolino.

'So you see,' Lissabelle finished, 'the man is obviously a simpleton, and hasn't a clue where our palazzo is, but he won't budge.' She put on her helpless look for Miranda, thinking how English and capable the woman looked, with a sensible white shirt tucked into her sensible length skirt, a sensible clip tying back her long brown hair, a sensible fringe covering her sensible forehead. Lissabelle, if those sort of women had not bored her, would have pitied Miranda, for being so sensible, but right now she needed help, so she tried to look meek rather than condescending.

It did not quite work. Miranda, taking an instant dislike to the woman, said brusquely, 'Your taxi driver's right. This *is* the Palazzo Bobolino.'

In the boat Simon and April looked at each other and rolled their eyes. The Italian driver rolled his eyes too, wishing they would get off his boat so that he could go off duty and see his sweetheart, who was arriving home from London today. She was a Sicilian, and given to hot flushes of temper, and would be fiery if he kept her waiting. Though perhaps that was not a bad thing, he thought, salivating with anticipation.

Lissabelle began to rant. For one so tiny, whose skirt was so miniscule and whose hair was so cunningly short yet able to be twirled around so flirtatiously, she had an amazingly big voice when she chose. 'But the estate agent here assured me the palazzo was near the Accademia Bridge, not the Rialto. This is San Polo! I asked for an apartment in Dorsoduro.'

'Tough,' Miranda called down.

'But one can't possibly live in San Polo,' Lissabelle whimpered, dropping the big voice and becoming irritatingly girlie.

This made Miranda curious, and much against her better judgement, she leaned down over the stone railing of the balcony to ask, 'Why not?'

'Because it's full of Venetians,' Lissabelle wailed. 'You know, people who *do* things, Venetian things. Like make masks, or glass beads. Shopkeepers, that sort. And, like, gondoliers. They all live in San Polo.'

Since both Jessica and Piero were teachers of English (and only half of the couple were Venetian), Miranda opened her mouth to shout, 'Not *quite* everyone,' until she realized how outrageous the woman's remark had been.

'You'd better go back to Islington, then,' Miranda cried venomously instead, and Lissabelle thought how mistaken she had been, thinking the woman sensible. She was a witch, with her strident voice, that waist-length brown hair pulled casually back with a wooden comb. And a woman pushing fifty, too. Probably older; everyone was older than they looked, these days. Long hair on such a woman should never be allowed.

But the taxi man was holding out his hand charmingly for her to take as she disembarked, and flashing perfect, if overlarge, Italian teeth at her as he murmured, '*Bella.*' Lissabelle breathed a sigh of relief. It was all right then, she was still called *bella*, beautiful; she was still young, and Venice was still falling about at her feet. Out on the Grand Canal a fleet of gondolas came floating by, and snatches of 'O solo mio' wafted like drifting leaves across the water, directed, she was sure, solely at her. Lissabelle was conscious of a dozen cameras snapping her photo as she and the handsome taxi driver smiled at each other.

'She's acting like it were the paparazzi, rather than a gondola-full of Japanese tourists snapping the palazzo,' April growled, under her breath.

'Stow it, she'll hear you,' Simon snarled back.

'Darlings, we're home!' Lissabelle cried as she stepped on to the sludgy marble steps, slippery now that the tide had somewhat receded, and stumbled out into the courtyard.

The two white cats, Tommasina and Topolino, thrown out of Apt. 1 by Miranda after they clawed her skirt, looked disdainfully at the newcomers. They too had seen it all before.

Simon, in charge of the key that the estate agent had sent, unlocked Apartment No. 3, also on the canal but on the opposite side of the courtyard. Miranda waited, a slight smile on her face. Sure enough, in a moment or two she could hear howls of rage, no doubt caused by Lissabelle's first sighting of the wallpaper, or the cracked wobbly sink in the bathroom, or the rank kitchen with its ancient gas cooker.

You want Venice? Miranda thinks grimly to herself. This is Venice. Not Dorsoduro, home now to ageing American film directors and once-hip supermodels from England, not to mention mega-rich German industrialists and balding gallery owners from New York. She wonders if the woman even knows what a Venetian looks like.

Miranda listens to the hysterics in Lissabelle's voice, lapping like waves across the water through open windows, and feels calmer. How soothing it is, to hear the discord of others. It makes one's own life seem so harmonious in comparison.

A half-hour or so later, a banging on the door downstairs startled Miranda as she unpacked her bags in the small bedroom facing the courtyard. Opening the door of the apartment, she saw the crocodile lady again, who said, 'Another one. Trying to get into the main door from the *calle.*' She pointed accusingly at a floppy-haired youth standing beside her. He had a rucksack the size of a cathedral on his back, and leather sandals on his pale feet. He was fair, with freckles. 'You'll burn in this sun,' Miranda said. 'It's hotter than you think.'

The crocodile lady said, 'He says he lives here.' She looked doubtful, as well she might. Miranda was doubtful too.

'I've rented a room, Apt. No. 1, Palazzo Bobolino, San Polo, Venice,' he said, reading from a crumpled letter he pulled out from his pocket. He spoke in God-awful Italian; Miranda could barely understand him. 'From someone called Piero and Jessica . . . I can't read the last name, it's too long and Italian.' He had lapsed into English, a great relief to Miranda.

14

She wearily let him in. She had forgotten, until she had seen the immaculately prepared bedrooms, that Piero and Jessica sometimes rented out the unused bedrooms in their large apartment, to help with the extravagant rent.

'I'm Marco. Marco Polo,' said Markian Polonski, not at all abashed. Miranda looked at him strangely, but made no comment. She showed him to his room, down at the end next to hers. Marco sat down on the bed, and expressed his approval. He was an artist, he said, and used to living in a spartan manner, used to hardship. Miranda began to feel insulted, then decided it was too much of an effort and sat on the bed next to Marco. The crocodile lady, who was following them about, sat on the bed too, and nodded sagely. Miranda wondered how she had crept in, but did not much care. She was begin to feel weary.

They all trooped into the kitchen, where Miranda showed Marco how to light the cantankerous gas burners, and where he could keep his provisions for cooking. The crocodile lady took off her black knitted cardigan, to reveal a black bodice which clung like cellotape to her skinny, scrawny body. She announced that she too would have a coffee, and advise Miranda on the perils and pitfalls of the Palazzo Bobolino.

Or that was what Miranda thought she said; she was tired, and the woman had lapsed into Venetian dialect, which was impossible to understand. Marco was going on about Culture, and the world-famous Biennale, mecca of Contemporary World Art which was opening later this month in the city. He talked with many capital letters and hushed syllables.

'And not only the Biennale,' he warbled on, 'but we also have here a compact history of Art, from Byzantium to Renaissance. My God, the Gothic! Take for instance Ca'd'Oro, the palazzo right across the canal. Why, you can even see it from here, if you stick your neck right out the window. And to think that we're part of it.'

15

Miranda couldn't figure out exactly what part of what they were all supposed to be, but she let it slide. Crocodile nodded wisely, and said, 'When the water rises, and the *acqua alta* comes, the courtyard gets flooded. Believe me.'

'Oh, I do, I do,' Miranda said fervently.

'And then, oh God, the wealth of history, the church of the Frari, with that Madonna of Bellini's, and—'

'And sometimes we have power cuts. When there are thunderstorms. Many thunderstorms in Venice in summer, believe me.'

'I certainly do,' Miranda repeated, as the door began to bang again.

She left them in the kitchen to go down the stairs to open it, and found herself wondering if time had reverted to last summer when she was visiting Stonehenge instead of Venice, for standing in front of her was a Druid.

Or so it looked like. But the white-robed figure cried, 'Jessica, my dear, at last. We meet at last. Oh, I say, you are exactly as I pictured you, so . . . so *Venetian*. My dear, I hope we can be chums; after all, though we come from different cultures, we are after all both European. And may I compliment you on your English? You have mastered it perfectly, which I did indeed notice during our telephone conversations.'

The Druid look-alike shook Miranda's hand heartily and went on, 'Oh, how dreadfully rude of me. I have not introduced you to Silvano.' A bald Italian with two fluffy bits of cotton wool stuck in his head above his ears, which on closer inspection turned out to be hair, smiled enchantingly. 'I met Silvano at the airport, and he most kindly accompanied me here. Would you believe he lives in the Palazzo Bobolino too? In Apartment No. 4, is this not right, Silvano? Silvano, this is Jessica. Jessica, this is my new Venetian friend Silvano, and neighbour too, but surely you must know him, since he lives in the palazzo? And what a bello, uh, I mean bueno, no, *bella* palazzo, it's fantastic, amazing. Oh, and I am Netty. Of course.' She bobbed her head and the red curls bobbed too, as did her healthy cheeks and her wobbly chin.

'Hello, Netty. And Silvano. I'm Miranda.'

'My dear, I am so delighted to meet you, after all the letters and phone calls. I had so very many questions, what to bring, what the weather would be like . . . you are *who*?'

'Miranda. Jessica's mother. She's at the seaside. I'm house-sitting.'

'You're the landlady?'

'I suppose you could call me that.'

'But you're English.'

'Snap. So are you. And so, for that matter, is Jessica, though of course her Italian is excellent.'

Netty's face fell. She looked ten years older when she let it drop like that, more like the age of the elderly Silvano, who was looking furtively around him. Damn and drat, Netty thought, how would she ever learn to be Venetian, living with an Englishwoman?

But as she and Silvano followed Miranda into the apartment, her spirits lifted. She had only been here a couple of hours, and already she had met not only a real Venetian, but a gondolier as well. This she announced proudly to Miranda. 'Did you know Silvano here is a gondolier? Truly, he *is*. I feel so totally immersed in Vee-nee-cee already. Do you know, I have always wanted to meet a gondolier.'

Miranda giggled, thinking of the sleek blonde in the Armani suit on the other side of the courtyard.

'I'll have to introduce you to the Englishwoman in Apt. 3,' she said sweetly to Silvano. 'She'd love to meet her new neighbours.'

They all, including the cats, followed Miranda into the kitchen, which seemed like a vaporetto at rush hour, so crowded had it become. Tommasina was busily swatting every bare leg in sight, while the other cat, fat Topolino, hid in the kitchen cupboard and

17

stared malignantly, hissing whenever Miranda tried to shoo him out so that she could reach the cups.

'What an extraordinary kitchen,' Netty exclaimed. 'So Italian,' she burbled on, noticing the funny odd-shaped stainless steel coffee maker on the hob, and the pasta pans hanging on hooks all over the wall, alongside numerous graters for, she thought excitedly, Parmesan cheese. 'How ethnic,' she warbled, seeing the garlic hanging in their clumped cloves above the cooker. Netty felt rather ethnic herself, if truth be told. Though born and bred in the Home Counties, she felt there was a streak of rebelliousness in her. She was rather hoping Venice would embellish this, for she did so want an adventure.

'Oh good afternoon; I am so very sorry, I did not see you there. How do you do?' Netty held out her hand to the crocodile woman, thinking she was a relative of Miranda's.

Silvano saw the woman at the same time as Netty. '*Dio mio, mia moglie*,' he gasped, unleashing Netty's hand from his arm, where it seemed to be clamped permanently.

Netty thought she would swoon with emotion: he had spoken to her in Italian. Unfortunately, she could not make out a word. This was obvious the way she turned to him and kissed him twice on each cheek, in a delightfully spontaneous manner. Netty prided herself on her spontaneity. Sometimes it took her hours to get it right, but she did not mind practising.

Miranda said mildly, 'What your gentleman friend said was, "Oh my God, my wife".'

But Silvano looked as if he were ready to throw himself at the crocodile woman's feet, much in the same way that Netty had thrown herself on the scuffed tiles of Arrivals a few hours earlier. '*Bella*, forgive me, I didn't see you there, I tried our apartment, but it was empty; I was devastated when you weren't at the airport . . .'

'Is what's-her-name, Bella, his wife? He never told me he had a wife,' Netty said huffily.

18

'She is obviously his wife, yes, but I doubt if her name is Bella. Italians call all women *bella*; it works every time.'

'It doesn't seem to be working much for *him*,' Marco remarked, trying to stroke the cat in the cupboard, for he prided himself on being good with animals. Topolino stiffened, and opened his pink mouth as if to say: you dare.

Marco, withdrawing his hand, wondered if it would work if he called Nina *bella*, next time he saw her. He was sure that he would see her again; she was his fate, his destiny, his muse. He knew it the minute he set eyes on her, in that dusty, lumpy bus coming from the airport. Venice was working its old magic again, he thought ecstatically, bringing him inspiration, pumping him with creativity, with passion, with testosterone . . . well, no, not that. Marco hastily scrubbed out that last thought. He was here in Venice to paint, to achieve Art, to become Famous. Not to get laid.

The crocodile lady, whose name seemed to be Elena (Silvano was chanting it like a prayer, to make amends), was shouting a lot in a guttural Italian. After a time, when the invocation of her name did not seem to soothe her, Silvano began to shout back. Netty felt a stirring, a thrill, go through her: they were fighting over her! How thoroughly Italian, how shiveringly Venetian! She knew she was right to come here, to this city of her dreams and imagination. Here was passion, here was Life, and here she was, in this thrillingly Venetian kitchen, an intense young man – an artist! – called Marco Polo sitting and brooding melancholically in the corner; and in front of her, a man and his wife nearly coming to blows over her, Netty Sweenson-Page from Buckinghamshire.

If this wasn't Life, then nothing was.

Miranda, watching the theatrics in her kitchen, sighs. This is why she dislikes Venice: it is so messy. All that Vivaldi, all those gaudy palazzos, all those dreamy reflections in lazy back street canals.

And all that Attila the Hun influence, everyone getting all excited about things and getting het up about them.

Miranda, metaphorically stopping up her ears, decides to ignore them all, just as she will ignore Venice too, this time around. Had she had done that years and years ago, when she first set eyes on the place, she certainly would not be here now. But she has learned since then. The city will not, this time, have the slightest effect on her.

But Venice, *la Serenissima*, the Most Serene Republic, has different ideas. *La bella Venezia* eavesdrops on the various musings of all these little souls clamouring for attention in her city and breathes a tiny, capricious sigh, causing a slight ruffle on the waters of her lagoon and a small lilt and rock in her gondolas as they bob about on the water. How many times has she heard all this before, but like an old tart, she's tickled to hear it again. How she loves flattery, loves the fawning and adulation, and yes, she even loves the Mirandas of this world, who think they can get away from her.

They won't, of course. Any more than they can make Venice *theirs*, no matter how they bow and scrape, and write her epic poems, and plaster on their canvasses her canals and cathedrals over and over again. *La Serenessima* will tease them, tempt them, maybe even sleep with them, old whore that she is, but she will never belong to them.

Pity the residents of Palazzo Bobolino have not learned this yet. It would save them one hell of a lot of grief.

Chapter Three

Twenty-four hours later, not much had changed at the Palazzo Bobolino, except the clothes in which our heroes and heroines were attired. Miranda was wearing a long loose cool skirt, of a green the colour of the Grand Canal this morning, and a sleevless blouse the colour of the stone steps leading into the water. She had slept twelve solid hours, and was feeling far perkier.

Netty was perky too, in another flowing skirt and tunic top, this time of a Franciscan brown, causing the little sparrows on the balcony to fly dangerously near her ample frame thinking they were near the great saint himself. Her beads today were like *bacci*, the chocolate kisses so beloved of Italians, and which Netty herself was stuffing greedily down her gullet. Silvano had told her yesterday that he adored women with large and fleshy bodies; no wonder, she thought, after years of living with that scrawny Elena who claimed she was his wife.

Sitting on a folding chair, Marco Polo (or Markian Polonski) was importantly painting the Grand Canal from the mossy marble steps leading to the water, next to the rickety landing stage. He too had changed his clothes; no longer the jeaned and t-shirted youth of yesterday, he had metamorphosed into An Artist. True, he was wearing a t-shirt, but it was black, black as the dark night of the

21

soul, with a turtle-neck and long sleeves. The shirt was festooned carelessly with a splash of paint here, a nip of a rip there. Over this he wore a crimson waistcoat of the softest leather; he had found it in a skip in Soho. It had black buckles and straps which he left casually unfastened; it resembled something worn in a bondage fantasy and probably was, but Marco, of an unimaginative English mother and a good Catholic Polish father, thought it merely rather Bohemian. The waistcoat brought him luck; he had sold his first painting whilst wearing it.

Miranda, missing her home, her quiet life in Shropshire, the country cottage where she lived alone quite happily without so much as a cat to keep her company (she hated cats, if truth be told), wished Marco would smile sometimes. With all those freckles and clean floppy hair, his face looked made for smiles. But then, looking at his painting, she could understand why he didn't: it was grim and grey and meaningless, like nihilism gone out of control. She wondered if a proper framing would help, and eyed it professionally. This is what Miranda did, back in green and golden Shropshire; she had her own shop and did picture framing.

'Aren't you hot?' She felt herself come up all prickly in a heat rash, just looking at him. As well as the long sleeves and the turtle-neck, the lad was wearing a waistcoat the colour of blood, with as many lines and wrinkles as an old used road map, not to mention the various chains hanging from it, as if to tether a half-dozen Rottweilers. His fair hair was loose and dishevelled, flopping artlessly very nearly to his shoulders. If Netty looked like St Francis today, Marco, despite the bondage waistcoat, looked like a clean-cut young Englishman with artistic pretentions and freckles.

From inside the courtyard, Miranda could hear the drones of the crocodile lady, or rather Elena, and her husband Silvano. They still seemed to be hurling abuse at each other, in a desultory kind of manner. Miranda thought how wearisome it must be, all that emotion. She was delighted that her friends back home, kindly gentle souls who dabbled in country crafts or ran vegetarian restaurants or immersed themselves in self-sufficiency, never indulged in much of it.

Marco was indeed hot; he was profusely hot, the sweat pouring in little streams and rivulets and what-have-you inside the blackness of his clothing. 'No, I'm not a bit hot,' he said glumly, taking out a black handkerchief and moping his brow. Couldn't Miranda see that it was the creative process, making him so fiery and agitated? His was not an ordinary sweat.

There was a flutter of flapping sleeves and the rattling of wooden things, beads as it turned out, as Netty swooped out into the courtyard and on to the pier, threatening to sink it without a trace. But the wooden structure held up, the moment of danger passed, and Netty cried, 'Oh Marco, I say! How fearfully intense you look.' She peered from the landing stage to where Marco sat at the edge of the water. 'Oh, do let me see! I am so frightfully passionate about Art.'

She wriggled about to get a better view of the painting. Before she could comment, which was just as well because she did not think it looked a bit like the Grand Canal, or any canal *she'd* ever seen, the door of Apt. 3 flew open and out came Lissabelle, followed closely by her entourage of two.

'Who are you?' she demanded. Then she remembered that he could be anybody, so she made her voice girlie again, until she was sure. 'I mean, do I know you?' What she meant was, are you famous?

Marco glanced at her, then away. Netty said, 'He's a well-known artist from England. Marco Polo.'

'You must be joking,' Lissabelle said, but gently, until she could positively ascertain just how important the artist was. She looked at Simon and April and winked, mockingly. But not so as the others could see.

23

'What a coincidence,' April said, 'Lissabelle here is a well-known artist from England too, in the literary circles.'

April knew it was part of her job to say these things, though they were not, of course, specified either aloud or in her contract, but understood. She was Lissabelle's personal assistant, as was Simon, though the title was never mentioned by any of them. Their wages, in cash, were left in surprise packages on their dressing tables or pillows, often wrapped in ribbons or inside boxes with tiny treats, like a pair of cuff links or a necklace. This was so that Lissabelle could continue calling them her nearest and dearest, her very best chums, her darlings, and pretend that she did not have to pay them to be her friends, of which she did not have many.

'Yes,' Simon went on smoothly, 'Lissabelle Clarence here, our dearest friend, is a Famous Novelist.'

The others looked blank. Netty tried desperately to remember if she had ever seen the petite blonde novelist on a talk show, for the face was certainly familiar. Lissabelle had indeed been on numerous chat shows and was profiled often by the tabloid press, not to mention the odd gossip snippet in the broadsheets. Though quite why this was, no one was really sure. It certainly was not for her novels, which as a matter of fact had never been published, which would have been difficult as she had not yet written one. She had begun writing her first book several years ago, and had, to be honest, not got very far, finding the whole tedious business of sitting alone in a room with only a laptop and a gin and tonic keeping her company a tedious business indeed. Luckily, she had managed to become famous first, before even finishing Chapter One, which would make everything far less difficult later.

Marco said glumly, 'I'm sorry, but I don't think I've read any of your books.' He wasn't glum about not reading her books, but because they wouldn't all go away and let him get on with his painting.

'No doubt you haven't,' Lissabelle snapped. 'My novel is not accessible to just anyone.'

'Heavy-going, is it?' Miranda asked.

'Not for intellectuals.'

Simon said, 'Lissabelle's book is not mainstream commercial.'

'It is highly literary,' April went on.

'Literary mainstream.'

'But commercially literary.'

'Widely discussed in certain academic circles.' Or might be, Simon thought, if Lissabelle ever gets off her butt and writes it. Though sensational press was more the order of the day.

Lissabelle listened to her darling friends and thought, how loyal they are! She must remember to give them each a little special gift this week, to show them how grateful she was.

When the litany of praise had stopped, Netty cried, 'My dears, how perfectly splendid,' only because she could not think of what else to say. She was not much of a reader.

'D'you make money?' Marco asked, turning his attention to Lissabelle at last. He did not think the question at all blunt. As a C.P., a Creative Person, who only occasionally made money out of it, he was always interested in those who did, if only to find out how it was done.

'Money is secondary to literary merit,' Lissabelle said loftily, which Marco understood as meaning that her books, whatever they were, did not make a penny.

Lissabelle was fortunate enough not to give a toss whether her book, when published, made even a ha'penny, for she was exceedingly rich without having to bother about such trivia as making a living. She had been married to a wealthy industrialist who had died just before she was about to leave him for a poet half his age, a poet who called her *bella* even though he was not in the slightest bit Italian. The husband died before having a chance to change his will, leaving Lissabelle with pots of money and plenty of time to become famous, which she seemed to do ever so well. She had a knack for it.

Marco went back to his painting, losing interest. This annoyed Lissabelle, who felt that anyone losing interest in her was someone who should be taught a lesson. 'If you're really interested in being an artist,' she said ominously, 'then I'd suggest you dress more like one. All that black raggedy stuff went out in the 60s, darling. Not to mention that waistcoat, which looks like it came out of a Soho sex shop.'

Marco raised one pale eyebrow, but did not look up. He may have been pale, and freckled, and a shade pompous and yes, dreadfully out of date, but at least he made money from his paintings. If only very occasionally.

'At least I am a professional,' he said coolly, indicating by raising his second eyebrow that Lissabelle was not.

'Oh?' Her voice dripped with disbelief. 'I don't think so, darling.' She was fast losing interest, for it was obvious that Marco was not a true C.P. These days creative persons wore Versace garments and carried Gucci handbags, to show how large their advances were. The days of the bag-lady, candle-burning, cheap skunk-smoking, alcoholic and starving artist were long gone, thank God.

Netty was wriggling about like a mouse under a cat's paw, so delighted was she by all this arty conversation. Her flyaway curls, red as traffic lights, shone blindingly in the late morning sunshine, slowing down the various barge boats and motorboats and vaporetti on the Grand Canal, as if they were waiting for them to turn green.

A gondola crammed with Japanese went by (as they very often did), nearly tipping the boat right over as they fought amongst themselves to get the best vantage point for a photograph. A Famous Venetian Artist at Work, surrounded by his glamorous and creative friends in the lush courtyard of their palazzo on the Grand Canal. How exciting it all was, what treats Venice bestowed on those who loved her!

After they had all finished posing – Marco looking furiously furrowed and intense; Lissabelle lifting her chin high so that her adorable profile would be evident; Netty putting one plump cheek in her plump hand and looking out at the Grand Canal with a look (spontaneous, of course) of dreamy contemplation – after the Japanese had snapped away, and then applauded mightily from their gondolas (so delighted were they), a sleek motorboat roared down the canal, nearly capsizing the Japanese and several other gondolas.

'*Ciao!*' cried the driver of the water taxi as he stopped abruptly at the landing stage.

'*Ciao!*' Netty cried, though she had not a clue who the stranger, who seemed to have more than his fair share of teeth, was. Venice was turning into everything she had fantasized about, and this was only her second day. She could feel the years fly off her ample body as baby birds from a cosy nest; she could feel her rosy round face lift higher than it was even after the cosmetic surgery she had had some years ago. One charming Venetian had held her arm yesterday, and today another, dishier one was shouting *ciao* at her and splashing her new brown skirt and top with salty water from the Grand Canal itself.

'*Ciao*, darling,' Lissabelle cried, in a bored and languid voice, though secretly delighted that the taxi driver to whom she had given a substantial tip yesterday had not been able to resist coming back to see her.

'*Ciao, bella*,' he grinned at her, toothy and tanned and gorgeous.

'Mm, darling, now don't be too cheeky.'

'Wait for it,' Simon hissed to April. 'She's going for an affair. An Italian job.'

'But he's only a taxi driver,' April whispered back. Lissabelle's lovers, since the poet had long gone, were people like herself, writers and artists and creative to the core. But rich. Very rich. And able to flaunt it with style. Naturally.

Lissabelle was thinking that perhaps her latest (and first) novel, the one she was here to write, could do with a Venetian or two in it, since it was set in Venice. Though not, she shuddered, in San Polo, but in Dorsoduro, where there were not many natives. She was not actually quite sure that they would fit into her book, but on the other hand, it would be a novelty.

'Now that you've moored,' Lissabelle called sweetly from the landing stage, 'why don't you come in for an *aperitivo*?'

But before the water taxi driver could answer, Marco was standing up, nearly tipping over his paints and easel as he rushed from the marble steps to the landing stage and peered into the boat.

'Nina, it's you. I've found you! Or you've found me, more like it.' He laughed, from nerves, and they all looked at him strangely. His laugh was like the call of a mynah bird in a hot tropical jungle, screechy and evocative of hot eerie nights and things that go bump in them. Privately, they all decided that they preferred Marco when he was glum.

Everyone peeked into the water taxi. From out of the small cabin a curvy figure emerged, dressed in shorts and a halter top, her short dark hair ruffled prettily as befits an attractive girl who rides on hefty boats. 'Marco, *ciao*,' Nina called, scrambling up to the front. 'Meet Paolo, my fiancé.'

Paolo scowled. 'You know this man?' He said it as if knowing someone meant fucking them until they howled, so black was his look, so hidden behind tight lips was his toothy smile.

Nina laughed defiantly. Miranda, watching all this despite herself, needing to go shopping but unable to tear herself away from all the goings-on on the landing stage, thought that it was a very defiant laugh indeed.

'*Si*, Paolo, I know the Englishman very well. We met on the bus, coming back from the airport.'

Lissabelle, not to be outdone by this presumptuous young thing, said, 'What a coincidence, darling. You know our English artist, and I know your fiancé, very well too as a matter of fact. We met yesterday as well, but in his taxi. Not in a *bus*.' The emphasis she laid on bus was frightening to hear.

'Oh? You must be the English *lady*' — she managed to make the word sound both old and suspect — 'that my Paolo had to drive from the airport yesterday.' She looked Lissabelle up and down dismissively. 'Well, it's a job, poor man.'

The two women glared at each other. Paolo, to get even with Nina for daring to talk to a stranger, foreign and male, on the public transport, looked at Lissabelle with a full monty of teeth. It was dazzling to behold. 'So nice to see you again, *bella*.'

Nina, not to be outdone, blew a kiss to Marco. 'See you again soon, *bellissimo*.'

Paolo revved the engine. As the boat roared off towards the Rialto Bridge, at a greater speed than was strictly necessary, or even legal, the others shook themselves, to get rid of all the water.

Miranda left the Palazzo Bobolino through the courtyard and out the door at even greater speed, thinking how melodramatic and blowzy Venice was, making everyone so bad-tempered and aggressive, or else soppy and sentimental.

Shropshire, thank God, was never like this.

A couple of hours later, Netty sat alone, drinking gin and tonic at an outdoor table in one of the expensive cafés in St Mark's Square. She had just walked about the narrow *calli*, the streets and alleyways of the city, in a blissful haze, in love for the first time in her life. Not with a man, but with Venice herself, *La Serenissima*, the city of artists and poets, of Wagner dying in his wife's arms, of

Browning – well, dying; of Byron's mistresses flinging themselves into the murky water of the Grand Canal; of Turner painting that very same canal, just as Marco Polo, her housemate for goodness' sake, was painting it this very moment, at the Palazzo Bobolino. It was awesome, and she was part of it.

She sighed, watching the pigeons shitting on the great Piazza, the tour guides shouting through their microphones, the day-trippers sweating and swearing with irritable exhaustion, wondering if they should queue for an hour to try to get into the Doge's Palace, or get caught in a traffic jam in a gondola under the Bridge of Sighs.

But Netty was not a tourist. Netty was a traveller, an adventurer. Netty was waiting for someone. She had an assignation. With a Venetian.

Trembling, she munched on the crisps that the waiter had placed on the checked tablecloth and ordered another gin. *English*, the waiter thought. The Americans wanted whisky, and Australians sat at his tables and drank bottled water that they had brought along in their rucksacks, until he shooed them away. The Germans drank beer, and the Japanese – well, they did not care what they drank, as long as they could take a *maledetto* photograph of it.

In the Piazza, the bells of the campanile peeled and hollared, a bit discordantly. Netty thought they sounded like the trumpets of angels. But then she thought the singing of the gondoliers was like opera, and the waiter, who was now serving her a second gin and tonic, a jolly little Italian fellow indeed. She had not had the bill yet.

'Netty, *bella*,' murmured a voice in her ear, nearly frightening her out of her wits. Silvano, the Assignation himself, had crept up on her from behind. He had been fortifying himself with a stiff grappa in a much cheaper bar down a side *calle*, before facing Netty. Not that he had not wanted this clandestine meeting; it

30

was just that the Englishwoman was so . . . so very much *there* somehow. Rather like the Basilica itself, he thought, staring at the magnificent old cathedral in the heart of the Piazza: flamboyant and gaudy, a bit old, a bit over-the-top, but overbearingly gorgeous.

'My dear Silvano!' Netty broke out in a crooked smile, rather like a rash spreading over her face, so red was her lipstick, so vivid were her blood-red curls falling over her face as her cheeks quivered with excitement.

He was in his *gondoliere* kit, the black trousers, the striped jersey, the straw hat which he took off ceremonially and laid on the table between them. His white tufts of hair stood up like fat little Eskimo huts.

'Netty, *cara*. My little darling, my treasure chest.' Silvano put his silvery gondolier's hand over her own pink plump one. A Japanese chap in a three-piece suit took a photo of them, to show his Auntie Yoko what a gondolier looked like in his off-duty hours.

In the short time since meeting at the airport, romance had bloomed. Silvano could not help comparing Netty's reckless red hair to the helmet-like Gothic of his wife's dead locks; Netty's ample body, as full and rounded as the domes on the Basilica itself, to the body of his wife, as straight and narrow as an anorexic Greek column.

Though they were meeting by stealth today, they had met by accident, a couple of times after that first airport meeting. First they had met on the vaporetto, pulling away from the Rialto Bridge stop. Netty was off to see the sights, and Silvano, to San Marco and the piazzetta where his gondola was moored.

'Oh ho,' chuckled Netty, 'how frightfully amusing, meeting you on the waterbus. I thought you would paddle yourself to work on your gondola. How terribly disillusioning.' She smiled to show that this was a little joke.

She too had got off at San Marco, and had her first glimpse of the Doge's Palace, the great Piazza, the Basilica, whilst clutching the arm of a real live gondolier, in full dress. It was the moment she had been living for all her life.

Another meeting had taken place later one night, again unplanned. Silvano had gone out to have a last fag before bed, and to get a bit of peace from Elena's haranguing. Netty had gone outside to see the moon reflected in the Grand Canal, a phenomenon she had read about in many of the novels, essays, poems and stories she had devoured about Venice during the past ten or twenty years. She had loved Vee-nee-cee for years; it was her hobby, her passion. Not a newspaper article had been written on The Serene Republic that she had not devoured, nor a guidebook she had not perused. Not a film nor documentary was released, that she did not watch. She belonged to the English branch of Save Venice; she wrote letters, passionate pleas to charitable institutions, wealthy aristocrats, foreign governments, to beg contributions to stop her beloved city from sinking into the sea.

Unfortunately, this work kept her so busy that she had no time to actually visit Venice. Not before now. But it was all just as she had imagined it could be; more, even. She had certainly not imagined someone as . . . as *Venetian* as Silvano, and on her own doorstep.

Silvano ordered another grappa from the waiter, who was a third cousin and would fiddle the bill for him, one way or another. If the Englishwoman paid, it would be more, naturally; if Silvano were required to do the settling-up, it would be *niente*, nothing at all, a pittance. It was what families were for, *naturalmente*.

'Oh Silvano, I cannot, simply cannot believe that I am truly here. What would my chums at the bridge club think of me now?'

'I cannot say, *cara*.'

'They would say . . . well, never mind.' She smiled at him

32

vacantly. She could not imagine England right now, could not remember what it was like to be English, though she came from a family of worn-out ancestral squires who knew nothing else. Netty herself knew nothing else, except what she had read and heard about Venice.

Silvano, drinking his grappa quickly, said, with as much casualness as he could muster, 'And, uh, your husband? What would he say, if he could see you now?'

'Good heavens. I say, do you think he can?'

Silvano looked around furtively, wondering if one of those burly Englishmen at a nearby table was her husband, spying on them. It was the sort of thing the English would do, if they suspected a wife of an affair, rather than acting with honour and resorting to violence as any decent Italian would.

'I wouldn't know,' Silvano muttered, releasing her hand and pushing his chair well away from the table, so as not to seem too intimate.

'But of course; you are Italian, and Catholic, and believe in such things.' Netty laughed, a horsy English laugh of the kind Silvano adored, for he was a passionate Anglophile. He had just spent a week in London, as he did every year, hanging around in Trafalgar Square and eating fish and chips and bacon butties. But he was nonetheless confused.

'What things, *tesoro*?' he asked cautiously, keeping his voice low so that in case there *was* a husband lurking around, Silvano would not be overheard.

His third cousin, the waiter, passed their table and gave him a wink and a victory sign. The whole family would know that Silvano had scored again, despite his advanced age and the fact that Elena was becoming more demanding the older she became. They would keep this knowledge from *her*, of course: Silvano's wife. This is what families were for, *naturalmente*.

Netty looked fondly at her gondolier, so Venetian, so Italian, so

33

Catholic. She would become a Catholic, she decided impetuously; the new vicar in the Anglican church back home, where she did the flowers every week, was becoming tiresome, all that young fresh enthusiasm and guitar playing during Evensong.

'Yes, I believe you are right, Silvano; I believe my husband is at this very minute, watching us both.'

Silvano sprang from his chair, just as the musicians on the outdoor platform of the café burst into something lively by Vivaldi. He was about to bolt when he felt the familiar clamp on his arm again. For a fat woman, Netty's hand was amazingly claw-like, rather like an English Christmas turkey.

'And approving of what he sees, Silvano! Giving us his blessings. I am quite, quite sure of it.'

Silvano slunk back down in his chair, weak with the aftermath of fear. This entirely made sense to him; he knew the English were unrepentantly mad. This was why he was so smitten with them. They were both cool and mad, unlike Elena, with whom he had lived in hellish marital discord for forty-odd years. She was both hot and sanely cunning, tracing down his sundry infidelities with the cold logic of a sleuth, and then exploding violently over them. He had had enough of it.

Silvano said, cautiously taking down his gondolier's hat which he had put in front of his face in the first moment of terror, 'Where, exactly, *is* your husband?' He looked surreptitiously around the Piazza.

Netty beamed. 'You should know that far better than I do, by Jove. I'm only C of E.'

Luckily, the musicians had finished their first piece with an abundant flourish, which required much applause and shouts of 'More!' which gave Silvano time to think. But fortunately Netty, after throwing herself enthusiastically into the clapping and shouting 'Bravo' like the Venetian she was at heart, said, 'He died quite young, God rest his soul. Well, relatively speaking.'

34

He had actually been seventy-four but Netty was not about to say so. It would make her seem so old, having a husband, even a dead one, of that age.

Silvano, relieved, fanned himself with his straw hat and signalled his cousin to bring them another round of drinks. The musicians romped through another Vivaldi, as if there was a prize for the first instrument that finished. Crowds of tourists milled behind the tables, standing and listening, while richer tourists sat comfortably and drank cappuccinos the price of their monthly mortgage repayment.

'How sad,' Silvano said politely, referring to the dead husband. He felt some comment was called for.

'Hm,' Netty said non-committally. Life was so much more *fun* as a widow. Instead of cooking proper meals every night, and having to entertain his retired naval chums and their dreary wives several times a month and for weekends in their fine home in the Buckinghamshire countryside, Netty, extravagantly pensioned, agreeably connected and with a mind of her own, was able to indulge in her own whims. These included, besides Venice, bridge, luncheons and the occasional foray around one of the better golf courses. The latter was to keep her figure in trim.

'Oh quite. It *was* jolly sad, but life must go on, of course. Stiff upper lip and all that, what? Besides . . .' Here her extravagant voice lowered to a rumble as she leaned her mop of red curls towards his fluffy white tufts and went on, 'marriage is sometimes not all it is cut out to be.'

She implied, by the sudden lowering of her lashes, tragic occurrences, but Silvano knew exactly what she meant. Excitedly, he thought it time he honoured her confidences with one of his own. Taking her hand, he said, '*Capisco*. How well I know what you mean. My wife, Elena . . .' here he too lowered his eyes before going on, 'does not understand me.'

'Good grief.' Netty's soft compassionate blue eyes misted over. 'My dear boy, I understand perfectly.'

'I knew you would.'

'I knew you'd know.'

'I do.'

This breathy exchange overwhelmed them for a moment. Netty thought, how expressive the Italians are, not afraid to talk of their emotions, unlike the British. She found it almost too stimulating to bear.

Silvano thought, how blessedly restrained the English are, so phlegmatic. Such a relief after the excesses of his wife.

Netty said, 'I thought it odd, the way she did not come to the airport to meet you.'

This time it was Silvano's turn to be non-committal. 'Mm,' he said, the word reeking with unspoken pain. 'No, this is true. She did not.'

Netty squeezed his hand in sympathy. Silvano decided not to tell her that Elena was not at the airport because she was furious with him for having gone to London, leaving her behind. He had been doing it every year for ten years, holidaying in happy solitude in his beloved country. Every year for ten years Elena had ranted about being left behind, as she would no doubt do for the next ten years. Not that she wanted to go to England, not at all. It was the principle of the thing.

Silvano loved England for many reasons, not least of it being the fact that all the water was where it belonged, up in the sky and falling from it, rather than seeping up from below the way it did in Venice. Frankly, the constant damp was giving him rheumatism, and in winter he always had a touch of bronchial problems. But there were other things that delighted him about London. The city was in the twenty-first century, with cars and motors, buses and bikes, and an Underground that took you where you wanted to go in a straight line, instead of weaving back and forth on either side of a murky waterway like the vaporetti did, a most annoying factor when you were in a hurry.

There were other perks as well. Nobody troubled you, in London. In the public transport system, no one began animated conversations with total strangers, as they did in his gondola day after day, year after weary year. People talked and talked, and got excited like his wife, and told him all about their lives back in wherever it was that they came from. This meant, naturally, that he had to talk back, something he had once loved to do, but after years of living with Elena, talking back was wearing thin.

Just as Vivaldi was wearing thin. If he heard another *maledetto* musician playing another *cazzo* piece of Vivaldi music again, he would shriek.

'Oh, splendid!' Netty was looking towards the outdoor platform in eager anticipation. 'They are doing *The Four Seasons*. Oh Silvano, will you show me Vivaldi's church? Is it not around the Piazza somewhere? Are not there Vivaldi concerts at the church on weekends? Oh, do let's go one night soon.'

Silvano did not shriek, but instead said, '*Bella* Netty, I work every night, *che peccato*. Weekends especially are a busy time for us *gondolieri*.' He patted his straw hat importantly.

'Oh.' Netty looked crestfallen.

Silvano then did something that he had not done for some time, not since the first randy passions of his younger gondoliering days had at last begun to abate. Trying to whisper as intimately as he could, while still being heard above the raucous violinist, he said, 'Can I take you out in my gondola?'

Netty blushed. She had read stories of propositions such as these. Never, in her wildest dreams, did she think that she would be the recipient. 'Gracious. Oh my. I couldn't possibly,' she stammered, while at the same time, a little voice in her head, the same one that told her to dye her hair red, and abandon the Jaeger suits she wore when her husband was alive for the loose and flowing garments she now favoured, said wickedly, 'Whyever not?'

'*Per favore*,' Silvano pleaded. Not because his lust had been aroused, but because her very Englishness was so soothing. He imagined being a child, and having her as a nanny. Not, of course, in the way an Englishman might imagine it, with whips and spankings and so on, but quite literally, as someone who would look after him. Elena was too skinny and bad-tempered to look after anyone.

Netty was looking at him coyly. 'When did you have in mind?'

Silvano thought about when his wife was least likely to spot them. 'Saturday night?' He always worked till all hours on Saturday, in the busy season. 'But late. After the paying customers have gone.'

Netty giggled. 'But it is your work, my dear Silvano. I shall pay you too.'

'Netty, you insult me. I would not hear of it. You shall ride in my gondola for free. It would be an honour for me.'

Netty knew what the price of a free gondola ride was; my goodness! Things were happening so quickly; it all quite took her breath away. But she had longed for something other than overnight coach trips to London with her bridge club to take in a matinée, and here it was. *Carpe diem*, as someone once said, and she would, she would!

And besides, what better way of consummating her love affair with Venice, than by a romantic tryst, or thrust as the case may be, in a gondola with a Venetian?

'I'll do it!' she cried. 'Seize the day and all that, what?'

'What? Oh, good, good.'

Silvano was delighted. Just like the old days, he thought jauntily, only of course without the sex, for after visiting England, he felt too respectful of the English to try any hanky-panky with one of their women, especially one who looked and sounded like one of the Royals. Not the old-fashioned, Queen Elizabeth type, but one of the newer, more flamboyant versions that seemed to be all the rage nowadays.

Not that there hadn't been an Englishwoman or two in his younger, more virile days. Not to mention American, French, German, Japanese and a fair sprinkling of Eastern Europeans to boot. But as somebody said – probably Dante, who said everything – the past was another country. He had, unfortunately, moved out of it some time ago, because the spirit, still as willing as always, had succumbed to the weakening of the flesh, and nothing had stirred (or perhaps a better word would be stiffened) for a year or two. Probably more; he refused to count.

Ah well. Silvano sighed, and smiled, and arranged to meet Netty, thinking philosophically how restful it would be, not to be called upon to perform in his gondola. There was as much an art to making love in the *maledetto* thing as rowing it, and it was a pity more people did not appreciate that fact. The life of a gondolier was exhausting, what with manoeuvring the damn things around the noisy vaporetti, and dodging the motorboats of the fire brigade and ambulance services, not to mention the *carabinieri* who thought they owned the Grand Canal. Then there were the tourists to put up with, all those foreigners whose language they expected you to know, and on top of everything, you were expected to be willing and virile, lusty and loving, long after everyone else in Venice had finished work and gone home to bed.

But Netty was different, *grazie a Dio*. Netty would want only moonlight, a smooth ride, and a glimpse of the Rialto Bridge all lit up, with perhaps a romantic word or two in her ear while he skilfully guided his gondola under a tiny stone bridge.

He smiled at her. Fondly.

Netty, shivering with anticipation and daring, smiled back. Seductively.

Chapter Four

Miranda, not at her best in the morning, staggered into the kitchen of Apt. 1 in the Palazzo Bobolino and opened the cupboard to find the teabags, only to have the door come off in her hand.

'That happened to me too,' said Marco, who was slumped at the table, his sensitive artist's fingers (so described once in a trendy Sunday supplement, after he had had a minor, but marginally successful, exhibition in London) wrapped around a cracked mug containing strong black coffee.

Miranda said nothing, but opened the double glass doors leading to the balcony. There was just about room for the two cats, a small table and a couple of chairs, if you shuffled everything about a bit. The sun struck the balcony with unnecessary force, Miranda thought, and flinched.

In front of her, the Grand Canal was hyperactive this morning, the water pulsating importantly as barge boats filled with casks of wine and olive oil, fruit and vegetables, chugged up and down, alongside vaporetti and taxis and the odd early morning gondola. It was noisy and chaotic, and made Miranda's head hurt. She thought of peaceful Shropshire and groaned.

'Vee-nee-cee, glorious Vee-nee-cee,' cried a voice from the kitchen. A flash of red beamed on to the balcony, as Netty stuck her head outside, and a boat carrying building materials slowed down, thinking it was a warning light.

'Venezia,' said Miranda sourly. She had not even had her first cup of tea, and the sun was far too flashy for her liking.

As was Netty, dressed as the Virgin Mary today, in something long and loose and very, very blue indeed. She crammed herself on to the balcony, threw her arms out towards the water, and breathed deeply. 'I have found my spiritual home,' she announced dramatically. 'I have found my roots.'

'Don't be so bloody silly,' Miranda said, with some asperity. 'And in Italian, you don't pronounce it Vee-nee-cee, but Ve-ne-zi-a. With the accent on the *ne*.'

Netty was so grateful for this Italian lesson that Miranda immediately felt guilty. 'I am frightfully bad at languages,' Netty cried. 'I always have been. For precisely this reason, I am beginning school on Monday.'

'School?'

'Language school. To learn Italian. I'm in the beginners' class.'

'Ah. Good idea.'

'That's how I found this accommodation, of course, through the school. They found it for me. I thought it would be much better than staying at a hotel, if I could live with a proper Venetian family, immerse myself in the language and culture.' Here she frowned at Miranda.

'Sorry about that,' Miranda said. She could see Netty's point. 'I had to take over as landlady at the last minute, or you would have had your Venetian family. My daughter's married to one, and the children were born here. And of course Jessica herself has lived in Italy for years, speaks the language perfectly. But unfortunately, they had to leave suddenly.' She said it sombrely, as if to imply tragedy and disaster. No need to mention it was a spur of the moment decision brought on by an early heatwave.

41

'That is quite all right,' Netty said graciously. As a matter of fact, she was relieved. Much as she loved all things Venetian, it would have been tiresome to speak in Italian first thing in the morning.

Marco's hand, the one with the sensitive fingers, reached out on to the balcony and handed out two mugs of tea, one for each of them. 'Why, how terribly kind,' Netty said. 'Do join us.'

Miranda wondered how he could possibly find room, but he was skinny enough to find a space in the corner, where he sat on the marble tiles of the balcony clutching his coffee. For a moment they were all silent, watching the activity on the canal. Further along down the waterway, the *traghetti*, the larger public transport gondolas, were ferrying people to the fish market and the open fruit and vegetable market of the Rialto. An ambulance boat, racing by with blue light flashing, made waves that rocked the *traghetti* back and forth like little plastic duckies in an overfull bathtub.

Marco said suddenly, 'I think I am in love. In fact, I'm positive of it. I couldn't eat this morning and I didn't sleep a wink all night.'

The two women stared at him with open mouths. What was he doing, blabbing such things at this hour of the morning?

Miranda groaned, and put her head in her hands. She really did not want to know.

Netty, pulling herself together, stared at the feckless youth and told herself that this was Venice now, not Buckinghamshire, and that she too was in love, with a gondolier. Though she did not think she would have the effrontery to spill it all out, as Marco did. But he was an artist, a Creative Person; that explained it. She had better get used to C.P.s; Venice seemed to be awash with them.

And so the three of them, Netty, Miranda and Marco, lost in their own thoughts, sit for a moment like a frozen tableau, indifferent to the shouts and noises of the water traffic below them. Venezia, city of dreams, of illusions, that Most Serene Republic, smiles wickedly to herself, and the soft breeze across the canal blows balmier, the sun's glare softens. Oh what fools these mortals be, she says to herself smugly, thinking perhaps someone should write that down: it's a good line.

But so much has already been written about her, most of it bollocks, of course. Not that the *Serenissima* is about to let on: she adores flattery.

And now another one has succumbed. Marco Polo. Well, the first Marco Polo brought riches and honour to his fair city – let's see what this second one can do.

What this second Marco Polo was doing at this moment was running his sensitive fingers through his pale floppy hair and twisting his face into a grimace of despair, looking quite suicidal.

Netty was shocked, but thrilled. Here was the other life, the one beyond bridge clubs and golf and the odd committee meeting for the church and the village hall.

Miranda was not so much shocked as horrified. Venice was bad enough without a lovesick young Englishman mooning about, wanting to talk about it all the time. The love-life of the young was so boring.

Marco looked ready to cry, but then he always did; it was something to do with the way his face was set.

It was Netty who said the words Miranda had been deeply, deeply dreading. 'My dear boy!' she cried. 'Tell us *all* about it.'

As Miranda's heart sank, Marco's expanded. Obeying Netty's imperious command, he did.

An hour later, Marco stopped talking.

'Good gracious,' Netty said. 'You had better find this Nina at once, ask her straight away to marry you.'

'He can't, remember? She has a fiancé, that taxi driver, Paolo,'

Miranda said wearily. Her head hurt, and she had wanted to go inside ages ago, but it seemed so callous, turning one's back on the agony of love.

'She is my muse,' Marco said. 'My inspiration.'

'Yes, yes, so you said. Several times.'

'I thought you said Venice was your inspiration?' Netty asked curiously. Artists were so difficult to understand.

'She *is* Venice. The two are indivisible. If I lose Nina, I lose Venice. I shall be ruined as a painter.'

'Oh really?' Netty was impressed. 'Dear boy, that would be such a pity.'

'Don't you feel, Marco,' Miranda said briskly, deciding that this was getting out of hand, 'that perhaps you may be just the teeniest bit exaggerating?'

Marco looked at her with wounded eyes and shook his head mournfully in denial. Miranda was beginning to lose patience when a loud thumping could be heard on the courtyard door.

'Ah, *eccola*, here she is,' cried a voice from the kitchen. 'Your landlady.'

It was Elena, looking less like a crocodile and more like a mammal today, for she was wearing something brown and sleek, like the skin of a mole, and she had a little tan felt helmet-like hat over her black helmet-like hair. Her jaw and teeth seemed not so prominent today, and Miranda thought that perhaps she was getting used to the woman. Amazing how you got used to everything, in the end.

Elena was going on, 'We knocked, for ages. First I find this young man trying to get into the front door, but of course the bell does not work. So I let him in. Then, we knock on Apt. 1, and no reply. But it was open, *fortunatamente*, and we came in.'

The others peered around her to see who the 'we' was, and found themselves staring into the bold blue eyes of a stalwart chap in cream-coloured shorts, a beige short-sleeved

44

shirt and a pristine haircut. '*Buongiorno*,' he said in a strong German accent.

Elena said, in Italian to Miranda, 'His name is Frank, and he's Swiss – German Swiss, not one of *us* – and he speaks no Italian, but he tried talking to me in English, which as you know, I have a slight understanding of.'

'Oh God. The new tenant. I forgot there was one more.'

'*Buongiorno*,' Frank repeated, louder, his accent even more prominent.

'Oh goody,' Netty said. 'An Italian. From the North, no doubt, with those eyes and that blond hair. We could do with an Italian in the house. Seeing that we are all in Italy.'

Frank began protesting in German that he was not Italian, nor even Italian Swiss. When no one understood him, he switched to a rather peculiar English. Netty went on, 'But how guttural he sounds. Is it the Venetian dialect, Miranda?'

Marco was eyeing the newcomer suspiciously, wondering if he were an artist. At the Biennale, which was opening in a couple of weeks, the Germans were tipped to take all the glittering prizes, for their contribution to modern art. Their pavilion was said to be completely empty, the walls and floor and ceiling uncovered, unadorned. No sculptures or paintings, no installation, nothing. It was brilliant, a profound commentary on the emptiness of modern society. The other countries were seething, wishing they had thought of it first.

But Frank was not an artist. Miranda was talking to him in English, explaining who she was, and why the landlady with whom he had originally made contact was not on the premises.

'But is not good, is not right,' Frank was protesting. 'I am to be here with family Italian. To learn language for business.'

Netty said, quite sensibly, 'My dear, you obviously speak absolutely no Italian at all, except for good morning, nor do you understand a word. Consider yourself fortunate to have ended up with us.'

'But that is why I go Monday to school which learns me to speak the Italian. To teach.'

'I think you mean the school which teaches you Italian, to learn. And that proves my point, Frank, that you are far better off with Miranda here, and the rest of us Britishers, for you could do with some practice in English.'

Frank, bewildered, listened while Netty introduced herself and Marco, and explained who Miranda was, and why they were all there. When she said that Marco was an artist, a painter, Frank perked up. 'Ah, the Biennale. I here for June to make course in language Italian because of Biennale. The German pavilion is to make big revolution for the modern art. And win prizes also, so they talk.'

'So they *say*, dear, not talk. Good gracious, you do have a lot to learn.'

'You are exhibitionist for Great Britain? In the Biennale?' Frank looked at the surly Marco with respect. He had never heard of the Biennale before, but this year the popular press was full of it, what with Germany set to astound the world. Suddenly, Art was splashing on the pages of the newspaper and on the screens of the tellies even more than pop stars and football heroes. It was the new rock'n'roll, Art, even to people like Frank, who did something in computers. Or, to be more precise, *to* computers. He was a repairman.

Marco, who pretended he had not heard the question, was irritated when Frank asked again if he were one of the British exhibitors, or exhibitionists as the Swiss German put it, for the great Biennale. What was it with foreigners, that they loved asking embarrassing questions? And not even speaking in decent English, which was the duty of every European.

The truth was, Marco was secretly, bitterly, agonizingly upset

46

about the Biennale, that he had not been the chosen one for the British pavilion. Last year he had received favourable reviews from one or two art critics, and his work had been reviled by the tabloids, all a sure mark of success. He had sold his latest painting for a sum enabling him to return to Venice, albeit on a budget. He had found the room in the Palazzo Bobolino through a friend of a friend, who had once been a student at the language school and had stayed in Apt. 1.

'Why are you studying Italian?' Netty asked Frank, as a way of making the young man, who was in his mid-thirties but looked younger than Marco, who was a mere twenty-six, feel at ease and at home. 'But I suppose that is a foolish question. All of us who adore Venice must eventually learn her language, *n'est-ce pas*? I understand perfectly; you need say no more.'

Miranda, stifling a grin at the thought of Netty learning Italian, let alone Veneziano, did not have the heart to tell her that she had lapsed into French.

Frank, who had no feelings about Venice one way or the other, said, 'I am needing to know the Italian because of my work.' He had landed a contract to repair and maintain the computers for a large and prestigious telecommunications business, but unfortunately the company was not German but Italian. A sprinkling of a few *ciao*s and *va bene*s would go down well, he thought, when he began the job in a month's time. Ambition was to Frank as Art was to Marco.

Miranda decided it was time to show Frank his bedroom, and took him down the stairs to a cubbyhole behind the scrofulous marble staircase. 'Mm. Small,' Frank said doubtfully.

'Ah, but you are paying less lire than the others,' Miranda said, having at last read the list of tenants and room allocations that Jessica had left.

Frank, being thrifty, found the room suddenly to his liking.

Upstairs, Elena had remained behind and was eyeing Netty

contemplatively. Netty was about to say something jovial and friendly when she suddenly remembered that on Saturday night, she would be bonking the woman's husband in his gondola.

'Ah, uh——' she began. But could not go on. It was a situation she was unprepared for, and it made her uncomfortable. She had not, in thinking about her forthcoming rendezvous, given much thought to Silvano's wife. Perhaps this was amiss? Perhaps she should feel guilt? But it was so Roman Catholic, guilt. Being Anglican, she was not quite sure what guilt felt like.

Bother, she thought. She had been so looking forward to a bit of – well, fooling about, as they used to call it in her youth. After all, it was a year or two since her poor husband had died. And besides, everyone fell in love in Venice, and had affairs and whatnot, it was all part of the show, and a jolly good show it was.

Elena was still eyeballing her. Netty, for perhaps the first time in her life, panicked. 'Ta, ta,' she cried. 'Must dash, Vee-nee-cee summons me and I must away and explore!' With that, she ran out.

Elena watched her retreat grimly. Silly woman, what was Silvano thinking of, beginning this ridiculous flirtation? But then, look at Silvano. Shaking her head in disgust at the stupidity of men, she flounced down the stairs.

This, then, was breakfast time in the Palazzo Bobolino, in Apt. No. 1.

In Apt. 3, on the other side of the tangly courtyard, it was much more civilized.

'Darling, another Bucks Fizz please. Oh, and Simon do, do, help yourself to another drink, and April too. Open another bottle of champagne, will you, darling? April, you star, you squeezed more oranges. Nothing like fresh Italian oranges, straight from the Rialto market, for breakfast. Ah, Venezia, what a city. The only place on earth that does not bore me.'

Lissabelle, reclining on the sofa in the drawing room of Apt. 3, had momentarily forgotten that she hated the Rialto market, and the Rialto Bridge, for that matter, for they were in San Polo, home of so many Venetians. All those merchants and artisans, all those gondoliers and common folk. Thanks to the bungling of her estate agent, it was her home too for the month, but for the moment she had forgotten that too.

Apt. 3 was very like Apt. 1, only scruffier, for at least in Jessica's place, it had been tarted up and made home-like, even cosy and funkily arty. Lissabelle's apartment, however, was used for short lets, a couple of weeks or a month or two perhaps, but not for permanent residencies. It therefore had all the features of Apt. 1, such as vile wallpaper, ancient plumbing, a suspect kitchen and hideous furniture, but without the plants and posters, throws and cushions, and lightness of spirit that made Apt. 1 quite pleasant, when one got used to it.

Simon and April went into the kitchen, ostensibly to get more orange juice and bubbly, but really to make plans. April, throwing open the double doors to reveal a balcony exactly like the one in Apt. 1, said, 'I've got to have a day off. I'm knackered. It's your turn to have her today. Besides, I want to do a bit of sightseeing; I've never even been to Venice before.'

Simon, who had, said, 'There's not much to see. When you've seen one gondola, you've seen the lot.' He opened the cupboard to see what provisions there were, if any. The door fell off in his hand.

'Anyway,' he went on, 'we don't have days off. We're friends, not employees.'

He smirked. April snorted. They stood looking out over the canal and thought about Lissabelle.

'Ah well,' Simon said, 'it's best to be philosophical about it. We both took on the job, knowing what she was like.'

April nodded. 'Why exactly *did* you take it?' she asked, looking at him curiously. He had been with Lissabelle for several years, while she had just come aboard, so to speak.

'Not sure, now,' he said, trying to fix the cupboard door. 'Something different. A chance to travel. Mix with the beautiful people. Thought it'd be easy, y'know?'

April knew. 'Cushy,' she said. 'With lots of perks, meeting celebs, posh do's.' They both laughed. There was some of that, of course, but mostly it was hard slog, and boring to boot. It was arduous work, being a professional sycophant.

'Ah well, we can move on whenever we feel like it,' April said. They were both young enough, and clever and attractive, though not quite so attractive as Lissabelle, naturally. That would not have done at all.

A shout from the drawing room interrupted them. 'It's the F.A. herself,' Simon grinned.

'Fat Arse?'

'Famous Author, ninny. We'd better get in there.'

Lissabelle, looking out the window at the Grand Canal, said, 'Darlings, I am bored. Can you believe it? I am in Venice, the city I adore, and I am bored.'

April said briskly, 'Well then, you'd better get started on the book. I've set up the computer in the bedroom with the view.'

Lissabelle took no notice. She wrapped her pale silk dressing gown tighter around her pale silky body and said, 'I don't think I can bear it, darlings. I was bored in New York, in Sydney and in Paris. Even Rome. Venice was my last hope; for the first time, it has failed me.'

Simon and April looked at each other and rolled their eyes. April cried, 'Darling, you poor thing! What shall we do to cheer you up? Shall we go to Harry's Bar for lunch?'

Simon watched with admiration. April had picked up the job amazingly fast. 'That's a marvellous idea,' he said. 'Shall I phone for a reservation?'

'Oh yes do, Simon. April, have you unpacked my rose skirt? The short one?'

Aren't they all? April said to herself, but aloud she said, 'Yes, and ironed it too.'

'You treasure.' Lissabelle held out her arms, and for a horrid moment April was afraid that she would try and embrace her. But she was motioning for the phone, which Simon handed her.

Lissabelle made her phone call, looking at a small white card she held in her hand. When she hung up, her face was radiant. 'Darlings, I've booked us a water taxi, to take us to lunch. And what a coincidence! Paolo's coming out, our driver from the airport. Can you believe it?'

Simon could, all right. And so could April. They both sighed, but not so loudly that Lissabelle would hear.

'It's going to be another one of *those* times,' Simon said dispiritedly when she had gone off to have her bath.

'Mm. I suppose it was inevitable. Italy and all that. And it's been a few months since the last one.'

'Yes, but a . . . a nobody? A taxi driver?'

'Well, it could be worse. A London cabby, say.'

'Same sort of thing. April, I'm seriously worried about this one.'

'About Lissabelle? That's sweet of you to be worried about her, Simon, but she's old enough to look after herself.'

'No, no.' Simon shook his head impatiently. 'I'm not worried about her, I'm worrying about us.'

'Us?'

'At least the others were *somebody*. Booker Prize short-listers, or ex-patriot Eastern European ballet dancers. Controversial musicians, outrageous rock stars, that sort of thing. Men on the cutting edge of the media, right?'

'Well, yes, but—'

'Oh April, can't you see? There're no perks for us in this one.

51

No need to keep a diary, take notes, look through the wastepaper baskets for the written word, in case the *Sun* or one of the others wants to buy the story.'

Comprehension dawned on April's face. 'I see. Yes, I do see. Exactly.'

Simon was pacing the floor, agitation pouring from his body like smoke from a faulty exhaust. 'And worse. Shit, April, think of it!'

'What?' April racked her brain, but could not think of anything worse than what Simon had already said.

'The boredom. The awful, incredible boredom of a liaison with a . . . a *commoner.*'

'Ah.' April thought about this. 'But not for Lissabelle, right?' She was beginning to get the idea.

'Right. The only time Lissabelle will see him will be in bed. The pair of them don't need to do more than grunt a few times, then fall asleep. But we'll have to hear about it. Talk to him, pour him drinks. Listen to her go on about him.'

'Shit.'

They pondered this awful prospect until Lissabelle came out of the bath, clean and scented inside and out.

Midday. Venice sits, hot and sultry, like a mother hen with all her chicks. Not a feather is ruffled; there is no breeze, not even much movement on the Grand Canal, just one drifting gondola and a slow-moving vaporetto.

It is time to stir things up a bit, *la bella Venezia* murmurs, and suddenly, as if by an Act of God, a summer storm races with the speed of the *carabinieri* along the aquamarine water. The skies darken, the wind whirls and chops up the waves like propellers, thunder rolls and lightning flashes.

In the midst of this glitzy, theatrical panorama, a racy *motoscafo* zoomed through the roughened canal to come to an admirably sharp stop at the rickety pier of the Palazzo Bobolino.

To add to the drama of the scene, the two people in the motor taxi were shrieking at each other in voices that matched the thunder in vehemence and ferocity. Their light waterproof jackets flapped and slapped around their slim beautiful bodies and their angry faces dripped with rainwater.

The door of Apt. 3 opened, and a black umbrella, held by a young, pleasant nondescript young man, emerged. Dry and cosy underneath the umbrella was *signora* (but who preferred to be called a *signorina*), immaculately coiffed, groomed and polished, and showing a great deal of leg barely covered by a Versace frock. Behind the *signora* was another attractively nondescript young person, female this time, who was holding the other woman's Gucci handbag, mobile phone, and other items necessary to a luncheon at Harry's Bar in San Marco.

The three Englishpersons from Apt. 3 stepped into the boat, and the young Italian woman leaped out, closely followed by the Italian man, who unfortunately was the driver of the boat. Another argument followed, with much gesticulation and swear words in Veneziano, while the umbrella-lady hollared for the driver to come back, and the motorboat, tied to the pier, bobbed precariously in the water.

In the midst of this fiasco, the door of Apt. 1 was flung open and a man in black, with wild hair and a crimson waistcoat dangling with leather buckles, ran out into the rain and cried, 'Nina! I love you!'

The dark-haired woman, with a sob, flung herself into the bondage-clad man's arms, her thin waterproof tearing to shreds on the buckles of the waistcoat, and cried, '*Anch'io.* Me, too.'

The driver of the water taxi, trying to decide which of the two to strangle first, was distacted by a shout from his boat. The blonde woman with legs and Versace cried, 'Paolo,' and held out her arms. The rain, despite the black umbrella, had drenched her flimsy frock, and a full and blowzy bosom, as befits a literary lady novelist of great fame (though no books as yet), stood awaiting him. Along with the legs, of course.

Paolo hesitated. Then, shouting 'Sod the two of you,' or words to that effect in Italian, he turned his back on Nina and Marco and jumped back into his boat.

Miranda said, 'You *what*?'

She was sitting in the kitchen with Marco, giving him a drop of whisky she had found in the cupboard, and a strong hot coffee, for he was all a'shiver. She had just towelled his hair dry, and given him one of her daughter Jessica's dressing gowns to wear, for he appeared to have none of his own.

'I told her I loved her,' Marco said miserably.

Miranda poured herself a whisky as well. 'Fine. So what's the problem? You spent an hour this morning telling me and Netty you loved her, so now you've told her. That's great.'

'It'll ruin everything.'

'*What*? Why?'

'She said she loved me back.' Marco sneezed, and a most depressing little sneeze it was.

Miranda was getting impatient. She had had enough of the angst of young people in the last few years, when Jessica was pondering whether she was in or out of love with Piero, whom she had met on a school trip when she was a practice teacher. Miranda did not need another round of existential crises from a virtual stranger.

'Have you ever thought of anti-depressants, Marco? I hear there are some state of the art ones about these days.' She gulped her whisky.

He shook his head. And began to shiver uncontrollably. Despite herself, Miranda was beginning to feel sorry for him. She could not for the life of her think why.

Another whisky soon had Marco's eyes filling dangerously with tears. 'After I saw Nina that second time, on the water taxi, something happened to me.'

'Yes, yes, I know,' Miranda said, patience running thin. 'You fell in love with her. As you said this morning. Over and over.'

'And it transformed my life,' Marco went on, oblivious to Miranda's tone of voice, as obsessives usually are.

'It often does.' Ironic and wry, this was, but no chance of Marco noticing such subtlety.

'I want to . . . I want to . . .' Words failed Marco.

'I know, I know.' World-weary, slightly jaded. 'It happens to us all. You wanted to go out and buy your beloved the moon, give it to her on a gondola, throw yourself at her feet and make love to her over and over again, and then, when you were sated, stay at her side for ever.'

Marco looked up from his whisky in surprise. 'Er, no. Actually. All I wanted to do was to run out and paint a picture.'

'Oh. Ah, I see. Of Nina.'

'No, no.' Now Marco was impatient. That was the trouble with non C.P.s; they never understood you. 'I wanted to paint Venice. The Grand Canal, the sky, the Rialto, the Church of the Salute – anything. I just wanted to paint.'

'Oh. And did you?'

'*Did* I?' Marco's face took on the radiance of St Paul on his way to Damascus. 'I painted the best painting of my life!'

There was a pause. Miranda said cautiously, 'Well, that's good then, isn't it?'

At that, the tears really did begin to flow down Marco's freckled cheeks. Miranda blamed the whisky.

'It's fucking awful. The painting was good because I was in despair, I was in agony. Nina, my beloved, had just told me that she was engaged to that Paolo, so naturally my heart had broken.'

'Naturally. Excuse me for asking, but how can you say it so matter-of-factly? Just curious.'

Marco chose to ignore this. 'And this morning. When I woke and realized how overwhelming my love for her was, and how desperate it was, how she would never be mine—'

'But she is!' Miranda cried, trying to cheer the poor boy up for the tears were threatening again.

'I went out on to that pier and began another painting, even better than the first,' Marco went on, ignoring the interruption. 'Oh, Miranda, wait'll I show you, it's exquisite, it's the kind of work I've always wanted to do. From the depths of my despair, my terrible, unconsummated love for Nina, came a painting that would be worthy of any Biennale. God, how I wish that I'd met Nina years ago, I'd be right in there.'

Miranda was beginning to see where all this was leading. 'Marco, let me see if I've got this straight. You're in love with Nina, right?'

'Right.'

'And it's inspired you to paint your best pictures ever.'

'Uh huh.'

'But if Nina loves you back, you won't be in despair any more – as a matter of fact, you'll be happy, right?'

Marco nodded his head unhappily.

'So you'll no longer be inspired to paint masterpieces.'

'Got it in one.'

Miranda stood up. She paced around the little kitchen and opened the double doors to the balcony, then shut them again quickly as the wind and rain rampaged in. Then she sat down again and said, 'But there's one compensation, Marco. One grand, wonderful, amazingly terrific compensation that most people would be happy to exchange ten years of their lives for.'

'Oh?' Marco's face brightened slightly. 'What's that?'

'That the person you love truly, madly, deeply, is also in love with you.'

The freckles on Marco's face drooped again. 'I'd rather have a painting in the Biennale,' he said dolefully.

While this conversation was taking place, another was going on in Apt. I as well, only downstairs, in the bathroom which was situated next to the small bedroom which was now Frank the Swiss German's domain.

Nina had just taken a hot steamy bath, as ordered by Miranda, for the temperature had dropped considerably with the storm and she was not only soaked to her underwear, but also blue with cold. Netty had been despatched to find some dry clothes for her, while Miranda towelled off Marco. Now, Nina was dressed in something patterned and flowing, wrapped around her several times, and was sitting, hair turban-like in a towel, on the edge of the bath. On a small stool near the sink, squatted Netty, who was saying, 'Now see here. You musn't, you know. Cry like that. Oh, *do* pull yourself together, for goodness' sake.'

Nina sobbed harder.

'You *do* understand English, don't you?'

Nina nodded.

Netty found a handkerchief and after much blowing and snorting, Nina pulled herself together. 'I'm sorry,' she whimpered. 'It's all gone so wrong.'

'You mean the weather?' Netty could not think of anything else the girl could be complaining about. Netty had been peeping from the window and saw her in Marco's arms, and all was exactly as it should be, in Venice. Excitement, love, passion, romance – even a thunderstorm, to add to the drama.

'No, not the weather. Marco.'

'Marco? But he loves you, I heard it all. Thrilling, it was, absolutely thrilling!'

57

'But I don't love him,' Nina wailed.

Netty frowned. How un-Venetian of the child. Whatever was she thinking of? 'But you must. Love him.'

'I love Paolo,' she howled, and burst into tears again.

It took another fifteen minutes, but Netty finally understood that Nina had come along with Paolo for the ride, as she often did when she had a day off, only to decide to stop off at the Palazzo Bobolino when she found that the taxi was headed there.

'But why?' asked Netty.

'To see Marco, of course.'

It took another ten minutes to figure out why Nina wanted to see Marco, if she did not love him, or even, at this moment, seem to like him much. It was because she had just been to London visiting her sister, who lived there. Nina loved London, and wanted to marry Paolo and take him there where he would be a London cabby and she could be a well-paid waitress in a trendy Italian restaurant in Covent Garden, and they would all live happily ever after.

'That makes as much sense as a dog's dinner,' Netty said, not sure if that was quite the appropriate remark for this occasion, but what the hell. This was Venice, and anything went.

'Marco spoke to me so nicely in English, on the bus,' Nina said. 'I want to speak English with him all the time, to learn better and better.'

Netty agreed that this made sense, but that it was rather hard on Marco.

'I know,' Nina said miserably. 'Especially as I told him I love him too.'

'You *what*?' Netty was incredulous. She had not heard *that* bit. 'But why?'

'Because Paolo is jealous. Very, very jealous. He tried to forbid me to see Marco, even though I explained why. So I am angry. In fury. I show him, I say to me. I go anyway. You not boss man of I. Paolo say I sleep with Marco.'

'Do you mean you slept with him, or are planning to sleep with him? Past or future tense? My dear, you must calm down. Your English disintegrates appallingly when you are distraught.'

Nina regained possession of herself, or of her English at any rate. 'He said I wanted to have sex with Marco. Because he was English. Because I love England.'

'Oh.' This idea was so novel to Netty that she asked curiously, 'Would you like to sleep with an Englishman?' Having done so herself, with one or two (discreetly) before she was married, and then for all those years with her husband, she was quite curious to know.

'Only if it can help my English,' Nina said, without hesitation.

'Oh. Ah.' This was getting all too sophisticated for Netty, despite her dyed disco hair and her lust for foreign ways. She very nearly walked out of the bathroom. But then she thought about the cosmopolitan life *she* was leading. A great artist for a flatmate. A famous novelist in the same palazzo. A gondolier next door, and an assignation on a gondola for Saturday night. She sat firmly where she was.

Now Nina was becoming morose, and wracked with guilt. 'Ah *Madonna*, I should not say to Marco, that I too was in love. You agree?'

'Oh yes.' Netty nodded her head fiercely, and many red curls, damp and frizzy from the steamy bathroom, fell in her face. 'Unless, of course,' she went on with a tiny giggle, 'you want to learn English properly. They say that the best way to learn a language is with a lover.' She giggled again, thinking that she would begin speaking Italian with Silvano, when they became lovers. As soon as she learned a few rudiments of the language, that is.

Unfortunately, Nina did not possess a sense of humour. 'I see.

Veramente, what you say is true. Think how good it will be, for Paolo and me in London, after I have had Marco for a lover. My English will be perfect. I will do it, for the sake of Paolo. For his career in England.'

She stood up, thanked Netty warmly for the use of her clothes, and swooped out of the bathroom, a green towel still draped regally around her Roman – or Sicilian, in this case – brow.

Netty, awash with astonishment not unmixed with admiration, sat a while, and thought.

When she could not find fault with Nina's logic – due, no doubt, to the influence of The Most Serene Republic – she too left the bathroom.

Chapter Five

When Miranda was at last alone in the house, she began to fret about things. It was what she hated most about Venice, how it made her fret.

It was evening; the rain had stopped, the sun shone grandly on the Grand Canal. Miranda sulked.

Opposite her on the right of the balcony, the stunning Gothic facade of Ca' d'Oro, the palazzo known as the House of Gold, gleamed in the clean, washed sunlight. Miranda stared at it, unimpressed. Give her the solid no-nonsense fortified walls of Ludlow Castle any day.

The downstairs door banged, steps bounded up. A blond Germanic head peered on to the tiny balcony where Miranda sat, desultorily plaiting her long brown hair. She did this often when she was fraught. Jessica's father had smiled fondly at this, said he always knew when she was on edge by the state of her hair. A long plait meant stress; a loose pony tail, that she was both contented and in control of her life. How the hell he presumed to know these things, Miranda thought bitterly, when he only knew her for ten days, was beyond her. It showed an arrogance beyond words. Thank God she had never seen him again.

It was when her hair was loose and wild that he loved her

best, he had said. It had been that way the night they met, which happened to also have been the night Jessica was conceived.

It had happened here in Venice, in a small hotel by a deep green canal, and though Miranda loved her daughter, she loathed watery places. They made her feel flaky, as she had when she was nineteen, and in the city for the very first time.

A clipped voice chipped at her reverie like a brisk woodpecker on a plane tree, pecking her back into the present. 'Miranda, you are here.' Frank, she had noticed during the short time he had been at the Palazzo Bobolino, was quite clever at stating the obvious.

'This is true,' Miranda said, voice rich with irony. She wanted to be left alone to brood.

Irony was lost on Frank, as humour was lost on Nina. 'Yes,' he said, acknowledging the fact.

Miranda waited. The two white cats, Tommasina and Topolino, walked daintily along the balustrade, snarling at passing sparrows, seagulls and *gondolieri*. Miranda wondered sometimes how they managed not to fall off into the green and sparkling (and often murky) water. Sometimes, when they hissed and spat with rude bad temper, she wished they would.

Frank was dressed in practical shorts and a crisp cotton short-sleeved shirt. His feet were in sandals that looked as if they could climb every mountain, stride up any hill, however pebbly. He said, 'Tonight, I make the dinner.'

'Oh?'

'My turn. I understanding.'

Since in the few days that everyone had been living together in the Palazzo Bobolino, nobody had really had dinner but seemed to be living in an unorganized manner of takeaway pizza (Marco), a thrown-together salad with lettuce leaves and various sundries from the Rialto market (Miranda) and exotic Venetian treats from the tiny shop around the corner (Netty), Miranda wondered what Frank was on about.

He went on. 'I have boughten many wondrous things from the Standa *supermercado*. Italian things. We here to learn things Italian, all. So we eat Italian.'

It was a statement that left no room for argument. Frank went on, 'I see that in kitchen, there is no rota.'

'Rota?'

'For Duties and Responsibilities.'

'Ah.'

'So I have made one.' Frank held up a pristine sheet of white A4 paper. On it, in black felt tip, and very neat indeed, was a list of domestic chores, such as Washing the Dishes; Emptying the Rubbish; Cooking the Dinner; and so on. Under each heading was one of their names, and the date and the time.

'Oh,' Miranda said weakly.

'Tonight, I cook. See?'

He pointed proudly to his name. Miranda saw. 'He who cooks, shops,' Frank said sternly. 'Is only fair, yes?'

'Uh, I suppose so.'

'And this is pot.'

For a moment Miranda thought that he meant dope, especially when he disappeared for a moment. 'Here,' he announced. It was not gear after all but an empty sugar bowl with a lid. 'We all put share for dinner here in pot.' He plonked it ceremoniously on the kitchen table. Several thousand lire notes poked out from under the lid. 'My share,' he said.

Miranda thought she should make some kind of protest. She was, after all, the landlady, and theoretically in charge. But trying to stop him seemed to require more energy that she had at the moment. And besides, he was beginning to hum a tuneless tune, happily pottering in the kitchen, creating his Italian meal. She decided to let him be.

The next person to shatter Miranda's mood, which was just

as well since she was beginning to get maudlin, was Netty. 'Oh Miranda, it is perfectly splendid, splendid!'

'What is?'

Netty looked at her in some surprise. 'This!' she cried, sweeping her arms out and nearly knocking Topolino off his perch on the balustrade.

'Oh. You mean Venice.'

Netty went on at great length about gondolas, cathedrals, Art and Beauty. Miranda yawned. She had heard all this before, when Jessica fell in love with both Venice and Piero. She had not been impressed then, either, having done the same thing when she was even younger than Jessica. Luckily, her daughter had the sense to hang on to the father of her baby, and even marry him beforehand. Miranda had nothing against Venice, except that it was foreign. She had nothing against foreign *per se*, except that it had made her pregnant, when she was quite young, and quite, quite unmarried, at a time when it was frowned upon to be both.

And it was a foreigner who had done it to her. Though, strictly speaking, they had done it to each other, and quite happily too, not to mention joyfully. Though he was not Italian, he was certainly European. Eastern European, but what the hell, they were the same thing now. Europe was Europe; she wanted no part of it. Nor of Europeans. She was glad England was putting up a fine defence against it all.

Frank popped his Teutonic head outside the balcony to say, 'Everything on the schedule. Dinner is to be had at the seven o'clock.' His head popped back into the kitchen, from where wafted the smell of burning garlic.

'Schedule?' Netty looked bewildered.

'Oh yes.' Miranda nodded tiredly. 'And your turn to-morrow.'

'Turn?'

'Yes. To cook.'

64

Netty looked bewildered. She had not cooked a meal for years. Marks and Spencer were quite adequate, thank you very much, even before Herbert died. And bless him, he never could distinguish between one of their meals and one of her own. She saw no reason whatsoever to clue him in.

Miranda went on, 'The rest of the week's rota is pinned up on the fridge. Frank's idea.'

Netty went pale. She did not come to Venice to be on some kind of a rota; there was enough of that at the church committee meetings. 'We'll see about that,' she said darkly, and stomped off the balcony and into the kitchen.

Several hours later, Marco, Netty and Miranda were crowded around the small kitchen table crunched up in the corner, while Frank dished up an odd sort of pasta dish, comprising tomato paste, burnt garlic, tagliatelle and not much else. 'Eat, eat,' he encouraged, finally taking his place at the head of the table and wolfing his portion down with immense energy and, apparently, enjoyment.

The others ate, because they were famished. Netty, who had bought several bottles of Pinot Nero earlier in the day, brought them out, and after that the meal improved. Marco even asked for seconds, but then his day had been so intense, it was no wonder.

Netty asked first, after her second glass of the red wine. 'I say, Marco. Where is your young lady? I don't want to pry, of course. I merely ask because she was wearing one of my tunic tops when the two of you went out. I have dried her own clothes, and I thought she could change back into them when you brought her back here.'

Marco said nothing, but kept stuffing his face with pasta and garlic.

Frank looked up from his plate and said, 'Nina? I have not

heard of this Nina. Is not on rota. Why did someone not tell me of a Nina? Now, I have to change rota all again.' He leaped up from the table, preparing to do it then and there.

Miranda said, 'Nina doesn't live here. She's, ah, Marco's *ragazza*.'

'Pardon?'

'What?'

'Excuse me?'

'Sorry, I forgot you two haven't started your Italian lessons yet. And Marco, she *is*. Your girlfriend. Whatever you say.'

Miranda was impatient with Marco. The cheek of the man, putting his paintings above the woman he was supposed to love, and who loved him. The man she had once loved, Jessica's father, had been an artist, one of those horrible creative types who had left her for a lump of stone. He was a sculptor.

But she did not want to think about him. Frank was busily writing down, in a little notebook he had in his shirt pocket: *ragazza* – girlfriend. Netty was saying to Marco, 'Anyway, I suppose you'll be seeing her tomorrow?'

Marco nodded glumly. 'We're meeting for dinner, at the trattoria where she works.' It had been Marco's tentative idea, this meeting. He had felt that something was called for, after that declaration of love in the courtyard. Nina seemed to expect something too, and took up his suggestion with such alacrity that it depressed him for the rest of the afternoon. Much as he loved her, he would have preferred it if she had found some obstacle, such as Paolo, or a vow of celibacy, or whatever. Not something that would have prevented her being entirely devoted to him, but an obstacle or two that could have kept them tragically apart, at least until he finished the painting he had started in the first blaze of passion.

Netty waited to be further enlightened on the Marco/Nina affair, but Marco had clammed up. So instead, she turned her attention to Frank.

'Oh, I say, Frank. About these dinners.'

'Yes. Good, no?'

'Oh, ah, yes. Delicious.' Netty was nothing if not polite, and the lad after all had tried his best.

'Tomorrow – you.' He beamed at her, rosy face shiny with heat and the aftermath of burnt garlic.

'We must talk about these dinners, Frank, and this rota you have set up. I am not entirely sure—'

'Oh Netty, you are displeased?'

'It's just that I do not think—'

'Is because I have give to you the rubbish disposal duty for two days straight?' Frank tore the piece of paper from the fridge to look at it frantically. 'Say nothing more, I understanding.'

'I assure you, it is not—'

'You are justly within rights. I do understanding. I am having your point.'

'No, listen—'

But Frank was beyond listening. He was taking his black felt tip pen and crossing out lines, adding squiggles. 'There,' he said triumphantly, waving the paper about the table. 'I have it done. Better now, for you.'

Netty opened her mouth but before anything could come out, Frank went on, 'I myself have taken on this rubbish job. For one of two days, so. You will me forgive, please, Netty, I hope very much.'

He looked at her with such sweet steely blue eyes that she gave up without a further struggle.

In Apt. 4, Silvano and Elena were eating *sarde*, fresh sardines cooked in olive oil, onions and garlic. There was no smell of burning garlic here, only the pungent aroma of the very best virgin oil, along with the fish and onions. Elena might be a witch and a shrew, Silvano thought fondly of his wife, but she was also a wonderful cook. Her risottos were especially fine.

Silvano was eating hurriedly, for it was a fine summer's evening, after the storm, and the city was teeming, with not just the normal amount of June tourists, but with those coming to either set up, participate in, be seen at, write about, talk about, be seen to be seen at, the Biennale. All sorts of government officials were pouring in, and museum officials and art ministers, and people who gave grants and ran foundations. Cherie Blair was flying in for a private viewing, and so was an Italian porn star who was running for arts minister.

And of course those few genuine art lovers who were nobody, but who came along anyway because they wanted to see what was going on in the contemporary world of modern art.

Not that any of this had any interest for Silvano. He had never been to the Biennale, even though it was on in Venice once every two years. But he had seen enough of it round and about the city. Neon-splattered on the walls of ancient palazzos with things like IMAGE IS ART or BIRDS FLY written in huge lit letters, God knew why. Even on the vaporetti, slogans like: If this wall was not here, a buffalo could walk through. *Allora*, how obvious can you get? If a wall was not there, anything could walk through. And *per l'amore di Dio*, when were there ever buffalo in Venezia?

No, the point of the Biennale was that it was a decent money-spinner. After all that dull art, the punters were ripe for a gondola ride. Most of them who came for the Biennale were rich too, and would pay top prices, especially if they wanted a clandestine midnight ride with partners who were obviously, and furtively, not part of their entourage.

'*Delizioso, Elena.*' Silvano smacked his lips. He got up, dropping his napkin on the floor, and casually kissed her cheek, leaving her with half her dinner on the plate, and a pile of dishes in the sink ready to be washed.

'By the way,' he called out to her as he walked out the door, 'I've left my white gondoliere shirt on the bed, could you have it washed and ready by tomorrow? And there's another striped one as well.'

He bounced out jauntily, belching as he went.

Elena sat. She sat for a long time. She stared out the window of the kitchen, which looked out over an alleyway and another building, as their apartment had no views of the Grand Canal. Those were far too expensive for the likes of them, born and bred in Venice; they were rented out to foreigners, or to the odd lucky Venetian like Piero in Apt. 1, who had an English wife.

Elena shuddered, not at the idea of an English wife, but at the idea of wifehood in general. Marriage to Silvano was not much fun, now that he was too burnt-out to do anything more than grunt goodnight before falling into a snoring sleep. Elena was into fun; it livened up her home town considerably. She loved Venezia, but it was like any other small town: dull at times if you didn't make an effort.

She got up and wandered into the courtyard, where Tommasina and Topolino were waiting for scraps. She threw the leftover sardines on the cracked stone wellhead and sat down on the wobbly bench under the old and neglected fig tree, watching the cats scrabbling for the food.

By and by, Netty came out.

Elena eyed her boldly, as she had been eyeing her for the past few days. Netty, springy with guilt, bounced over to her with over-familiarity, to compensate for the fact that she was about to betray her, on Saturday night with her husband.

'*Buona sera, signora*,' Netty cried. 'Lovely evening, after all that rain, what? Cleared the air beautifully.'

She was not quite sure how much English Elena could understand or speak, so she babbled on some more, thinking that if she repeated it enough times, the woman would catch on.

Elena listened, apparently attentively, and Netty was encouraged to carry on. 'I do believe we will have a most pleasant night. Not so hot and sticky as last night. But the rain has been so good for the jasmine, don't you think?'

Elena watched her unnervingly as she talked. Netty had changed into trousers, but unlike the straight tight black trousers the Italian woman wore, Netty's were wide and flowing and very, very orange. She had a loose long-sleeved top of the same colour, which came down to her knees. Around her neck she had four or five strands of wooden beads, a duller, saner marmalade colour. It all clashed terribly with her hair, and the purple of her lips, but nonetheless Elena was impressed. Bizarre the woman might be, looking today like a member of one of those obscure Indian sects that occasionally floated around the city, all those amber flowing things flapping about like some great orange bird. Yes, bizarre she was, and outrageous, flaunting all that un-dieted flesh, but it had to be said, Netty was swanning about sightseeing and flirting with another woman's husband while Elena sat home.

And did the washing-up, and then the soaking of the gondolier's shirt so that it would be pristine for tomorrow. And later, while Netty went off for a Prosecco in some amusing campo or another, with lively foreign friends, she, Elena, would be at her son and daughter-in-law's place, baby-sitting her three grandchildren. As she was called upon to do several times a week, while they too went off for sparkling wine and a fun night out with friends.

Elena thought about these things. Light began to dawn.

Netty, assuaging her guilt, talked on. She could have assuaged it far quicker by calling off her rendezvous with Silvano, but if that annoying little thought zizzed into her brain, she slapped it away as she would a mosquito.

Elena thought, *The Englishwoman is free. Independent. Husband-less and therefore Having Fun.*

Netty said, 'The wisteria this time of year – stunning. Odd, you know, I thought wisteria was so English, yet here it is, on all the old Venetian walls. Astounding.'

Now if I got rid of Silvano . . .

'And the colour, my dear! Against the brick of the buildings. Superb.'

Or better yet, got him to leave me . . .

'I wouldn't like to lose the apartment,' Elena said aloud, unthinkingly. Fortunately she spoke in Veneziano and Netty did not understand.

'Oh, you agree? About the wisteria?' Netty cried eagerly, clutching at straws.

'Oh yes,' Elena replied, in decent English indeed, though spoken with a strong American accent. She had learned from Silvano, who had learned from the Americans, his best customers.

The Italian woman put her arm through the Englishwoman's. 'You must come to our apartment for an *aperitivo* one evening. Silvano speaks so well of you.'

'He does?' Netty smiled, flattered, quite forgetting that it was his wife she was talking to.

'Oh yes. And I am so pleased.'

'You are?'

'Very much.'

She too smiled, fondly and conspiratorially at Netty, who, remembering who Elena was, felt most uncomfortable.

'So. That is settled. We are friends, *vero*?'

'Uh, yes. *Vero, vero*. Why yes, of course we are. Chums, ha ha.'

How very foreign the foreigners were, Netty thought in wonder. She could get used to them. And to Venice. Especially to Venice.

I could live here, she thought. I could live here and be a . . . a courtesan, she said to herself, with a tiny thrill of excitement. But only for Silvano, of course, she added primly. She could

71

sell her house in Buckinghamshire, buy a tiny apartment here, be available for gondola-tripping at all times. Why, she would be part of the great history of the Venetian Republic, when courtesans flourished, had power over the men of state that no mere wife ever had.

The best of it was, Elena approved. Who could misunderstand that wink, that nudge? That little squeeze she was giving, to Netty's elbow. By Jove, they seem to have come to some kind of understanding, the two of them: Silvano's wife and soon-to-be mistress. How sophisticated the Venetians were!

Elena, as she waved an effusive *arrivederci* to her new English friend, was thinking how interesting life would be, how exciting, when Netty went back to England, with Silvano in tow. No cooking, no ironing those pesky gondolier's shirts, no snoring husband next to her in the double bed but perhaps some younger, friskier gentleman friend who didn't mind a bit of fun now and again.

She went back inside the apartment, and ignoring the washing-up, and her husband's shirt, she began to plan a new, younger wardrobe, for when Silvano finally became no longer an Anglo-phile, but English.

Netty, in the estate agent's, was planning on home furnishings, for when she finally became wholly Venetian. The estate agent, handing her brochures and price listings, looked bored. People like Netty were not uncommon, wanting to live out their fantasies unmindful of the fact that it would bankrupt them (house prices being what they were in Venice), give them permanent rheumatism (the damp and the *aqua alta* being what it was in Venice) and completely cut them off from all Venetians (even if, unlike Netty, they spoke Italian), for everyone in Venice spoke Veneziano, which no one but Venetians could understand.

But a sale was a sale after all. The man agreed to show

72

Netty some properties later in the week, in salubrious areas, for the Englishwoman seemed well-heeled. He himself lived on the mainland, in Mestre; there was no way he could afford to buy property in the city where he was born.

The estate agent's was just off St Mark's Square, so Netty wandered across the great Piazza, admiring the curvy contours and gilt and froth of the Basilica, with the long queue of discontented visitors waiting to get in. She wove past pigeons and pigeon shit, and sellers of pigeon food guaranteed to make the pigeons shit even more. Finally she was at the edge of the lagoon. To her left was the Doge's Palace, in all its Gothic glory, and in front of it, a flotilla of gondolas, the *gondolieri* touting for business.

'Yoo hoo, Silvano!' Netty cried.

It was now Friday, and she was well aware how close this was to Saturday. She was wearing trousers again, wide and floppy and as yellow as her sunhat, which perched merrily atop her gleaming curls. She felt daring, a free spirit.

Silvano's mates, the older *gondolieri*, watched her tripping skittishly towards them, her eyes only for Silvano, and spent several enjoyable moments poking him in the ribs, making ribald comments and indulging in some playful mock-jealousy. Secretly, they were torn between envy and relief. It was one thing to shout, Good old Silvano, you haven't lost it, women still hang out around your gondola, you old dog, you! But silently they remembered that the poor fellow would have to pay the price, and at his age, it wasn't quite the carefree lark it used to be when they were all in their lusty youth. All that gondoliering in the middle of the night – it didn't get easier, when you got older. And then, after a silent dark tour alongside the more romantic back canals (hard work, that), Silvano would be expected to be Italian, and macho, and croon nonsense words that sounded like words of love into the woman's ear while at the same time taking off her clothes and trying to keep the gondola from tipping over, and – *porca miseria*, when you thought about it, it was enough to give you a heart attack from the stress. Not to mention the actual performance, which had to be of the highest calibre, in order to maintain the reputation of the league of *gondolieri*.

'Netty, *bella*, hello my dearest, *ciao, tesoro*,' Silvano called to her, well aware of the admiring looks of his colleagues. He kissed her enthusiastically on both cheeks. He decided he adored her. How good she was for him, for his reputation amongst his fellows, for his morale, his self-esteem. She would grace his gondola with her feisty presence, yet would demand nothing in return, merely a *bella* or two in Italian, the occasional cappuccino in Florian's, and perhaps an unstressful cuddle or two on the Rialto Bridge at midnight now and again.

Netty had, in the past couple of days, been hanging out a great deal around the gondola mooring stage at the piazzetta. It made her feel so Venetian, hobnobbing with gondoliers. She felt she knew the city like no one else, standing there bantering with them all. But then she had always felt she knew Venice better than anyone else, even before she had been there.

'Silvano, I've something to show you.' Netty, after she had flirted coyly with the other gondoliers for a bit, opened her capacious yellow handbag, to show him the leaflets from the estate agent. But before she could get them out she suddenly shut it again.

'What is it, *cara*?'

'No, I've changed my mind. It must be a surprise for you, Silvano. You will know when the deed is done.'

Silvano nodded. He did not think it of any importance. He knew how whimsical the English were; it was only one of the many reasons why he adored them.

'*Bellissima* Netty, may I take you to Florian's? For a cappuccino?' It was mid-morning, and time for his break. Business had been particularly good already; there were huge parties of Japanese there for a long weekend before doing the Gucci and Armani shops in Florence; and other parties of Americans having a quick tour of Venice before descending on the Colosseum in Rome. Both groups were early risers — there was so much to do in Europe, and so little time! — and his gondola had been out a couple of times already. It was only just past eleven.

'Oh, that would be splendid. But I insist upon paying this time. I know what the prices are at Florian's.'

But Silvano would not hear of that. He respected Netty too much to let her take the bill.

Especially as his cousin was on duty this morning.

They were not the first ones at Florian's that morning. As Netty and Silvano sat themselves at a table outside, at a prominent place where Netty felt they could be most envied and admired by all the tourists, of whom she, of course, was not one, a shiny blonde with impossible legs eased into a nearby table. With her were two younger, though less attractive, people, dressed discreetly to the point of blandness.

'Good gracious, Silvano, is that our neighbour?' Netty cried. 'It is. The famous novelist who is renting Apt. 3.'

Silvano had already noticed Lissabelle. He was too busy tarting up his fluffy tufts with deft fingertips to reply to Netty, who went on, 'She is such a creative person, my dear. So wrapped up in her work, like Marco. I've passed her once or twice in the courtyard at the palazzo, but she must not have seen me; her face was a picture of concentration. Very intense indeed. Creative people have to be, you know.' She inclined her head sagely.

Simon was ordering iced champagne for Lissabelle, and of course for themselves as well. They were pretending to be celebrating the fact that the famous author had spent a half-hour this morning actually writing, but in reality they were posing for the tourists. Lissabelle thought it her duty to give the common day-trippers and coach parties and three-day holidaymakers a bit of Venetian glamour, which she, of course, could provide much better than the natives. Venice, like New York last year and Paris the year before that, was her creative and artistic home; it belonged to her, far more than it did to the tourists. Or the Venetians themselves, for that matter.

'Yoo hoo, Lissabelle! Remember me? Netty? Your neighbour in Apt. 1.'

Lissabelle glanced at the next table and shuddered. That was the trouble with San Polo, they let such riff-raff into places like the Palazzo Bobolino. She pretended she did not recognize Netty and turned to April, who had raised her glass of bubbly and was congratulating Lissabelle on the completion of her fifty scintillating words of literary merit for the day. The trouble was, those words had so worn her out that it would be weeks before she could face her laptop again.

Netty, having herself snubbed many a cheeky over-familiar shopgirl or a curate who did not know his place, recognized a rebuff when she saw one. She bristled. And prepared her attack.

'Lissabelle, hallo! I waved at you yesterday, when you and that taxi driver were madly kissing each other goodbye at the pier, but you must not have seen me, just as you didn't see me just now. Lucky old you, to find a handsome beau so quickly.' Netty stopped, pleased with herself. Famous author and creative person the woman may be, but that was no excuse for snobbery.

She smiled sweetly at Lissabelle, who had whirled around at this, making little mewing and gasping noises to get the woman to shut up. Paolo with the teeth was hunky, true; and no, the teeth certainly did not get in the way when he put his smooth Italian tongue erotically down her throat and then ran it gently across her lips as he kissed her goodbye yesterday. Lissabelle had high hopes from him; as a matter of fact, she had decided that she was besotted with him. It was no fun being in Venice without being besotted, what was the point? But that was another problem with San Polo. In Dorsoduro, there were the better sort to choose from, men who were very very rich, and often famous, as she was. Lissabelle knew that as much as she was intensely passionate about, and crazy in love with, Paolo, there was no need for the world to know it. It would not do her media-cred one column inch of good.

'Netty, darling, how positively marvellous to see you here!' she cried, as the older woman was opening her mouth to go on about the scene she had witnessed on the water taxi. 'Do join us, darling; no, don't say another word until you've moved over here to our table. Waiter, another glass, please. And another bottle, why not?'

Netty, satisfied, said regally, 'Thank you, my dear. My friend and I would be happy to join you.'

Simon and April grinned at each other as Silvano followed Netty to their table. Lissabelle had turned pale. To be seen in Venice in the company of a gondolier! She would be the laughing-stock of the style police, of everyone she knew. A gondolier's proper place was in a gondola, discreetly gliding his craft from the Hotel Danieli to the opera at the Fenice theatre; or, now that it was burnt down, to some place equally as exclusive. With the rich and the bored and the famous in the gondola, of course. Like Lissabelle herself.

Gondolieri did not know their place these days. They paddled up and down the canals with flocks of Japanese and Germans inside, or, far worse, sat in places like Florian's as if they were somebody.

Netty was settling in nicely at their table, as was the horrid gondolier, his straw hat placed brazenly on the table next to the ice bucket. Netty said loudly, in her brash and braying voice, 'Lissabelle, this is our neighbour in Apt. 4, Silvano Gemilinni.'

Silvano held out his hand grandly, always ready to impress another tourist. Lissabelle said blankly, 'Neighbour?'

'Yes, at the Palazzo Bobolino. Silvano and his wife Elena live in the apartment next to ours, opposite you. Apt. 4,' she repeated patiently, as if to the simple-minded.

Lissabelle had no choice but to shake, limply, the hand offered to her. She looked horrified. Netty thought, serves you right, you silly creative person, you. Famous or not, she was strongly inclined to loathe Lissabelle, after the snub. Giving herself airs like that. Well, Netty showed her. All Lissabelle could hook was a taxi driver with teeth, but she, Netty, had landed a gondolier.

Smugly, she scoffed her champagne as if it were Guinness, which she was partial to after a brief but jolly holiday in Cork after Herbert had died. Silvano preened. He talked a great deal, deliriously happy to be in the company of all these delightful, friendly Anglo-Saxons. He must live there, he decided in the middle of his third glass of bubbly; the English were extraordinary. So kind, so up-front, so genteel and gentle. All those afternoon teas. And everyone sitting around in lush green and golden gardens drinking champagne with their morning cappuccino, as they were doing now. Everyone, that is, but Elena. The most beautiful thing about England was that his wife was not on that green and misty island, nor ever would be. She hated the place.

Silvano looked at Netty with his swimmy brown eyes, prepared to follow his newly found beloved to the ends of the world.

Which was, of course, England.

Chapter Six

Saturday afternoon in June. Venice, gem of the Adriatic, glistens gaudily in the sunlight, the beams bouncing off Byzantine mosaics with the same insouciance as they do off the tourists and pigeon shit in Piazza San Marco.

Venice, the old tart, twinkles mischievously in Campo San Polo too, where little Venetian children on tricycles pedal furiously around the public benches, ramming into red-faced Germans and freshly showered Americans, who tell them snappily to watch where they are going. How pleasant Venice would be, think the tourists, as their comfortable walking shoes step into another dog turd and they trip over another tiny tot on the trike, if there were no Venetians with dogs and children.

La Serenissima smiles sunnily, and sends down more hot sultry sunbeams. How she loves being loved. Luringly, she tempts the hot disgruntled tourists back into the fold, with *gelato* like they have never tasted before, under shady awnings of grapevines in sweet outdoor cafés filled with amiable waiters and tall iced drinks. And then, to top it all, with a glimpse of the most perfect sparkling green canal floating beneath an exquisite Gothic window.

The Japanese and Australians, the British and French, the Germans and Swiss, fall for it every time, and once again fall in love with *la bella Venezia* as they sit in the shade and watch the world go by, in gondolas of course, against a backdrop of architectural splendour. How Venice laughs at this. But fondly.

'Nina, *Dio*, will you calm down? I didn't go to bed with the *maledetta* Englishwoman, I only kissed her goodbye. On the *maledetto* boat. *Porca miseria*. In the rain, *per l'amore di Dio*.'

'Stop swearing so much, Paolo. And why did you kiss her goodbye, eh? What d'you think I am, *stupida*? She was only your passenger. Or do you always kiss your passengers goodbye?'

Paolo and Nina, sitting on a bench in Campo San Polo, were enjoying the sultry afternoon's siesta having a flaming row before going back to work. Nina had heard about The Kiss from Marco who had heard it from Frank who had heard it from Netty.

Paolo said that no, he did not usually kiss his passengers goodbye. The Englishwoman, Lisabelle, had been particularly friendly, and he had been after a good tip. This was not strictly true; what he had been after was making Nina jealous, after she had rushed into Marco's arms. Though he had to admit, though not to Nina of course, that the kiss was not unpleasant. It tasted of expensive after-dinner mints and smelled like hothouse flowers.

'And what about *you*?' Paolo said accusingly. 'Rushing into the Englishman's arms?'

'Only because you were so unreasonably jealous, just because I wanted to see him to practise my English.' Nina did not add that she would probably sleep with him too, for the very same reason.

They slumped into a glum silence. A few stray cats wandered around the campo, looking for shade under the leafy trees. A pigeon settled next to one of them, but the cat merely lifted a jaded eye and ignored it. It was too hot.

A French couple on the bench next to Nina and Paolo looked at each other in disappointment. They were sorry that the row seemed to be over. They had been enjoying the spectacle of

Italians shrieking at each other in public. It made them feel so superior, which of course they were.

'*Allora*, I forgive you,' Nina said, because she had another appointment and wanted to get rid of Paolo, for the time being. 'Only don't let it happen again.'

'It's the furthest thing from my mind,' muttered Paolo through his gleamy white teeth, though it was actually the only thing in his mind these days, ever since he had taken the sleek Englishwoman (with those two other friends of hers whose faces Paolo could not remember) to Harry's Bar. Not that he particularly fancied the woman, though she did taste nice. It was just that he had never slept with someone who was famous before. He knew that she was famous because those two who were always with her had told someone in the Palazzo Bobolino who had told Elena who was married to Silvano, who was a friend of Paolo's father. Nobody was quite sure what exactly she was famous *for*, but that was unimportant. Fame is fame, after all.

'Anyway,' Paolo went on, '*I'll* forgive *you*. For embracing the Englishman with all that unfashionable hair. If you promise you will never go near him again.'

Nina shrugged, and began kissing Paolo passionately so that he would not notice that she did not promise anything.

The French couple exchanged lofty looks and condescending smiles at this new display of Italian vulgarity.

As arranged, Marco and Nina met in the Campo Maria Formosa, well away from the Campo San Polo. She met him inside the Ca' Nostra Trattoria where she worked, so as not to be spotted by Paolo should he chance to come whizzing on his boat down the narrow canal at one end of the campo, on his way to pick up or deliver a passenger.

There were few people inside, most of them tourists choosing to remain outside despite the heat, huddling under gaudy umbrellas and bright awnings at their tables. Inside it was far cooler. Marco, spotting Nina, said, 'Shouldn't we go outside? While there's sunshine?' He was not a mad dog, but he was an Englishman.

'Don't be *stupido*,' Nina said. 'Sit down.'

Her tetchiness gave him hope. Perhaps she was going to break it all off? He looked at her with new longing, with fresh passion. God, how he adored her.

'God, how I adore you!' he cried, taking her hand.

She whipped it away quickly. 'Don't do that,' she hissed. The bartender, Gianni, knew Paolo, knew she was engaged to him.

'But why?' Marco asked, frantic now. He felt his heart would break, if he was not able to clutch her hand, hold it to his throbbing heart.

'Paolo!' she cried theatrically. Gianni, behind the bar and craning to eavesdrop, dropped a glass of Campari. Nina looked furtively at him and lowered her voice. 'Because of my fiancé.'

Marco shook his head. 'I have lost you to Paolo? With the teeth?' The black dog of despair took him in its own sharp teeth and shook him to shreds. He shivered with excitement.

She nodded sombrely. 'I'm engaged to him. Remember?'

'But you love me!'

She lowered her eyes, nodded tragically, obviously too moved to speak. Her fingers were crossed underneath the table. If she did not say it, it was not quite a lie.

Marco said cautiously, 'I don't understand.'

'It is honour, Marco. I cannot break off my engagement.'

Marco knew about the honour of the Italians. He had seen *The Godfather*. 'I see,' he said, looking at the bartender nervously, wondering if he came from Sicily. Gianni, drying a wine glass, narrowed his eyes.

Nina looked up at Marco, her eyes soft. Christ, how he loved her! God, how he was suffering.

She said, 'But it need not mean goodbye, *caro*.' She looked at Gianni, to make sure he was well out of hearing.

'It *can't* be goodbye.' Marco tried to clutch her hand under the table, casting sly glances at the bartender. He did after all love Nina. He did not want his heart broken to such an extent that it stopped working properly, and he could no longer paint.

Gianni, gazing out the open doorways into the campo, shouted something to Nina in Veneziano, scaring the hell out of Marco. Nina whispered to Marco, 'Quick, out the back door. Hurry.'

'Why?' But he was already up.

'Paolo's on his way here. Quick.'

When Marco was safely gone, and as Paolo was approaching the trattoria, Nina said to the bartender, '*D'accordo*. All right, I owe you one.'

Gianni grinned. 'Half your tips tonight.'

'Steep, isn't it?'

'Protection money. Worth every lira.' He was a Sicilian.

'Done.' Nina and Gianni shook hands. It would be a good investment, Nina thought, satisfied. For peace of mind, while she pursued her English lessons.

'No use ringing the bell,' Miranda said to the fresh-faced man standing at the Palazzo Bobolino. 'It doesn't work. None of them do.'

The man smiled at her eagerly. 'Hey, that's real cool, letting me know. Thanks for that.' He waited, expectantly.

Miranda looked warily at him, for traces of heavy sarcasm. There appeared to be none. The face was as bubbly and open as a baby, and with the same expression of infant blandness. It was as chubby and clean as a baby's too. The eyes were innocent. *Naïve*, more likely, Miranda thought. The man was forty if he was a day, but his face looked six months old, as if it were waiting for life to catch up with it.

Miranda said cautiously, 'I have a key, if you need to get in. Who are you looking for?'

The man looked as if angels had come to rest on Miranda's shoulders. 'Neat. That's real nice of you, I sure do appreciate this. The name's Bruce Brinson.' He held out a clean and honest hand. 'I'm not looking for a who,' he went on as they entered the courtyard together, 'I'm looking for an apartment. Number 2. This *is* the Palazzo Bob, isn't it?'

'Pardon?'

'The Palazzo Bob-something-or-other. Didn't get its last name.' Bruce giggled. It sounded like the tinkling of baby wind chimes.

'The Palazzo Bobolino. Yes. You're, ah, renting an apartment?'

'You bet I am. Right on the Grand Canal, or so the real estate guy in New York promised.' For a moment Bruce looked worried. His face took on the expression of an infant with wind. 'Say, he wasn't conning me, was he? That bit of water over there looks kinda pokey.'

'That's the Grand Canal all right.'

'No kidding.' Bruce looked doubtful. Then he perked up. He looked at Miranda eagerly. 'You my landlady?'

'No, but I live below your apartment, in No. 1.' Miranda told him briefly who she was. Then she had no choice but to invite him in, so that she could phone the estate agent here in Venice who was supposed to be meeting Bruce at the Palazzo Bobolino, to give him a key and show him inside.

'Well hey, look at this,' Bruce cried, as he and Miranda settled, with a cup of coffee, on to the tiny balcony to await the arrival of the Venetian estate agent. 'Jeez, it's so goddamn clever.'

'What is?' Miranda looked down at the vaporetti, the gondolas, the barge boats; then across at the splendid architecture of the palazzos opposite, and found them, to her surprise, pleasing. It surprised her because the first time she had been to Venice, she had been too young and in love to notice much, and the other times, visiting Jessica and Piero, too cross at them for dragging her back.

Bruce, standing at the balustrade, said admiringly, '*This*. Man, it's so cool.' He swooped his arm about, nearly knocking Tommasina, sitting on her perch, into the Grand Canal. The cat growled malevolently at him, but he soothed her with purring noises and then went on, 'It was a neat idea, this. Making Europe so small, so compact. This miniature waterway here, just right for those little gondolas, see.' He pronounced it gon-*doe*-la, the accent on the doe. 'It's so goddamned cute. Like Disney World, only better, see, because it's authentic.'

'Europe is nothing if not authentic,' Miranda said dryly. Then, to change the subject, she asked politely, 'Are you staying here long?'

Bruce turned from the Grand Canal to Miranda, face plumply eager. 'Now that's real kind of you to express interest. Europeans don't, as a rule.' He remembered that Miranda was one, so went on hastily, 'Not that that's a criticism, that's for sure. Hey, I *love* Europe. It's just that they're different from the rest of the world, see?'

'From Americans, you mean,' Miranda said, even more dryly.

'You got it.' Bruce smiled, grateful to be understood. 'But if you treat them okay, like, if you treat them with respect, why, down deep they turn out to be just like the rest of us.'

Miranda shuddered. She nearly said, I sincerely hope not, but then decided that she did not have the heart to grind the gooey smile off that baby face with such harsh words.

Anyway, she did not really have the time to reply, for Bruce, encouraged by the fact that he had been asked a question (he had travelled the length and width of England without being asked one) was telling her all about himself. It appeared that six months ago, he had sold the firm he had built up from scratch to a multi-national, surprising himself and everyone else by making millions. He was now rich, retired and still in his prime, determined to travel the world, starting with Europe, where he hoped to find a bit of culture. He talked about culture as if it were a commodity.

Miranda said politely, 'And what *was* your firm?'

'Information technology.'

'I'm afraid I don't know anything about that.'

Bruce giggled. 'Miranda, honey, I'll let you in on a secret. Neither do I. Wasn't it smart that I got out of it before anyone found out?'

An hour later, Frank walked in on Miranda, who was trying to read a bit of Jane Austen and pretend that she was in England. All these foreigners were becoming tiresome. It was not that she minded them, it was just that they exhausted her, with their endless enthusiasm.

She was in the courtyard, well away from the noise and water traffic on the canal, sitting in a deck chair she had brought out. The big leaves of the fig tree gave her shade, and the white cats supplied company of a sort, being in reasonable tempers after a saucer each of milk.

Frank said, 'Miranda.' He made it sound like a command.

'Yes, Frank?' She looked up reluctantly from English country manors and the genteel aristocracy to see Frank's face twisted in rage.

'The American.' It came out not as a statement but as an expletive, as violent as the outburst of a volcano. 'Miranda, do you know this thing? That this American he is here living, at the Palazzo Bobolino, in Apt. 2? With view over Grand Canal? The apartment above us, Miranda? Do you know that this very same American is took, is tooken, the whole complete apartment which is of the same largeness as Apt. 1? As Apt. 1, the one

86

in which we is living? In which four people do live? You, I, Netty and—'

'Yes, yes, Frank,' Miranda interrupted impatiently, 'I know exactly how many people are staying in Apt. 1, and who they are.' She did not quite grasp what Frank was so indignant about. That Bruce was American? That he had the apartment above them? That he was rich enough to have it all to himself, such a grand (if shabby and neglected) place?

Frank sat down, on the stone bench opposite. He ran his broad capable hand over his face, momentarily overcome with something or other, then said, almost in a whisper, so indignant was he, 'The American, this Bruce man, has made invitation for all, *all* of Apt. 1, to his dinner, tonight. In his apartment. Apt. 2.'

Miranda waited. No further exposition was offered. Frank sat mute. Miranda said at last, 'Why, that's rather nice, don't you think? So kind of him. So neighbourly. The Americans are like that, I believe. Neighbourly. Did you accept?'

Frank shook his head miserably. 'Very much I try to say no, no, no, but Bruce not let me.'

Miranda nodded sagely. 'Americans can be quite persuasive as well.' She still did not know what the problem was. It would be rather fun to eat out, even if it were just in the apartment above them.

She said as much to Frank, who by now was less agitated but sadly resigned. 'I am afraid, Miranda, that you is English,' he said, sounding quite accusing.

'Well yes, I am afraid I is. I mean, I'm afraid I am,' she answered. Dryly, again. She wondered why no one seemed to notice how parched her replies were just lately.

'You do not understand.'

'No, probably not.' Miranda was happy to concede this.

'You have forgotten rota. Tonight is Netty's. We were to eat gnocchi. With tiramisù. You know what is this tiramisù?'

Miranda shuddered. She hated the stuff. 'It is a sweet, a dessert. Reminds me of trifle, only Italian, and therefore richer.'

'Trifle?'

'Forget it. Too complicated to explain.'

'But the gnocchi. Tonight was gnocchi and tiramisù night with Netty.'

'You are repeating yourself, Frank. Well, we shall have them tomorrow night.' She picked up Jane Austen determinedly.

'But tomorrow is Marco and risotto.'

'Well, surely . . .' She trailed off, knowing it was hopeless. Frank looked so doleful that she found herself putting down her book and promising him that all was not lost, that she herself would help draw up a new rota.

'We're *what?*'

'Having dinner with the new tenant,' Simon said.

'American,' April said.

'Quite wealthy,' Simon went on. 'He's rented Apt. 2 all for himself.'

'Indefinitely.'

Lissabelle looked up at the chandelier with all the bits missing and said, 'Good-looking? Young?'

Simon and April exchanged glances. April said, 'In a scrubbed sort of way. Forty-ish.'

Lissabelle shed her usual expression of ennui to ask, 'Is he in films? Or perhaps an art dealer? There are many about, for the Biennale. I bet that's what he is, an international art dealer, from New York. They are usually from New York.'

April said, 'He did mention being from Manhattan.'

'There! Oh Lord, is he gay? So many of them are.'

'Not sure,' Simon said. 'Could be either. Perhaps both.'

'Oh, wonderful,' Lissabelle said, 'I like a challenge. We shall go tonight.' That would show Paolo with the teeth, she thought grimly. He had been far too vague, when saying goodbye. Lissabelle had been expecting a frantic 'When will we meet again?' speech, as befitted a besotted Latin. She was growing bored again with Venice. This new American art dealer would cheer her up considerably.

It was a merry table, in the shambolic grand dining room of Apt. 2. Around the walls the paper peeled, on the ceiling the chandelier hung by loose wires, but by this point nobody minded. Bruce thought the curling plaster and loose cupboards were exotically decadent and European, like Berlin was supposed to have been before the last war. He was charmed by them.

They did not bother Lissabelle either, for she felt in her own element at last, sitting at the wealthy table of someone as famous as she was. She absolutely *knew* he was, darlings, as she said to Simon and April later; it was the way he threw money about.

Bruce had, through large tips to the fawning estate agent, procured the services of a chef, who had swanned in with enormous supplies and produced a seafood meal fit for – well, for a New York Art Dealer of international reputation, as Lissabelle e-mailed all her London journalist cronies that very night.

'That was absolutely gorgeous,' Miranda said, replete amongst the debris of every imaginable form of shellfish the chef could find at this late notice. They had eaten fresh asparagus until they could bear no more; they had stuffed themselves on a first course of pasta rich with vine-ripened tomatoes and fragrant with Sicilian oregano. And the table was even now laden with fresh figs and strawberries and kiwi fruit the size of melons, and white Italian peaches and smooth delectable nectarines.

'Super!' Netty cried. 'Delicious!' she bellowed above the sirens of a *motoscafo* full of firemen rushing down the Grand Canal. The long windows of the dining room were open to the evening sky, peppery with black flakes of clouds now that the long hot day was coming to an end.

Netty patted her capacious stomach gently, indicating how full she was, but she had not eaten much. She was aware of her approaching assignation in the gondola with Silvano. She was not exactly sure how much weight a gondola could hold and did not want to take any chances.

She looked around the table at the smooth and illustrious guests sitting around it, in various stage of digestion. Venice was all she had dreamed it would be, for here was another star in The Serene Republic's most glorious firmament, the famous American Bruce Brinson. She did not quite remember how she knew he was famous; no one had exactly come out and said it, but it was in the air, it clung over them like cobwebs. Look how that dreadful Lissabelle managed to wangle the seat right next to him; look at how she was staring at him with that bold, bored look, as if he were solely hers, and not belonging to all of them at the Palazzo Bob, as the American so amusingly called it.

Yes, this was no Venetian fantasy; this was Venice herself, and she Netty, was at last a part of it.

Of course there were no Venetians here, which slightly troubled her when the thought fleeted skittishly through her head. Silvano was of course working, and Elena was baby-sitting her grandchildren. They had both been invited, though; everyone had been. So it was almost the same as their being at the dinner party. Perhaps even better, in a way, for despite Elena's recent friendliness, Netty still felt the occasional twinge of Catholic guilt, no doubt brought on by the proliferation of churches in the city. Adultery was not a thing to be taken lightly, not with cupolas and campaniles round every corner and all those infernal church bells belting out the hour in every campo.

But she reminded herself that this was Venice, where it was all right to be amoral. This thought cheered her, and she felt guilt vanish like the wine in her glass.

Bruce, perched cherubically at the head of the table, tapped his wine glass gently, to get everyone's attention. 'Hey now, you guys, I just want to say that I'm real glad to have found some neighbours as nice as you. Now I've been wandering around Europe for five months or so already, and I can say this, that I've never met folk as great and friendly as you Venetians. So thanks, pals. And I mean that from the heart, see?'

There were loud cheers, and a rendition of 'For He's a Jolly Good Fellow' from Netty, which no one joined in. But Bruce was thanked fulsomely by everyone, except Frank, who was still sulking about his spoiled rota.

Lissabelle said, as more wine was poured and no one made a move to leave, 'So tell me, Bruce darling, are you here for the Biennale?'

'Biennale? What's that?'

Everyone laughed. 'You Americans have such a quirky sense of humour,' Lissabelle said with a slight frown.

'Yeah? I guess maybe we do,' Bruce agreed, giggling. For some reason Lissabelle was reminded of the tinkly pink glass chimes in her girlie bedroom, when she was a pubescent, pre-famous girl-child. The memory was not unpleasant, to her surprise.

Marco said, 'If you've got any influence on the Biennale, Bruce, you'll make a protest about it.'

'Oh?' said Bruce, interested. He liked making protests; it was an American way of life, especially in Europe, which was often doing things the United States government had to protest against.

Marco poured out his fifth or sixth glass of Barolo and let the rich red wine slither sumptuously down his throat. He was more than usually expansive this evening, due not only to the wine and the food, but also to the fact that when he had left his beloved Nina (ignominiously sneaking out the back door of the Ca' Nostra

Trattoria), he had gone out and continued the painting he was working on, the one that his recent happiness had threatened to destroy. Now, deeply suffering, he was working like a Trojan on the painting. Large and wild, it was a canvas dedicated to the tragic defeat of love in a fraught modern society, based on his passion for Nina and its existential despair. It was solely grey, with pinpricks of more grey. A work of genius.

'What do *you* know about the Biennale?' Lissabelle said scornfully to Marco. She knew his type; psuedo creative nobodies, big on ego and small on talent. Poor, too.

'I know that it's supposed to represent the very best in contemporary art from every country in the world, but that grave errors have been made in some countries in choosing what artists should be exhibited. Some would even call it corruption, nepotism and even worse.' Marco looked defiantly at Lissabelle as he made this pretty little speech. He was not about to be cowed by her, rich bitch that she was. He knew her type: psuedo creative posers, big on ego and small on talent. And rich.

'Hang on,' Bruce said easily, 'those are mighty powerful accusations, Marco. You're not accusing the good old US of A of anything like that, I hope?' His baby eyes narrowed slightly.

'Don't know anything about the States,' Marco said, and Bruce relaxed, 'but I happen to know that the sculptor chosen to represent England is the grandnephew of a former prime minister and the second cousin of a model who married one of the Royals and the son—' Here Marco paused for effect. 'The son of a BBC tycoon and famous chat-show hostess whose name I will not tell you.'

Marco pressed his lips together, to indicate that he would rather die than reveal the name of both the BBC tycoon and his chat-show presenter wife, since he, Marco, was above gossip and corruption. Actually, it was because he could not remember either.

'No kidding,' Bruce said, leaning over the table to look at

Marco. He rather liked Marco's looks, so European, all those raggedy black clothes; so eccentric, that kinky crimson waistcoat with all the buckles and chains. They were weird, Europeans, but kinda cute too, and they certainly knew stuff about culture. Already he was learning about this Biennale extravaganza; he had never heard about it before.

Twinkling like the fairy on top of a Christmas tree, Bruce sparkled at Marco. Had he lusted for boys, which he didn't, he would have lusted for this young man, he decided. A true European artist, probably Italian, with that name, though he sounded English, and came from England. He would have liked to bring Marco home to his new posh penthouse in Manhattan, bought shortly before leaving for his world trip, and keep him like a rare pet, showing him off to friends, rather like Columbus brought back an Indian chief or two.

Perhaps he would anyway, he decided. One of the most delightful things about money, Bruce had discovered, was that it really could buy anything.

Before Bruce could inquire further about this Biennale thing that they all seemed so het up about, Lissabelle distracted him by saying that her last lover – and here she dropped the name of someone who was so seriously famous that even Bruce recognized him, even though he wasn't American – had lived on the better edge of Central Park for several months, and could it possibly be near Bruce's own place?

It was, and the fact forged an instant bond between them, or so Lissabelle told her dearest friends Simon and April later. (And e-mailed to her journalist mates, so that they could throw it nonchalantly into their columns.) Bruce said she must visit him in Manhattan one day, and she insisted he visit her in Islington.

Bruce had shifted his firm but chubby body the other way now, so that it leaned towards Lissabelle. Had he lusted for women, which he did not, he would have lusted for this one, with her

93

glossy blonde tresses, the Dolce and Gabbana sunglasses perched casually atop them. She looked so bored, so sated, so jaded. So terrifically European, like someone out of *La Dolce Vita*, which he had seen at a cinema in New York showing old classics. She was probably Italian too, despite what she said about being English; she looked every bit like one of the women in a film of Antonioni. Bruce could not quite get a grip that the English really were English. In America, Americans were Irish or Italians, or Norwegian or Ukrainians or what have you. The English seemed to be English, and that was it. Confusing.

He sighed, and reached across the table to either side of him, taking hold of Marco's hand with his right, and Lissabelle's on his left. 'What great buddies,' he said tearfully, for he too had been imbibing the wine freely, 'my goddamn terrific Venetian pals. I love you all, y'know that? Man, *I love you*.' He looked around the table beatifically, like a cherubic Christ with a scrubbed face and a neat haircut, presiding at the Last Supper.

Miranda, who had also drunk much more than she should have, sobered up instantly. Bloody hell, this was worse than America cinema, the soppy romantic comedy kind set in places like Seattle.

This was why she loathed Venice, she remembered. It brought out the grottiest sentimental crap in people, even sensible ones.

'I'm off,' she said, 'thanks for the meal, Bruce, it was delicious.'

And she was off, before the big American baby could burst into blubbing tears, embarrassing the hell out of her and every sensible English person besides.

If there was such a thing as a sensible person, English or otherwise, here in Venice, she thought waspishly as she looked back at them and waved as she made her escape. Lissabelle was slouched over the table, elbow in a fig in a most debauched manner, gazing at Bruce in a way that managed to convey both sophisticated boredom and downright seduction. Marco, on the other side, was slumped *on* the table, head in hands, doing a sad impression of the tragic artist. Or, as the case may be, a drunken sot; it was hard to tell which.

At the other end of the table, Netty was fluttering like a black flag, the sleeves of her latest robe-like frock waving fecklessly as she swung her arms in a paroxsym of ecstasy, going on about how she and Bruce were soulmates, for she too loved Venice and all Venetians, especially those dear ones sitting around this table. And Frank—

But Frank, being German, or Swiss German to be precise, did not count, for he was not English, and could not be expected to know how to behave. The others had no excuse.

At least she, Miranda, retained a bit of sense. She slammed the door on all of them, just as Frank was banging on the table with his shoe to announce the washing-up rota.

Later, in bed that night, she thought longingly of home. Outside she could hear the singing of the gondoliers; it was Saturday night, and festive. The song was 'Santa Lucia' and it sounded appalling, just as it had been that night in Venice twenty-eight years and nine odd months ago, when Jessica had been conceived. It had not been a gondolier who crooned the bloody awful song in her head, nor even an Italian, but merely another lonely foreigner, a student on a summer spree from the university in his own home town, his own home country. As she had been from hers.

They had had a day together, and imagined they were in love, as one does in Venice. The gaudy old city must have laughed her Most Serene Head off, Miranda thought later, ruefully and pregnantly. She and the young man, new to the city like herself, had met over coffee in the breakfast room of their cheap hotel near the railway station. By the end of breakfast they felt they had known each other all their lives, as lovers who are impossibly insane tend to do. By mid-morning cappuccino they were holding hands in the tiny campo of Santa Maria Nova, a gondola floating by as they dangled their feet on the tiny bridge over the tinier canal and watched the sunlight reflecting on the pink and green and ivory marble of the church by the water.

By lunch, they were soulmates.

At siesta time, they crept past the sleazy porter in their hotel, cowardly trying not to be seen (they were new at this sort of thing) to become lovers in Miranda's bedroom. (Hers was tidier.)

By evening, wandering around deliriously in Piazza San Marco, gazing at the glittering facade of the fairy-tale Basilica, they knew that they had been fated, kissed by destiny. That they were special. The only two people in the world. That they loved each other more than anyone had ever loved anyone else in the whole course of human history. Even divine history, if truth be told: they were descended from myth and mystery, from the gods and goddesses. They were that young and arrogant.

Miranda, thinking about it now as the excruciating discordant notes of bloody 'Santa Lucia' melt away down the Grand Canal, cringes as she remembers being nineteen, the horror of it all. Not so horrible then, of course; in fact, bloody marvellous at the time.

But later. She having to return suddenly less than ten days later, to her dying father in Shropshire, though she had planned to stay in Venice longer. Hasty tearful goodbyes and promises to meet. He returning to his own country, for his college course had begun. And then nothing. Not even her father dying, for he revived suddenly and lived another twenty years. Her lover, her soulmate, getting tied up in university politics and the excitement of the times and forgetting to write to her; and she, Miranda, coming to her senses on the soggy, sensible English turf, pregnant and alone.

She thought about telling him about the baby, when she found out she was pregnant. And discarded the idea at once. Quite simply, it was far too embarrassing. To reveal a love-child, when the love had quite died? She could not face it. The one letter she did write said nothing about a child. She was testing the water, so to speak, see if he were still interested. Apparently he was not, for he never replied and she never wrote to him again.

And so Miranda lies in bed tonight in Venice, thinking about how her young lover, silly young man that he was, sang 'Santa Lucia' in her ear in bad, bad Italian, mimicking the gondoliers as they sang outside the hotel bedroom. His bedroom, this time; he had tidied it up quickly after dinner.

And feels a tear trickling down her cheek, for such are the wicked games that Venice plays with her children, the twenty million or so visitors a year who come to her Most Serene Shores. Damn this place, this shit-hole, Miranda swears out loud. She does not miss her long-lost lover, the father of her child; she can hardly remember his face. No, what Miranda is crying for is herself, the girl she was at nineteen, in Venice and in love.

'Oh bugger,' she says aloud, and gets out of bed and puts on a dressing gown. Wandering out of her bedroom and into the kitchen, then balcony, she glares moodily at the dark steamy waters of the Grand Canal. A misty rain is beginning to fall. Down the canal, on the other side at the *traghetto* landing stage, now closed and shut as the public transport gondolas stop running for the night, are moored the regular gondolas. They too are silently tied and bobbing in the water.

But wait, one is moving out. A lone gondolier is stealthily rowing out into the misty water, a passenger sitting at his feet. With an umbrella, of all things.

Miranda stares, as the gondola heads out into the canal. The gondolier has ducked his head, as if he were trying to hide; so, for that matter, has his passenger, who seems to be some kind of priest in long black flowing robes.

But then, under the dark umbrella, Miranda catches a glimpse of fierce red curls, and the lights from the side of the canal flash on familiar glass ruby-red beads that tinkled merrily during dinner at Bruce's apartment. She wants to cry out, to wave, but she finds she cannot. She is laughing too hard.

Miranda goes back to bed, in a much jollier frame of mind. That old slut Venice can still surprise you, she thinks gleefully, can still pull her meretricious magic and charm the pants off anyone, make fools of anyone, no matter how young or how old.

She is amazed at how cheered she feels, knowing this.

Chapter Seven

'Ohhh, Silvano! Oh, good grief! Ohhhh!'

'Shh, Netty. We're passing the Palazzo Bobolino. We don't want to be seen.'

'I thought we were tipping over. It's swaying so.'

'It's supposed to.'

'I have never been in a gondola before.'

'So you have said. Many times. *Per favore*, do not move so much. Keep still. *Piano, piano.*'

For a wild moment Netty thought he was about to produce one, a piano that is, and start serenading her then and there. You never knew, with gondoliers; some of them played accordians, or violins or guitars. She had never heard of one with a piano, though. Then she realized he was talking Italian to her, which thrilled her so much she squealed again and joggled about dangerously.

Silvano frowned at her. At last he was able to pull off the Grand Canal into a side waterway, where he breathed easier. It would do no good for Elena to spot him. He wanted to go off to England with Netty in his own good time, not thrown out by his wife before he was ready. Besides, if he and his wife parted amicably, he would have a bolt-hole, a place to stay when he visited his grandchildren.

Netty had quieted down as they punted along the side canal, the buildings looming dark and crumbling on either side. 'Oh, I say,' she whispered, as the boat glided silently along in the black night, 'rather spooky, what?' But that was all. She was wondering if they were about to stop, and how they would go about it, making love in a gondola. Not only had she never done it before, she had never done it previously in anything but a bed, and a double one at that. How Bohemian it all was. How thrilling. How utterly Venetian.

The only trouble was, the rain was now coming down in torrents.

Silvano, getting drenched, was regretting the whole escapade by now. For one thing, he had lost his mooring in the piazzetta and had to pick up Netty right in front of the Palazzo Bobolino. Not only was he running the risk of Elena witnessing it all (luckily their apartment did not face the canal), but also, and more importantly, his mates, the other *gondolieri*, were not around to see the big, bright splendid Englishwoman getting into his gondola at midnight. What was the point of a romantic rendezvous, at his age, if there was no one around to admire, to envy, to call him a randy old bugger (or the Italian equivalent) and smack him with comradely affection on the back?

There was no one about to see him now, only the odd water rat or two.

He rounded another corner, and came upon a tiny mooring post on a narrow canal by a small campo in the deep bowels of San Polo, at the home of an old friend and colleague. He had done the friend a favour once or twice in the past, so Silvano did not hesitate. Steering the gondola skilfully to the edge, he threw his rope and tied it securely to the post.

This is it, Netty thought excitedly. *Here it comes.*

Silvano, going to her, to take her hand and help her out of the boat, was thinking about walking her home under the big black umbrella as soon as possible, getting her safely back into Apt. 1, and sneaking himself into his own apartment where he would drink a hot rich chocolate drink and slip gratefully into bed beside a snoring Elena. He had done his bit. He had given her a romantic gondola ride. She owed him one now. She owed him England. Fair enough trade.

'Netty, *cara*,' he said lovingly, for he was ever so fond of her, despite the pig-like noises she made when she was excited. 'Come to me, give me your hand.'

Now, Netty thought, and her knees went weak, her heart thumped. He grabbed her hand firmly, then her arm. She thought she would faint. 'Ohh, Silvano. I think I am going to faint,' she said faintly.

Then, to both his surprise and hers, she did.

Later that night, sitting in the kitchen with Miranda and pouring out the whole story to her (for Netty had lost her key, and had to bang on the door of Apt. 1 to be let in), she said mournfully, 'So you see, I could not, in the end, go through with it. The spirit was quite willing to indulge in a spot of Venetian fornication, but the flesh was too weak. I am too Anglican, Miranda. I thought I was such a liberal, such a rebel in my small way, but I am merely an Anglican. I cannot even indulge in a good Roman Catholic romp without fainting dead away.'

Miranda, stifling laughter, said, 'So what happened? After you fainted?'

'Apparently I was out only for a moment or two. Silvano revived me, untied the gondola, and rowed us back to our very own landing stage here at the palazzo. At great risk, of course. Elena could have spotted us at any moment.'

Miranda said that this was highly unlikely, since it was one in the morning by then, and Elena, if she had any sense, would be fast asleep.

Netty grew thoughtful, thinking of the great danger she and Silvano had been in. The dark sinister side canals. The rocking, dripping gondola. The danger of drowning, not to mention the proximity of the wife. 'Perhaps it was just as well,' she said after a bit. 'That I fainted. The rain, you know.'

'The rain? What does that have to do with it?'

'It would not have been at all romantic, all that rain. I mean, for my very first time.'

'First time?' Miranda was puzzled. She knew Netty had been married for at least forty years. 'Was Herbert, uh, celibate?'

'Good gracious no,' Netty said robustly. 'What a thought. No, I meant my first time at Fornication and Adultery.'

'Ah.'

'I would so like it to be romantic.'

'Quite.' Miranda paused before saying, 'So, you'll try again?'

'My dear, I'm British! Of course I'll try again. Now should we have a tad more of that brandy? I do believe I caught a chill, in that damp gondola.'

With a perfectly straight face, she poured herself another tot, while Miranda, unable to stop herself, rushed into the bathroom and stuffed a towel in her mouth for a full five minutes, trying to keep her howls of laughter from leaking out, like water from a gondola, into the kitchen where Netty sat on, guzzling brandy and wondering why it was so hard to be truly Bohemian.

The next few days were, both within and without, peacefully sunny. Capricious Venice benignly glittered in the sunshine, her arches and architecture, her waterways and alleyways, festooned with dusty moats of festive sunbeams, covering everything like a sprinkle of golden confetti.

The hearts of the residents of Palazzo Bob, as Bruce kept calling it, beat steadfastly and contentedly in their various bosoms, as did those of their acquaintances and hangers-on. Frank, every weekday, marched off to the language school in Cannereggio, where he arrived punctually at 8.55 every morning, sitting at his desk by 8.57 waiting for his nine o'clock class to begin. Unfortunately, the teachers, Italian all, never arrived before 9.10, which caused him no end of consternation. But Frank, ever resourceful, spent the time profitably organizing his writing pads, pens and notebooks, and thus did not complain.

Netty, on the other hand, suppressed the habits of a lifetime to arrive late, at 9.15, breathless and apologetic as she flew, or rather her clothes flew, to her seat. She was late because at exactly 8.30 every morning, when Frank left the apartment, Silvano walked out too, to have his first smoke of the day in the courtyard and thus to check the weather and the state of the canal. Netty, leaving Apt. 1 laden with dictionaries, phrase books, guidebooks and Italian grammars, passed Silvano under the fig tree at precisely 8.32, and whilst Frank, not to be deflected, muttered a curt *buongiorno* and proceeded on to school, Netty stopped for her romantic fix for the day.

'Ah, Netty, *cara, bella*! How marvellous you look today, how sparkly. Like Venice herself, this fine morning.'

Who could not resist such a lift, at 8.33 on a weekday morning? Not Netty. And, if truth be told, not Silvano either, for Netty, drowning herself in all things Venetian, soon became as adept in charm and flattery as her gondolier soon-to-be lover.

'I say, Silvano, how handsome you look today, what? I do believe that red and white striped shirt is made for you, my dear. It makes you look so perky.' She gave him a smile both wicked and seductive. Oh, how she loved this! Oh, how she was getting the hang of it! She was far better at being Venetian than being English, she decided. Besides, it was so much more fun.

This charming romantic tryst under the fig tree was invariably broken up by Miranda, which was just as well or Netty would have arrived at the language school even later, and never

103

learned Italian. Which she never did anyway, but that is beside the point.

Miranda, an early riser, liked to get out at a reasonable hour and walk the short distance from the Palazzo Bobolino to the Rialto market, to buy the fresh fruits in season and have a look around. She was finding that she could keep ancient memories at bay in this insidious city by doing things she never did when she was nineteen, such as shopping, basket over her arm, pretending she was an Italian housewife. She and Jessica's father had never shopped, for they hardly ever ate, living as they did on love, poor fools.

It was night-time that got to her. All those water lights reflected on the canal. All those lovers wandering with arms wrapped around each other, dawdling on tiny stone bridges to watch silent black gondolas drift by, a lone red light in the prow.

Hellish, that. It reminded her what an ass she had been, at nineteen.

And so, '*Buongiorno,*' Miranda called every weekday morning at approximately 8.50, to Silvano and Netty under the fig tree.

'Goodness, I must be off, look at the time,' Netty said every morning, and Silvano bobbed his little puffballs of hair and said, '*Dunque,* I too must be off,' though he had nothing else to do but to listen to Elena prattle before he went off to his gondola at about ten.

At about the time Miranda came home, basket filled with strawberries, cherries and fresh peaches, Marco had staggered out into the courtyard, to set up his easel facing the canal. Every weekday morning Miranda called, 'Hello there, Marco, work going well?'

Marco, not looking up, always replied, 'Fantastic,' for, these days, it was. Not only going well, but brilliantly. His huge canvas of grey on grey would be completed soon, and it was, he told himself modestly, a masterpiece. Provisionally entitled,

'Existential Nihilism in a Post-Technological Age', it was, of course, patently obvious that it was a reflection of his doomed and unconsummated love for Nina.

Which, as the week progressed, was becoming even more doomed and unconsummated, thanks to the presence of Paolo, who was beginning to hang around the Palazzo Bobolino like a mosquito with teeth. At around about the time Miranda was exchanging pleasantries with Marco, the deafening roar of Paolo's motorboat would drown out birdsong and conversation as the taxi driver pulled up at the wobbly pier. 'Aha, the great artist,' he would shout scornfully in Italian. Marco frowned, but was secretly pleased. He understood the words, but did not grasp the subtleties of sarcasm in a foreign language.

Sometimes Nina was on the boat, since she did not have to be at the Ca' Nostra Trattoria until afternoon. She blew kisses to Marco behind Paolo's back, and tried to make frantic secret assignations about meetings. Marco became so agitated that he invariably got them wrong, and spent hours waiting for her in sly hidden campos where little children gaped and housewives good-naturedly asked if he were lost. This of course caused him further suffering, which he poured out on his painting. Life was, all in all, perfectly splendid these days. Good old Venice had done it again.

With the first putt-putt of Paolo's motorboat in the distance, Lissabelle, who had a built-in sonar system like a bat for these sort of machinations, rushed outside, then appeared bored and surprised when she saw Paolo. 'Oh, *you* here, darling?' she said languidly every morning. Miranda, watching with her basketful of fruit, always waited with a small smile on her face for this bit; it was so wonderfully predictable.

Then Lissabelle posed herself, usually in something impossibly trendy, on the water's edge, to be gaped at. It has to be said that Paolo did. He still remembered the taste of those expensive mints on her breath the day he kissed her on his boat; a mixture of rich chocolate and cool sharp peppermint. His stomach rumbled whenever he thought of it, not to mention other parts of his hunky self which did other things relating to hunger, though not necessarily for food.

Lissabelle said, every morning, 'Now that you're here, I suppose you'd better have a coffee. I do believe Simon is in the kitchen making one right now.' Then she pulled her Dolce and Gabbana sunglasses down over her eyes, so that he would not be able to read what was in them. Actually, there was nothing much, for Lissabelle was vacillating between indulging in a little bit of rough with Paolo, or frolicking in a more sophisticated manner with Bruce, the New York-based international art dealer and media-darling of the trendy set such as herself; the man who was obviously here in Venice to hobnob with the stars of the Biennale and all their influential hangers-on.

In the kitchen, struggling with the cappuccino machine, Simon snarled at April, 'Who do you bet on? Paolo, or Bruce?'

'Oh both, darling.'

Simon looked at her in surprise. Now, why didn't he think of that? He had been with Lissabelle for a far longer time; he thought he knew her inside out.

But it made sense. Lissabelle was not one to deny herself anything she wanted. Simon looked thoughtfully at April. She was getting far too astute at this, predicting Lissabelle's moods and actions. *He* was the first in line as dearest friend and confidante, not April. He was paid the most too, or so he assumed. He narrowed his eyes slightly. April was a dear, dear girl, but he would keep an eye on her. He was not about to be usurped by a girlie best friend.

April smugly poured the cappuccino while Simon put the cups and saucers and tiny Venetian biscuits on a tray.

When the coffee appeared, as if by magic, in the courtyard on these blissful mornings, Bruce appeared as well, and after a few moments, Elena. She was there to nose around, and he, to delight in all his new-found Venetian friends.

'Well hey, cappuccino? Cool. Say, don't mind if I do,' Bruce said every morning, as cups were passed around. 'Man, this is the life,' he would say, at least once before the first cup was finished. 'Europe might be tiny, and kind of backward, and sort of fusty, like a museum that hasn't been opened for a while, but hey, it's sure got its compensations.'

He clicked his cup with Lissabelle when he said this, since it was her cappuccino, but the gesture drove Paolo to an insane paroxysm of jealousy so that he ignored Nina for a time and homed in on the famous Englishwoman.

This suited Nina, for it left her free to home in on Marco, and kiss him furtively behind his vast canvas. 'I love you,' Marco whispered hurriedly when the loud wailing of the *polizia* or the ambulance sirens came screeching up the canal, rippling the water and causing it to slosh precariously over the pier and the steps leading to the courtyard.

'Tonight?' Nina whispered back. She named an obscure campo.

Marco nodded. Nina hoped he would be there, this time. It was helping her English not one bit, these mute fumblings behind canvas.

Bruce always felt expansive after the coffee, and invited all of them to lunch somewhere, usually somewhere famous and expensive, like Harry's Bar or the Cipriani or the Hotel Danieli. Usually they all went, for various reasons, nothing to do with food, and Frank and Netty would join them, for their classes finished at one. Silvano too, in between customers, sometimes spotted them strolling across the Piazza San Marco and to the piazzetta along to the waterfront, and was hailed cheerily, and invited to come along.

Only Miranda went to eat, for she loved good nosh. The other foreigners went because they were afraid of being left out of anything, here in Venice. Silvano went because he loved being with the English. He took care not to sit next to Frank, who would not be the best luncheon companion for an Anglophile.

'Man, what a place, hey?' Bruce would say, as they staggered back home after lunch, tiddly and replete. 'It's impacted me, man. The Palazzo Bob. I feel like a crumbling aristocrat myself, living here.' His chubby face beamed. Maybe he could buy himself a peerage or something. Become a European count, or, better, a prince. He had the cash for it.

'It's what?' Miranda asked. 'Impacted you?'

Bruce looked puzzled. 'Yeah.'

Simon said, 'He means it's made an impression on him. An impact.' He knew the lingo; he had been to Washington not that long ago, with Lissabelle and her lover of the moment, a Clinton confidante who spilled secrets on nationwide talk-shows. Simon had taken copious notes on that one, for the politician spilled secrets in bed too, which Lissabelle discussed with her two dearest friends long into the early hours.

Miranda, pondering the strangeness of Americans and yawning mightily, thanked Bruce and unlocked her front door, saying she was going up for a siesta. Suddenly everyone was yawning, and deciding a siesta was a sensible idea, rushed off to their own separate bedrooms.

But not always.

There was a time, during that placid interval, when many found themselves not only in the wrong bedrooms, but in beds not their own.

Nina, for one. Somehow she found herself nakedly under the sheets with Marco, wishing that he would speak while he fucked, so that she could learn some English vernacular, this being the whole point of the exercise.

But that was her only disappointment. To her surprise, what

they (Italians) said about them (Englishmen) was not entirely true. Marco was tweaking her taut nipples with nimble and expert fingers with his left hand, and tantalizingly teasing other places with the right, so that after a bit she stopped fretting over the fact that he was so *maledetto* silent about the whole thing. Perhaps there would be post-coital conversation, she thought fleetingly, before finally going under without a thought for her poor betrayed fiancé.

Who was, at that very moment, also in the wrong bed, in Apt. 3 right opposite. With Lissabelle, looking nakedly bored, though not, *Grazie a Dio*, boringly naked. She had been pummelled by masseuses, primed by personal trainers; she had been rubbed down by creams and oils the price of a pied à terre abroad; she had had a nip or two here and there in Harley Street, a bit less to the buttocks here, a bit more to the bosoms there.

In short, she was perfect.

Paolo took her manfully, and she accepted his thrusts with what he assumed was pleasure, though the 'I've seen it all' expression on her face did not change throughout the exercise. However he enjoyed it thoroughly, and when finished, dropped his head on her naked belly and began to snore, his teeth making an indentation not unlike an appendix scar on Lissabelle's perfectly stretched and skilfully manipulated skin.

Netty seemed to be the only one in her very own bed that afternoon, but there seemed to be more than just herself in it. It had all begun after lunch at the Danieli, where that lovely American with the baby teeth and the hair like a baby angel had treated them to a most delicious repast. They had arrived in style at the private landing stage of the hotel, in Paolo's taxi. This was moored with a flourish and left, since naturally he had been invited too, Americans not knowing the difference between classes. This was perfectly fine with Netty, in her new role as international Bohemian; in fact she quite liked Paolo, though he was not as posh as a gondolier.

Instead of all piling into Paolo's boat to return to the Palazzo Bobolino for their usual siesta, Marco and Nina somehow detached themselves from the others, saying they preferred the long walk back to San Polo. Nina had muttered something to Paolo about English lessons, which would have ordinarily made him rage with jealousy except for the fact that Lissabelle was breathing mint chocolate in his face again. Paolo was, sadly perhaps, getting the taste of the Good Life, or rather the Expensive Life, and quite enjoying it.

So when Lissabelle murmured in his ear, 'Darling, let them go, we'll all meet again at the palazzo,' he followed her willingly into his taxi, thankful that Nina's back was already turned as Lissabelle's buffed and polished fingernails scraped gently on the bare flesh of his arm.

Miranda decided she needed a walk too, and because Elena was not there but in Mestre all day, shopping with her daughter-in-law, Silvano gallantly offered to take Netty back to the Palazzo Bobolino in his gondola. 'Oh, super!' Netty had cried, tossing her most pitying look on Lissabelle, who was merely travelling in a motorboat which you could do on the Thames, for goodness' sake.

Silvano felt he should ask Bruce, out of courtesy, as well, but Bruce was off to the Doge's Palace for his spot of culture for the day. That left Frank, who also refused. He was exploring Venice in order, one *sestiere* at a time, crossing off each region as he explored it with the help of a detailed map and a thick guidebook without one picture. This afternoon he was checking the Arsenale, where the great naval fleet of the Most Serene Republic had been built in the old days of the city's glory.

And so it was that Silvano, basking in the smutty Venetian innuendoes of his comrades as he escorted Netty into his shiny sleek gondola moored on the piazzetta, felt young and virile as he manfully rowed her down the canal, passed the glowing domes of the church of the Salute, under the bridge of the Accademia, around the bend and under the Ponte di Rialto until at last they were at the Palazzo Bobolino.

It was quite hard oaring, from the Hotel Danieli to the Rialto, and the Grand Canal wasn't what it used to be, all the traffic nowadays and Silvano not getting any younger. He found himself in a peculiar state, what with too much wine and food and all that rowing right on top of it. And so, not quite being in his right head, a fuzzy Silvano found himself following Netty into Apt. 1 and into her bedroom, where she seemed to be enticing him, a plump siren billowing clouds of frothy clothes and encouragement.

Luckily, for Silvano, for with his wife in the same palazzo it was best not to be seen or heard by anyone, it was on the other side of the drawing room from Marco's bedroom, where he and Nina were at that moment silently copulating.

Which was exactly what Netty wanted to do. The oysters for lunch had made her tingly with lust, though that may have been the power of suggestion; certainly, the wine she had drunk had loosened every last vestige of Anglican inhibitions.

Silvano, through no fault of his own, found himself in Netty's bed, with Netty beside him, in another one of her flowing things which he recognized as a nightdress, only because it was quite, quite sheer and she had nothing on underneath. Before passing out he had time to appreciate the fact that her great mound of a body looked quite delectable in its semi-nude state, being as round and firm as an air balloon.

Bruce, our genial American host, is the only one alone in his own bed right now, Miranda still walking and Frank still studying the historical charts at the Arsenale. Bruce had decided against the Doge's Palace when he got there because of the crowds, making

111

the wise decision that after a large lunch and a copious amount of wine, culture should take second place to a siesta. He took a vaporetto straight home to the Palazzo Bob, to put this to practice.

Now, he is where he wants to be, in his own cute lumpy dollhouse bed in toytown Venice, where he is having the time of his life.

But wait, he is not alone. Two pale white things have crawled into bed with him, and not for the first time. Bruce strokes their warm bodies, and falls into a gentle sleep whilst doing so. He is entirely happy, with his dozy entourage, whose company, it has to be said, Bruce prefers more than either that of woman or man.

As he sleeps, Tommasina and Topolino purr, happy to have sneaked away out of the window of Apt. 1 and the strange ménage there, into the peaceful shuttered colonial slumbers of Apt. 2.

Somehow, everyone got back to their proper places without undue embarrassment, or even without being seen by those whom they preferred not to be seen by.

And everyone went home happy too, not a mean feat these days.

Marco had been momentarily distraught, when he came to his senses, feeling that he would now be too sated and contentedly in love to paint, but after burbling about this for an hour or so (he was never laconic, post-coital), Nina jumped up and cried, '*Dio!* I am late for work! Gianni my boss at the trattoria will be furious.' She began pulling on her clothes frantically. 'And so will Paolo, if he finds out about this,' she added darkly.

This caused Marco much anguish, not only because it reminded him that his one true love was promised to someone else, but also because of the Sicilian connection. Gianni the bartender made him agitated. He was nervous around Sicilians anyway, after *The Godfather*. 'Go,' he cried to Nina. 'Leave me lying here, after making love to you, and go back to your fiancé!' His voice dripped with pain.

When Nina left, well satisfied after an hour of post-coital non-stop English, Marco leaped up and with a great surge of energy went back to his 'Grey-on-Grey' (the working title of his painting, the real one being too difficult to remember). He worked like a man demented for the next couple of hours.

Just as Nina was rushing off, Silvano woke, and, feeling guilty about falling asleep so ignominiously, kissed Netty all over quite thrillingly. 'Netty, *bella*, how I adore you, how tasty you look, how delicious you feel in my arms.'

Netty squealed.

'But, *cara mia*, much as I would love to stay here and kiss your rosy nipples indefinitely, my wife will be home at any moment. I must fly, *subito!*'

Which he did, at once. But Netty, far from being nettled, was more than contented. The afternoon had been Bohemian enough, thank you very much, without full consummation, what with lunch and ordinary tourists snapping her photo as she sailed grandly down the Grand Canal and under the Rialto Bridge with Silvano. Then the wickedness of it, changing deliberately into her nightie, her summer one, and being kissed all over by a Venetian gondolier, the cotton wool hair-balls tickling her belly when he passed out on her stomach. This passing out business could have been an embarrassment, except for the stroke of fortune that decreed that Netty too overindulged in wine during lunch and so fell asleep as well, at more or less the same time as Silvano.

Honour intact, Silvano walked jauntily to his apartment, arriving home only minutes before his wife.

Miranda was almost happy that afternoon, but not quite. Lulled by the wine and the food, and the company that, despite their peculiarities, she was beginning to enjoy, she had let herself do something she had never done before. She walked up the Strada Nuova, in the direction of the train station, until she found the hotel where Jessica had been conceived.

To both her delight and despair, it was still there. Spruced up and smartened, it was three-star now, instead of the half-star or whatever it had been when she was there.

She was happy that it still existed, because it proved that Jessica was indeed conceived normally, or as normal as anything can be, in Venice. Sometimes Miranda wondered if she were crazy, and had imagined it all, and that really Jessica had been planted in her womb by some mischievous Roman god or a naughty Etruscan satyr. Or Venezia herself, in a particularly capricious mood.

But it also made Miranda desolate, finding the hotel. She was beginning to doubt her own long-ago decision not to tell Jessica's father that he had a daughter. Jessica knew about him, of course, and Miranda still had an address, twenty-eight years old, should her daughter ever want to make contact. But Jessica said she did not; she was not bothered, not now. One day perhaps, but not now; she was far too busy living in the present, with two children of her own and an Italian husband.

Miranda knew she was doubting now because she was lonely. Venice always made her lonely, the seedy old place. All those sodden canals and ridiculous beauty.

She was never lonely in Shropshire. In Shropshire she had books and a job and occasional lovers who lasted a few years and then disappeared on a shelf, much as her paperbacks did when she finished with them. She never missed either books or men when they were put away and done with; Jessica's father had sated her appetite for great passions; and *War and Peace*, which she read while nursing Jessica, had fulfilled her lust for great reads. Anything that came after, she could take or leave.

To pull herself together, Miranda walked for three hours,

stopping only once for a quick espresso before charging down the alleyways and mazes of the city again.

When she finally got back to the Palazzo Bobolino, wrecked with self-pity and weariness, she found Marco walking up and down the courtyard, ignoring his easel and the overwhelming canvas he had been so dilligently working on up to now.

Miranda tried to edge past him – he looked tortured; and she, having tortured herself all afternoon, felt she could not cope with anyone else's whips and lashes – but Marco cried, 'It's not fair!'

I'm not, Miranda said determinedly to herself, *going to say, What's not fair?*

But before she could run like hell, a voice cried, 'Hey Marco, you're all upset, man. What's not fair? C'mon over here and tell Uncle Brucie and Aunt Miranda all about it.'

'I'm not an insect,' Miranda said crustily, then felt so guilty when Bruce looked confused that she did not have the heart to run away and leave them to it.

Instead, she sat down on the stone bench with Bruce, with Marco fretting and frantic between them. 'Hey now, cool it, man. What's the prob? Not your picture, goddamn it, is it? Not going well?' His smooth pink face wrinkled in concern; these poor artists, he thought; one minute they're hollaring hosanna because they're on a roll, the next minute they're in the pits. He was glad his field was Information Technology. And even gladder that he had got out at just the right time, so that he could be here now, consorting with artists. He didn't want to be one, but it was pretty whacky, hanging out with them. Despite their bouts of manic-depression, they were quite fun, and Bruce appreciated that. He himself, American through and through, did fun exceptionally well, and liked others who did too.

'It was,' Marco said, biting his fingernails. 'Going well. The painting. But I can't do another thing, I'm finished, finished.'

'Oboy.' Bruce whistled knowingly. 'Girlfriend, am I right?

Nothing stops creativity more than a ding-dong, ja-zoo fight with the ole girlfriend.'

'No, no, not Nina, she's not the problem.'

'Well, what is?' Miranda said, becoming impatient again. She was hot and tired and wanted an ice-cold drink and a nap.

Marco gnawed on his lower lip, pulled a lock of his floppy hair to shreds, and groaned, 'My father.'

'Oboy,' Bruce said, instantly sympathetic. 'Tell me about fathers. I was in therapy for ten years because of mine. He changed sexes when I was eleven. Hey, is yours gonna do the same? Gosh, no wonder you're a mess.'

Marco shook his head dolefully. 'I wish it was just a sex change. No, it's worse. He's coming here.'

'Here? To Venice?'

'To the Palazzo Bobolino,' Marco said miserably. 'He just phoned, asked if he could stay. Said he'd sleep on the sofa, anywhere. I tried to put him off, but . . .' His voice trailed off miserably.

'Hey kid, lighten up, Uncle Brucie'll take care of everything. If it's accommodation that's the problem, I got this mega big apartment with more bedrooms than I can count. Your pop can have one of them, no prob.'

Marco accepted this offer gratefully, with effusive thanks, but Miranda could tell he was still unhappy. 'What else is the matter, Marco?' she asked wearily. How trying were the problems of youth.

'*Him*,' Marco said despondently. 'Him, him, *him*. My father.'

'Uh oh,' Bruce said and rolled his eyes.

'You, uh, don't get on with him?' Miranda asked cautiously, wondering if Jessica ever talked that way about *her*.

Marco began to laugh hysterically.

'Uh *oh*,' Bruce said again, and both whistled *and* rolled his eyes.

Marco said, 'Oh yes, we get on all right. He's quite okay, as parents go. And I think he's fond of me. In fact, I know he is. He's proud of me, as a matter of fact.'

'So what's the score? Why the wailing and gnashing of teeth? I know, he's one of those that hate Venice, loathes the place. Am I right?'

'No, Bruce, you're wrong. He loves Venice, comes here often, spends hours, days, roaming the old familiar streets.'

'Well then,' Miranda stood up to go, 'that's all settled then. Your father's proud of you, he loves Venice, no prob. I mean problem. He can stay at Bruce's, and I'm sure Frank will be overjoyed to make up another rota to accommodate him for evening meals, and . . .'

But Marco was not listening. 'He was especially proud of me when he learned I was exhibiting in the British pavilion at the Biennale this year. So proud that he took a couple of weeks off from work, booked a flight, and is arriving in time for the opening.' Marco put his head in his hands and groaned.

Bruce and Miranda looked at each other. Bruce spoke first. 'Call me a dumbo, Marco baby, but I didn't know that. I could of sworn you said you weren't in this Biennale thing.'

'I'm not!' Marco's voice was barely audible, with his face still buried deep in his hands.

'Aha. I see the problem.'

Miranda said gently, 'Marco, how did your father ever get the idea that you were representing Britain at the Biennale?'

Marco lifted his head slightly and peeked out between his fingers. 'Because I told him,' he said in a tiny muffled voice.

It took some time to get the whole story out of Marco. A year or so ago, when Marco's father and mother were splitting up for the third and final time, Marco, noticing a paternal drooping of

117

spirits, decided to cheer his father up by boasting of his successes in the art world.

'Dad was chuffed,' Marco said now, 'always was, when we talked art. He was a kind of artist himself, when he was young, but ended up in advertising. But he always encouraged me, far more than Mum.' He did not add that his mother, one of the bright young things in the early days of hip advertising, was scathingly discouraging. 'Go into marketing, Mark, if you've got any sense in you at all. Or PR. That's where the money is.'

One thing led to another, during this trying period of divorce and acrimony. Marco, closer to his father than to his mother, tried to divert him from this painful period of divorce by talking painting and art. Marco was having a string of minor successes in London; his father was beside himself with hope and expectation for the Biennale.

'I just couldn't tell him,' Marco said now, head in his hands again. 'That I hadn't been chosen. It would have broken his heart. I never dreamed he'd actually come to Venice, because June's his busiest month at work. He's your original workaholic; he loves his job. He wouldn't even go to my cousin's wedding last year because it was in June, said he couldn't even afford one day off. Caused a huge family rift, but Dad wouldn't budge.' Marco groaned again.

Bruce and Miranda looked at each other gravely. 'And he's coming here,' Miranda said unnecessarily.

'Tomorrow.'

Marco nodded wordlessly. When he spoke again his words were terrible to hear. 'It'll break his heart,' he repeated with a desolate howl.

Miranda was getting fed up with all these broken hearts, wafting around Venice with the carelessness of pigeon guano. And as messy, too.

Yet for all that, she was sorry for Marco. It was sweet of him to be so concerned for his father.

'And there's worse,' Marco said, beginning to whimper now, a positive step, Miranda thought, after the howling.

'Oboy,' Bruce whispered. 'Worse?'

'Ever since Dad phoned, about an hour ago, it's been a disaster. I was nearly finished, putting the last touches on "Grey-on-Grey," and now it's gone.'

'The painting? Gone?' Miranda asked, but when she looked she could see it was still there.

'Inspiration. Passion. The muse. Wiped out by one phone call.'

This time Miranda really did have enough. 'Don't be so fucking daft,' she said briskly. 'Just pull yourself together, and finish the bloody thing. We'll worry about your father later. Go on, back to work. I'm off now, I need a nap. But I'll be down in an hour to see how you've got on. And you had better have done something.' With that, she was gone.

Bruce and Marco stared at her in wonder. After a moment Marco, meekly, did as he was told.

Bruce stared admiringly at the closed shutters and door of Apt. 1. If he were into women, he could go for that one. Real passion there, oboy oboy.

He shook his head, in awe and delight. As he went back into his own apartment, he glanced at Marco, who was painting with an intense concentration and fury, though the boy did throw the occasional worried glance at the door to Miranda's apartment.

So it's really true about Englishmen, Bruce thinks with a silent giggle: *The nanny syndrome.*

Europe was the niftiest theme park in the world.

Chapter Eight

For the rest of that afternoon Palazzo Bobolino was at peace. Well, in a manner of speaking. In Apt. 1 Miranda was lying on her bed reading *Wuthering Heights* and wishing she were on the Yorkshire Moors, or any Moors, or anywhere where it wasn't 30 something degrees and unnaturally humid for June.

Down the corridor Frank sat diligently at his table studying Italian verbs, while in the bedroom Netty snored, never being one to miss siesta time even though the language school had given them plenty of homework. This confirmed what Frank already knew; that the English were an undisciplined lot who let their cows become ill and their currency shambolic. They certainly had no sense of order. Already Marco had asked that his rota be changed, so that he could finish his painting. It was beyond Frank how they ever won a war, let alone two.

Marco was still at his canvas, and in Apt. 2 Bruce stroked the two white cats and pondered over what could be done about the distraught artist. Bruce liked Marco, wanted to help. He wanted to help everyone, actually, in that peculiarly American way that assumes everyone *wants* to be helped, whether they think they do or not.

It did not occur to Bruce that there was nothing he could do.

He was American, for goodness' sake; the Americans always came up with something when the rest of the world failed.

The first thing, Bruce mused as Tommasina and Topolino purred and snoozed under his caressing fingers, was to find out more about this Biennale stuff. For some reason everyone seemed to assume that it was something he was familiar with. But how was he supposed to know about it, when it took place in Europe? Now had it been New York, or Chicago, or Miami or Atlanta . . .

His thoughts were broken by a knocking on his courtyard door. 'Bruce, darling, are you in?'

'Lissabelle, hi, sure I'm in, for you, baby, if no one else, ha ha.' He winked playfully at her. One of the more pleasant perks of being filthy rich was that you could flirt outrageously with just about everyone, and never have to follow through if you didn't feel like it. Which Bruce never did.

'No, darling, thank you but I won't come in,' she said in reply to his invitation. 'I wondered if you would like to come with me to the opening of an art exhibition, all part of the Biennale. Private invitations only, of course, but I'm sure they wouldn't mind if I brought a guest.' She said it in such a way as to imply they would not mind if she brought a hundred guests and arrived on an elephant, so deperately did they want her attendance.

Bruce said without thinking, 'Wouldn't Marco appreciate it more than me? He's the artist.'

Lissabelle said without thinking, 'You must be joking. Why in God's name would I want to be seen with Marco?' How peculiar Americans were, she could not help thinking. Why would she want to go to the opening of an art exhibition with an insignificant minor artist when there was a prestigious New York art dealer to accompany her?

Bruce agreed to go, to find out more about the Biennale. And also because he was intrigued by Lissabelle, as he was by just about everyone. Europe was a foreign country, he was discovering. So was being rich. It was great fun, exploring both, and now he would have a chance to explore Being Famous, since everyone said that was what Lissabelle was.

The roar of a motorboat breaking the speed limit down the Grand Canal and shrieking to a noisy halt at Palazzo Bobolino coincided with the uproar going on in the courtyard of that same palazzo.

'I'm done! It's finished! I've finished!'

Out of the various apartments came the inhabitants, to see what was going on. Marco was jumping up and down, making victory fists and shouting, 'YES, YES, YES!' and embracing everyone who came near him.

They all crowded around to see the completed painting, 'Existential Nihilism in a Post-Technological Age', (working title 'Grey-on-Grey') and to congratulate Marco. There was a stunned silence, which Marco interpreted as awe for his work. He would not have been surprised to see them fall on their knees and worship.

The silence was, actually, because the painting looked exactly the same as it had on the very first day that Marco had begun it. It also looked uncannily like the other one he had done, when he had first arrived.

Miranda spoke first. She proclaimed it fantastic, though she knew nothing about modern art. But it looked as good as anything she had seen so far in the pre-Biennale exhibitions dotted around Venice, and as good as the odd contemporary paintings she had scrutinized in various galleries in Shropshire. She also did not want to see Marco go into a decline again; it was far too tedious for the rest of them in Palazzo Bob. So she said again, 'Fantastic, Marco. Well done.'

Frank nodded sagely and talked a great deal about what the Swiss German Art Movement was doing with Installations and whatnot; then he went on to rave again about the German pavilion which was expected to win all the prizes. Netty said, 'Oh, I say,' a great deal, and squealed, and looked frightfully impressed, which she was.

Silvano, who was not working that evening, announced that it was better than anything he had ever seen at any Biennale, and he had witnessed them all, being Venetian and right in the thick of things. Because he liked Marco, he did not voice his usual opinion that never had he seen such a load of crap as exhibited year in and year out at the famous art event.

Elena, pulling Silvano over towards Netty so that the English-woman and her husband could make surreptitious arrangements to meet clandestinely later, said yes, yes, she agreed. Though she hadn't a clue what she was agreeing about, for she had not been listening. She was becoming more and more impatient for her husband to flee the marital nest into the cloud cuckoo land of Inghilterra, so that she could have a life.

Paolo, who had pulled up in his water taxi while all this was going on, frowned and said he was not sure whether he liked it or not. But everyone knew that this was because he was jealous of Nina and Marco, so he was quite rightly ignored. However, Paolo did not give a fig about being ignored, for he had, moments ago, received an imperious phone call on his mobile from the beautiful, disdainful Lissabelle, summoning him to the Palazzo Bobolino at once. She was panting for it, he told his mates with a hearty chuckle as he zoomed off in his boat.

But at this moment Lissabelle came out, looked cursorily and dismissively at Marco's painting, and said offhandedly to Paolo, 'Bruce and I are going to the Museo del'Arte in Campo Santa Maria Formosa; you know it? There is a side canal directly at the door; you can take us there.'

While Paolo stared, speechless at this effrontery – Lissabelle treating him as if he were a mere taxi driver – Bruce came out of Apt. 1.

For a mad moment, Miranda thought she was seeing three white cats, until she realized that it was only Bruce, followed by Tommasina and Topolino. It was just that Bruce himself looked like their big brother, with a white linen suit, a Panama hat, and his round puffed face smooth and slightly pinkish, as if he had been licking it clean with his own rough tongue.

The crowd around Marco and his painting parted like the Red Sea, to let the great Art Dealer from Manhattan view the work of art. There was a hushed silence, as Bruce (and the cats) walked grandly to the easel.

Bruce stopped in front of the painting and stared. He turned his head this way and that. His eyes narrowed. He frowned, and the onlookers gasped inaudibly. He smiled, and so did they.

This went on for several moments. No one, not even Lissabelle, could keep his or her eyes from Bruce, waiting for his reaction.

Bruce, in fact, was hedging and shifting, hemming and hawing, because he hadn't a clue about modern art, or any art at all for that matter, and did not know what he was supposed to be looking at. He understood that something was expected of him; he could tell by the hushed expectancy around him. Even the water traffic seemed to have stopped as the very canal waited for his pronouncements.

Bruce, for he was an innocent man, assumed that this was because he was a friend of Marco's, and naturally everyone wanted their friends to approve of them. To love them unconditionally too, and cherish them and make allowances. Bruce knew this was every American's right; he supposed it must be an Englishman's right too.

So, though he could not make head nor tail of all the grey dots and swirls in front of him, he said at last, 'Well hey, Marco, it's terrif. A real masterpiece, man, I love it. I just really, really love it.'

With that, everyone cheered.

Except Lissabelle, who was looking at Marco in an entirely different light.

The flash of cameras, the whirr of television paraphernalia, the thrusting throbbing of journalists, all mixed with the eager hum of the cognoscenti as they milled about in the splendidly large and magnificent drawing room of the palazzo which housed the art museum. Chairs had been brought in and placed in rows, in front of which stood a long table with microphones, bottles of the best mineral water, pads of paper. Some very important people were already importantly shuffling these papers and sipping the water, but no one knew quite who they were. It was hard to tell the audience from the important people, unfortunately, so one had to be gracious to everyone, just to be sure.

Lissabelle was doing just this, in her usual I-couldn't-give-a-monkey's way, smiling at people in a kind of jaded, suggestive manner. Of what she was suggestive about, no one was sure, so they hung around her to make certain they were not missing anything.

Bruce, at Lissabelle's side, was impressed in that nonchalant, optimistic American manner, thinking how stage-managed Europe was, in a loose, slightly scruffy, eccentric manner. A great many people talked very loudly, both dignitaries and guests and those of the media. The voices that could be heard spoke Italian (several government ministers, a faded pop star who was a patron of the arts, a scattering of museum and gallery curators); and English. The English voices were divided roughly into the Americans (the artist and his entourage); and, well, the English. The latter were here because it had been rumoured that Cherie Blair would be present, and it would have been pleasant to mention this casually in postcards home.

Bruce was surprised and gratified to find people flocking around him too, talking to him in a babble of accents. He had not a clue what they were saying half the time, especially if their language was English; it was all to do with chromatic interplay of light and shadow, and spacial continuum, and Meaning as a figurative attribution in art. But it was heady stuff nonetheless, and ever so cultured.

When finally, three quarters of an hour late, the fifteen or so important people settled at the long table, and the hundred or so not-so-important people squeezed into seats or stood around the glittering salon of the palazzo, the event began. This, Bruce decided, was not quite so much fun. Everyone made a speech. Loudly, dramatically, and long-ly. Far, far too longly; they went on and on. Some in Italian, some in English, some in American. These last two were translated into Italian, to remind people that they were in Italy.

The artist talked last, and longest. He wore black clothes and had loose hair; he could have been Marco in thirty years time, with greying pony tail and sunglasses over bloodshot eyes. His eyes were bloodshot under the black glasses, Bruce assumed, because he had been working terribly hard on his latest installation, which was being dedicated tonight to the city of Venice and the Biennale. Bruce had seen it as they had entered the palazzo; it looked to him like a Christmas tree made of clothes hangers with bare 60-watt bulbs all over it which went off and on haphazardly. It was called 'Conceptual Realization'. Bruce tried terribly hard to like it, but after a bit decided it was not really necessary. After all, the artist wasn't his friend, like Marco was.

'Well, darling, what do you think?' Lissabelle asked, her hand tucked into his white-suited arm as they strolled out into the campo afterwards. They stopped for a moment to look back at the palazzo with the installation blinking like fairy lights in front.

Bruce searched around for something positive to say, so as not to offend Lissabelle, whom he had heard raving about the piece of work to everyone in sight just a few moments ago. 'Oh, uh, interesting,' he managed, but as she seemed to be hanging on every word, he felt forced to go on. 'Yep, it was, like, real conceptual, you know? Spacially connected, don't you think? And, um, full of continuum.'

Several people were milling around outside, and shamelessly eavesdropping. Word had somehow got about that the man who looked like a cherubic Tennessee Williams in his white linen suit and jaunty Panama hat was an influential art dealer from Manhattan, who was in Venice not only as one of the top judges of the Biennale but also to arrange for some of his best artists to exhibit at the prestigious Peggy Guggenheim gallery here in the city.

They were looking at Bruce and nodding and bobbing their beautiful heads with every word he uttered. Encouraged by this, and by Lissabelle's hand pressing his arm possessively, he went on, 'Yes, certainly. The, um, neon effect is a visual comment on the, ah, subjectiveness of, oboy, I would say the concept of . . .' Here Bruce looked around him, 'the concept of the dark interconnecting waters of the canal.'

As if to emphasize his point, a gondola came down the canal and drifted under the narrow stone bridge opposite the palazzo. The Japanese couple inside oohed and aahed over the Christmas tree made of clothes hangers and rushed to one side of the craft to take photos.

After the gondolier stopped shouting and the gondola had righted itself, Lissabelle, still hanging on to Bruce, and aware that more people were gathering round to hear his sage pronouncements on art, said, 'Go on, Bruce darling. You were saying?'

Bruce hadn't a clue what he had been saying, so he stared at the Christmas tree for inspiration. None came, so he said what he was thinking. 'It makes Marco's painting a work of genius.'

There was a buzz in the crowd as this was digested. Someone asked, 'Marco?'

Lissabelle said quickly, 'Marco Polo, darling, the artist. Don't tell me you've never heard of him?' She laughed in a light derogatory manner. Several others nodded their heads knowingly, and said that of course *they* had heard of him.

'Marco's a very dear friend of mine,' Lissabelle went on, 'but he likes to keep himself to himself. His work, you know. But you'll be hearing all about him very, very soon, I promise. Bruce here has taken Marco under his wing.'

With this Lissabelle blew a few kisses into the crowd, settled her sunglasses down over her eyes, and firmly steered Bruce away from the palazzo and out into the sweet twilight of a Venetian June evening.

And such an evening it is. Swallows and swifts titter, a setting sun makes orange and red paintings on the smooth surface of darkening green canals. Mosquitoes bite, but not too hard. Restaurants overcharge, but not too much. Venezia is mellow tonight. Soft and sensual, like the textures of the rich velvets and silks in the shops; glittery and mysterious, like the masks of Carnival.

While Bruce and Lissabelle stroll back to the Palazzo Bobolino ('Why not, darling? Walk? It would be such a Venetian thing to do!' Lissabelle had cried, as if she had only just discovered her feet), other people in this serene city are not so energetic.

In Palazzo Bobolino, Paolo, still enraged over having been treated as a taxi driver by the woman he so recently bonked (and so well!), waits in the courtyard for her return, the righteous fury of Italian machismo full upon him.

Unknown to Paolo, his fiancée Nina is also in the palazzo, but not in the courtyard. She is in Apt. 1, in Marco's bedroom to be exact. Nina is listening carefully to Marco as he has a post-coital flush of words, English words of course, which she tries to remember carefully. Marco is waffling on about his completed painting (over which he is ecstatic); and about the arrival of his father (over which he is not). He rambles on for a long, long time, while Nina, surreptitiously, sneaks out the notebook and pen she has hidden under the bed and makes notes in a column headed: English Expressions Useful to Know.

Frank too, in his cubbyhole of a bedroom downstairs, also has a notebook and pen. The column he is writing in is headed: Italian Irregular Verbs. Unlike Nina, he is not writing his list whilst lying moist and naked in bed with another person in the same condition, but sitting upright in a straight-backed chair at his tidy writing desk.

Most Serene Venice frowns slightly at this, causing a few clouds to mar the near-perfect sunset. Frank is not quite getting the hang of it, somehow. He may excel at Italian verbs, but he hasn't quite caught the drift of the city itself. He is too stolid somehow. Too plodding.

But elsewhere, things are more to Venezia's liking. People are making delightful fools of themselves all over the place: Netty, hanging around the gondola moorings near the Bridge of Sighs and flirting outrageously with Silvano every time he brings in a passenger; Silvano, flirting ridiculously back; even Miranda, walking along the Zattere, the wide walkway by the vast Guidecca Canal, mooning foolishly about things that happened twenty-eight years and nine months ago.

All is as it should be. Venice smiles, satisfied, and blows away the clouds, leaving the sun free to set over her waterways and palazzos in its usual blowzy splendour.

'Oh bloody hell. Now it's that American art dealer.'

'Well, I could have told you that, Simon. Did you see her clinging to him on the boat as they left?'

'Darling April, don't be such a know-it-all. Of course I saw; I was waving them off, just as you were. But there is clinging and clinging. Look there, out the window, under the fig tree.'

'Ah. I see what you mean.'

There was silence for a moment or two as they watched out the window of Apt. 3 into the courtyard. After a time April said, 'D'you think she is eating him? She seems to be doing something curious to his lips with her teeth.'

'Darling, don't be so provincial. I know you come from Dorset, but *really*. She's kissing him, April. That's how we do it in London.'

'It looks aggressive. Quite terrifying, I would say. Not much fun at all. In fact, Bruce doesn't seem to be enjoying it one bit. He's backing away as from a lion.'

As if conjured up by April's words, a roar such as usually comes from the throats of wild beasts came from the other side of the courtyard, where Paolo, having drunk a bottle of red wine while waiting to satisfy his manhood, had fallen asleep on some soft foliage under the other bench. He had woken to a hangover and the vision of his woman (well, one of them) devouring that pink chubby American as if she had not eaten for days.

At that moment Bruce shrieked, whether it was because he had seen Paolo rushing dementedly at him, or whether it was because he simply did not know how to get away from Lissabelle, was never fully explained. April and Simon thought it was the latter, but when Lissabelle discussed it at great length with them later, they assured her that Bruce had seen the mighty Paolo's fist about to crash into his sweet American face and it was only natural that he should scream bloody murder.

Somehow Bruce ducked, leaving the brunt of the blow to fall on Topolino, who was sitting on a fat low branch of the fig tree, Tommasina not far away, watching the amusing antics of the human inhabitants of the palazzo. Topolino, reflexes sharpened by night-time exercises catching the odd canal rat who strayed into the courtyard, yowled and struck and caught Paolo's cheek with an outstretched claw. Paolo yelped, and tried to swipe the cat who raced to another branch of the fig tree. Bruce, galvanized into action by this cruelty to animals, clutched at Paolo's arm, while Simon and April, who had come running outside, clutched the rest of him.

The courtyard was full of strange little noises during this shameful episode: Venetian curses from Paolo, growls from the cats, shrieks and whimpers from Bruce, and four-letter words from Lissabelle, who nonetheless was secretly marvelling at the fact that for the first time in years, she was not bored.

'You are a scumbag,' Paolo shouted at Bruce. 'And a whore and a man with no balls,' he went on, trying to remember the English he had picked up from various passengers. It was amazing how many couples had major rows on his boat, usually on the way back to the airport. On the way into Venice, it was all lovey dovey cooing and kissing.

'You are a shit-eater and a dog-fucker,' Paolo went on, 'and your mother wears Army boots.'

'Jeez, now where did you get *that* one?' Bruce asked with interest. 'Man oh man, the last time I heard that I was a kid; I remember my best buddy's mom—'

But he was stopped by another roar from Paolo. 'Oboy,' Bruce whimpered, 'you can sure scare a guy. Now c'mon, pal, this is a big, big misunderstanding, and if we kind of calm down a bit and talk things out . . .'

Bruce trailed off as Paolo's mouth was opening to roar again. 'You shit-heap son of a whore. I'll kill you, Englishman.'

'OH NO, GOD, PLEASE, DON'T.' Bruce hollared out the words while holding up his hands in front of his face. The thought went through his mind that he was not an Englishman, but he did not think now was the time to bring this to Paolo's attention.

When nothing happened to his face Bruce peered out from

between his fingers to see even more people in the courtyard. Frank seemed to be shouting brusque orders, like 'On count of three, I grab shoulders and you arms,' while holding down Paolo, who now seemed intent on murdering Marco, who had suddenly appeared in the courtyard. Paolo was crying, 'English whore! English scumbag and son of scumbag-whore.'

April said to Lissabelle, 'Doesn't have a very wide vocabulary, does he,' and Lissabelle answered, 'They never do, darling, not the rough ones. But that is often an advantage, believe me.'

'What's going on?' Miranda cried, also having just arrived and wishing she hadn't. Nina, who had been cowering behind Marco, rushed into her arms.

'I thought I could sneak away,' Nina wailed. 'Out of here, while all that fuss was going on with Bruce and Paolo and Lissabelle. I'm already late for work. Paolo's been lurking here for ages, I didn't think I'd ever get out.'

A scream went through the crowd as Paolo broke away from Frank, and Simon as well, to lurch at Marco, who kept bouncing away nimbly and saying things like, 'Here, steady on,' and 'Look, I can explain.' Not that he could, of course. He was also thinking what a waste all this good angst was, with his painting finished. Not only was he suffering emotionally, he was about to suffer physically as well, for Paolo was bigger than he was.

Suddenly a croaking noise, rather like a large reptile having a temper tantrum, made everyone look up and shut up. At least for a moment.

Elena said in a loud gravelly voice, 'What is all this nonsense? I could hear all of you from outside the main door; what kind of people will the neighbours think live at the Palazzo Bobolino?'

They all stared at her, abashed.

'How many years am I living here? Forty-one, that is how many. Always, this palazzo is fine, is respectable, until now. Never have

132

I heard such noise, such language. Paolo, you should be ashamed of yourself. Wait until I tell your mother.'

'*Zia Elena, per favore, no.*' Paolo, as miraculously changed as astringent water into sweet white wine, looked imploringly at her. 'Don't tell Mamma, please.'

'They know each other?' Miranda asked Nina.

'Oh yes, she's his aunt. Venice is a small place, remember.'

It was extraordinary how civilized the courtyard became under Elena's stony gaze. Bruce took out a white handkerchief and mopped his brow, while Lissabelle sat meekly with April on one of the benches. Frank reluctantly let go his grip on Paolo's shoulder, though he did instruct Simon softly to be prepared for more action if necessary. Marco scurried over to Miranda, while Nina braved Paolo.

'I was having an English lesson,' she said truthfully. Well, half-truthfully. 'Why are you so jealous of a simple English lesson?'

'Because I love you,' Paolo muttered, realizing as he said it, that he did. She was Italian, what more reason did he need? The Englishwoman had good legs but was unfaithful; look how she went off with the pink American as soon as his back was turned. Nina was honest and true and faithful.

She was also cross, now that Paolo was meek. 'And you?' she said, pressing her advantage. 'What were *you* doing, hiding in the courtyard? And don't tell me you were waiting for me; I saw how you began a fight with the American. Over *her*, eh? That English whore.' Nina spat contemptuously in the direction of Lissabelle.

'Darling, stop being so melodramatic,' Lissabelle called to her. She had not had such fun since the BAFTA awards, when she was going through her lesbian phase and dating a woman up for Best Actress. The woman won and made a militant speech for Gay Rights, dragging out of the closet several Cabinet ministers both male and female, a star footballer on the England team and an

Anglican woman priest, tipped to become a bishop. The resulting pandemonium and publicity had kept Lissabelle in the limelight for weeks.

Nina took a threatening step towards Lissabelle, who stood up defiantly from her bench. God, this was like the old days, she thought, exhilarated. Pity there were no paparazzi about, though. Not even a sad little journalist.

Realizing this, she sat back down, losing interest. Paolo had grabbed Nina by the arm and was whispering, 'Cara mia, the Englishwoman means nothing to me. She has been a passenger in my *motoscafo*; she is a customer,' he said truthfully. Or half-truthfully as the case may be.

Then, inspired, he pulled Nina further away from the listening throng. 'I will tell you the truth, *cara*. I was angry with the Englishwoman, and came here to tell her this. She gave me the wrong fare. Too little, understand? Far too little; I felt she was cheating me. I was trying to settle it, but you know me, a bit hot-tempered.' He looked coyly at the ground as he said this last bit, so as not to appear too immodest.

Nina decided that it was time to throw herself into Paolo's arms, for she did indeed love him, even though she didn't believe a word he said. And anyway, his Aunt Elena was watching and would surely tell his mother if there was a rift between them. Then Paolo's mother would tell Nina's mother, who would tell Nina's brother, who had been promised a job in the government office where Paolo's father worked for short hours and a good retirement scheme, not to mention life-long security and a top-notch salary.

Being Italian, one needed to keep these things in mind.

Paolo welcomed her in his arms because his *zia* was watching with those crocodile eyes, and his mother would kill him if he broke off with Nina after Nina's older brother promised his father's younger sister his old job as junior supervisor in a huge dry-cleaning establishment when he got in with Paolo's father at the government office.

Lissabelle watched with her favourite expression of bored contempt while she wondered if Paolo was worth prying off his silly little fiancée. She decided not.

She looked at Bruce but he was slinking away towards his apartment. He was probably gay, she thought, remembering how unresponsive he had been to her expert kisses in the courtyard. Not that that mattered one iota; she herself changed sides now and again; she was sure she could entice Bruce to do the same.

But then she spotted Marco, being comforted by Miranda for the loss of Nina. Lissabelle remembered what Bruce had said about Marco, about his painting. How brilliant it was.

'Yes,' Lissabelle murmured to Simon and April who were sitting at her feet (where they belonged) on the tiny grassy bit under the benches in the courtyard. Her eyes were firmly on Marco. 'Yes, yes, yes, yes.'

'No,' Simon muttered as they watched Lissabelle approach Marco. 'No, no, no, no, *no*.'

'Third time lucky?' April said softly. Then they began laughing, so hard that Miranda, having found herself unaccountably no longer at Marco's side, went and sat next to them to hear what the joke was.

'Oh nothing,' April giggled.

'Sort of a family joke,' Simon cackled. 'Not very funny to others.'

And they would not tell her, for they were far, far too loyal to Lissabelle, who was not only such a dear friend but paid them a whopping great salary to boot.

Chapter Nine

Elena was, as usual, the first to greet the newcomer.

'Bells don't work,' she said as the stranger pushed and poked at all of them, in very much the same manner as Miranda had, when when she first arrived. 'No good in even trying.'

Elena took out her key to the massive courtyard door and unlocked it, thrusting her various parcels of groceries and sundries to the man trying to get in. 'Who are you looking for?'

The stranger, struggling with a travelling bag, a camera bag and now Elena's fruit and vegetables and loaves of bread and several large bottles of mineral water, said politely, 'My son, Markian Polonksi. He's English. I believe he is in Apt. Number 1. This is the Palazzo Bobolino, isn't it?'

'Well sure, it's the Palace Bob!' The traveller was thumped on the shoulder in a friendly manner and given a huge welcoming smile by Bruce, who also had just returned from shopping. 'Did I hear you say you're Marco's father? Hey, how're y'doing? We've been expecting you. Marco didn't know exactly when you'd be arriving, or we'd all have met you at the airport. Now here, just hang on to these bags for me for a sec, till I find my key. I'm taking you straight into my apartment, where you'll be staying. Now don't worry about a thing, it's all arranged. I got rooms coming out of my ears, and your son's apartment, Number 1, is kinda crowded. But, like, it's right next door, how does that grab you? C'mon in. Marco's gone out to breathe in some vibes, get a handle on the lagoon, or whatever it is artists do in Venice.' He laughed lightheartedly, and Mr Polonski wondered why he was reminded of the tinkling of tiny baby rattles, and little wood chimes, the kind you hang over a pram.

A few moments later Bruce was still searching for his key, while Elena gave suggestions and Mr Polonski stood helplessly laden down with shopping. 'Sorry about this, Mr Polo. I do this all the time, I'm afraid. Getting a bit cheesy in the head in my old age, hey? Happens to all of us, I guess.'

'Polonski. My name is Polonski. Mark shortened it for his work. Polo comes from Polonski.'

'What? Goddamn, thought I had it then. False alarm, it's the key to the mailbox. Now what were you saying, Mr Polo?'

'Never mind. Just call me Radek.'

Privately, Bruce thought Mr Polo a whole lot easier to remember, and get your tongue around, but was too polite to say so. 'Great to meet you, Mr Radek.'

'Just Radek. My Christian name.'

'Hey, I'm slow today. Hi, Ray, pleased to see you. I'm Bruce Brinson, and this is our good neighbour here Elena.'

They both held out a hand for Radek to shake, and looked perplexed when he made no move to respond, until they realized he was laden with packages. Then everyone laughed.

From the courtyard window of Apt. 3, Lissabelle said, 'Now who is that rather dishy man standing out there with Bruce and the gondolier's wife?'

Neither Simon nor April knew.

A moment later, Bruce was saying, 'Oh hi, Lissabelle. Meet Ray, Marco's father.'

'Radek. Nice to meet you, Lissabelle.'

Lissabelle was disappointed; she had expected some well-known and influential friend of Bruce's from one of the trendier international circles of jet-setters and beautiful people. Pity, for he was good-looking in a chunky kind of way, with a mass of hair the colour of polished steel and an amused emerald glitter in his clear bright eyes. 'Are you an artist yourself, Radek?' Lissabelle asked, a slight gleam of interest in her voice. Perhaps he too, like Marco, was a man with great talent which she, Lissabelle, could make use of.

'No, I'm afraid not, though I had pretensions of being a sculptor in my youth. I had no talent, though, but luckily I was astute enough to spot that early on.'

'But surely that's where Marco gets his creativity from.'

'I doubt it. It most likely came from his mother. She was a painter too, like Marco.'

Bruce noted the 'was' and bowed his head in a sympathetic manner. 'She's, ah, passed over?' he said sombrely.

Radek's green eyes twinkled. 'Yes.'

'I am so, so sorry.' Bruce squeezed Radek's elbow in sympathy. 'That is so sad.' Bruce immediately felt sad himself, in empathy. He was taking a shine to Marco's father, who was quite a handsome man, for a European. He even had good teeth. Bruce for a moment regretted that he was not into men, but got over it quickly. Life was far too much fun without the complications love and sex could create, no matter what the gender.

'When did she pass away? Your wife.'

'Over a year ago, nearly two now. She passed over to another man. And another career. He is a dentist, and she is his assistant.'

Bruce did not quite know what to say to this. He supposed the man was being droll; the English were known for this. Though the man was not quite English; there was a tang of accent in his voice, something smoky and evocative of rickety wooden tables

138

and hushed secret meetings. Something Eastern European, like straight shots of vodka and the hoofbeats of Cossacks thundering over the plains. Bruce hoped he was not a Communist, until he remembered they were no longer the enemy.

He said cautiously, 'I'm sure sorry to hear that. About your wife.'

'Heavens, don't be,' Radek smiled. 'They seem quite happy, from what Marco tells me. Though it *is* a pity she gave up her painting. She was quite talented.'

For once, Bruce was at a loss for words. This sometimes occurred when he was in the dangerous swamp land of marriages and coupledom. It was all mud and murky substances to him, and he stayed clear of it.

At last Bruce found his key, which had fallen somehow into an unknown shirt pocket, and they all proceded to go inside, Elena and Lissabelle as well, Elena because she always went into everyone's apartment, and Lissabelle because she was bored witless with just the company of Simon and April, who had tagged along as well.

Radek was given tea and a view of the Grand Canal from the drawing room. Bruce said, as he was passing about biscuits, 'Have you been to Venice before, Ray?'

Radek nodded. 'The first time was years ago, when I was a university student. Almost thirty years ago. I come back whenever I can find an excuse, and Marco's painting in the Biennale gives me a terrific one.'

At this, Lissabelle, who had been looking listlessly out the window at the boring old gondolas going up and down the canal, looked up. 'Marco's painting? In the Biennale?'

Behind Radek's back Bruce was making furious gestures, holding his fingers to his lips in a secretive manner, shaking his head silently no, no, no. Lissabelle opened her mouth and closed it again when Bruce said hastily, 'We're so proud of Marco, all of us here at the Palazzo Bob. Why, it's as if one of *us* were exhibiting at the Biennale! I guess it is, in a way. One of us, that is, heh heh. One of us in the good old Palace Bob, neat, eh?'

He went on in this inane manner for quite some time, until Lissabelle said sharply, 'No one told *me* Marco was an exhibitor.'

Bruce looked at her sternly. 'Oh? The boy is too modest, too shy.' He frowned at her in what he hoped was a don't-you-know-anything? look.

Lissabelle felt foolish, and reprimanded. She had not felt like that since schooldays, and did not like it then. She decided it was time to say something scathingly, woundingly, witty to Bruce, cutting him down in front of Radek so that he writhed in tiny bleeding pieces all over the cracked tiles of this blasted run-down palazzo.

But as her mouth opened, Simon, standing by the window next to her, said very softly, 'He's a mega art dealer, remember, and influential too,' and Lissabelle's mouth shut firmly.

April whispered admiringly to Simon, 'You've earned your wages this week.'

Radek listened to Bruce praising his son with a face radiating pride like a piece of uranium radiating radiation. He glowed with it. Bruce could feel it zapping around the room like a nuclear reactor gone wrong.

'Oh, Elena, there's your husband.' April, who had moved from the window over the canal to the one looking out over the courtyard, waved to Silvano. She did not mention that he was canoodling with Netty under the fig tree; discreetly, of course, being well aware that his wife may be lurking nearby. April felt Lissabelle was looking bored again, and needing a diversion. April also wanted to prove that she could be as much an asset to their employer as Simon.

Bruce ran to the window, for Elena seemed quite uninterested in either seeing, or communicating with, her husband. 'Hey you guys, come on up,' he shouted down to Netty and Silvano. 'Come meet Marco's father.'

Lissabelle shuddered at this, and wished she were in Dorsoduro, where the gondoliers stayed in their gondolas on the edge of the canals, where they belonged. Simon and April eyed her, for signs that they must leap up and announce that Lissabelle's agent was ringing her shortly with important details of million-pound contracts and advances, and she must return to her own apartment at once. Simon was better at reading the signs than April, and he relaxed and kept quiet. Lissabelle was looking bored, but not bored enough to leave.

'She's waiting for Marco to get here,' Simon whispered.

Netty and Silvano came up the marble stairway of Apt. 2, giggling like adolescent lovers. They were delighted that Elena had not seen them scurrying up to Bruce's place together. Silvano pinched Netty's bottom surreptiously as they entered the drawing room. It was just like old days, he thought deliriously. He felt youthful blood begin to simmer and boil in his veins, until he looked up and found himself face to face with his wife.

Bruce cried, 'Meet Marco's father, Ray Polo.'

'Radek Polonski. Pleased to meet you.' He shook hands with them both.

Silvano began a babbling, near incoherent speech, welcoming him to Venice, La Serenessima, the Most Serene Republic, going on about her colourful and magnificent history and her glorious tradition, exemplified by the *gondolieri*. It was roughly the same sort of thing he gave his customers on his gondola, to impress them and be assured of big tips. Here, he was merely trying to avoid having to speak to his wife.

'I thought you were supposed to be working,' she muttered in Veneziano, when he stopped welcoming Marco's father and tried to breathe.

'Lunch time, my dearest. I thought I would come home for lunch today, and see you, my treasure.'

Elena was cross, and Silvano could tell. She must have seen the pinch on the vast bottom that belonged to Netty.

Elena had, and she *was* cross. Running off to England with the silly Englishwoman was one thing, but making a fool of *her*, Elena, right here in Venice with the fat tart of a woman was another. Elena had her pride, her self-respect to consider. If Silvano did not intend to run off and leave her a merry single woman again, then he had better behave with dignity and restraint.

She was about to open her mouth to speak when Bruce asked, 'You guys didn't see Marco, did you? He hasn't even seen his father yet.'

Netty, recovering from the shock of seeing Elena, who had mysteriously dropped her pretence at friendship and was glowering at her, cried, 'Radek, what an interesting name! It's not English, of course.'

'No, I am from Poland. I went to England after my student days, and remained.'

'How frightfully interesting!'

'Say,' Bruce said, 'you'll have to meet Frank. You'll have a lot in common; he's from your neck of the woods. In fact there he is now, just coming back from his morning at the language school.' Bruce leaned out the courtyard window and yelled, 'Yahoo, Frankie, come on up. We're having a little party here.'

'I cannot. I have much work to do. Ten irregular verbs to learn by tomorrow.'

'Hey man, loosen up,' Bruce said good-naturedly. 'I'm making some lunch, you've got to eat.'

Frank, torn between hunger and discipline, decided he could alter his afternoon schedule of a quick snack, a half-hour siesta, one hour of intense study followed by a half-hour brisk exercise, to accommodate a free lunch.

Bruce introduced him to Radek, saying, 'You're both from the same area, more or less,' in a pleased kind of way, as if he had brought them together himself for the sole purpose of their pleasure and delight.

Frank said indignantly, 'I am Swiss.'

Radek said, more mildly, 'I was born in Poland, but I've lived in England longer than I did in my native land.'

'There!' Bruce was beaming with good-will. 'Same thing, right? I knew you'd have a lot in common.'

Netty turned to Radek and said, 'I say, you must be exceedingly proud of Marco. His last painting was so . . . so . . .' Words failed her. She did not have a clue how to describe his last painting, or indeed anyone's painting. 'So very compelling,' she finished enigmatically.

Once again Radek began to glow. 'Yes, that's why I'm here, of course. To see his work at the Biennale.'

Frank said, 'But I did not know—'

Bruce shouted, 'It's Ray's dream, his lifelong dream, fulfilled, seeing his son's work at the Biennale!' He began frantically gesturing behind Radek's back.

'Well, I *am* rather pleased. In fact I have to confess, I've never felt so proud in all my life.'

'Ah,' said Silvano. He could understand the dreams of fathers. He too, had had a dream, that his son would become a gondolier, like himself and his own father, but the young man had become an artist instead. A terrible step down.

April, at the courtyard window, suddenly said, 'Look, there's Marco, at last. Marco, here's your father!'

Marco, downstairs, said to Miranda whom he had met in the courtyard on the way in, 'Oh God. My father. I'll have to tell him, won't I. About the Biennale.'

'I'm afraid so. He'll find out one way or another.'

'Come up with me, okay? I want you to meet him anyway.'

Miranda followed Marco up the stairs. When they got into Bruce's vast drawing room, she saw a flurry of colour: Netty in a long white floating dress festooned with crimson and yellow poppies; Lissabelle in a jade silk trouser suit; Silvano in his red and white striped gondolier's shirt. And Bruce himself, in a rose pink shirt that matched his rose pink cheeks.

Marco, in black as usual but fortunately without his bondage waistcoat, was embracing a man in jeans and a dark blue t-shirt. There was a great deal of noise in the room, people chattering, Marco and his father gabbling affectionate greetings in a very un-English way, and outside the open windows of the drawing room, the water traffic sounds of boats and barges and the shouting of *gondolieri*.

Perhaps it was this that distracted Miranda, made her perceptions not quite as acute as they might have been.

Or perhaps it was only that twenty-eight years and nine months was a long time.

And so it was that a full two or three minutes went by before Miranda recognized the father of her only child.

'Miranda, where are you going?' Bruce grabbed her arm as she was about to bolt and run down the stairs. 'Here's Marco's father. Ray, this is Marco's landlady, kind of. Well, she's looking after her daughter's apartment, and so in turn is looking after Marco. Miranda, this is Ray.'

Radek, still beaming after the reunion with his son, looked up to see a woman he had once loved insanely, as one does when one is nineteen or thereabouts and in Venice. She was staring at him with a pale shocked face. 'Miranda,' he said dumbly.

'Radek,' she said stupidly.

'Neat, like we're all acquainted now, right? So how about some lunch?'

Marco knew that something was terribly wrong with his father

144

during lunch, as everyone dug into the parma ham and gorgonzola and fresh bread and vine-ripened tomatoes. Instead of falling all over his son's every word, as he usually did, Radek listened to Marco's chatter with an air of distraction, occasionally looking out into space in a most odd manner.

What Marco did not notice, for he was not especially observant of things that were not directly related to him, was that the space his father was looking out at, was in the direction of Miranda, who was sitting at the opposite end of the table.

This preoccupation on the part of his father did not annoy Marco today, as it would have ordinarily. An only child, he had been far closer to his father than his mother. Radek had interesting relatives, who spoke an exciting language, full of harsh zeds and vees and other fascinating, guttural sounds. These relatives often came to visit, and sometimes he and his father went to places like Krakow or Zakopane, where his father spoke all the time in the strange language which Marco never could quite master. Luckily, many of them spoke English as well, which seemed entirely as it should be.

Today, however, Marco was immensely relieved not to be the focus of his father's loving scrutiny. There would be questions about the Biennale, and Marco would have to confess. Oddly, Radek never even mentioned the Biennale at lunch, and no one else did either. Marco began to relax, like an ostrich whose head is so firmly in the ground that it has forgotten the boot about to kick its arse.

Miranda also was distracted, but no one noticed her because everyone was too busy with their own concerns. Bruce was enjoying playing the bountiful host, as he did so often in Palazzo Bob; he liked people, especially these adorable Europeans with their quaint little ways. He felt large and strong and avuncular as he did so, like Uncle Sam himself; or like one of the Pilgrim Fathers, perhaps. Thank goodness the European natives, unlike the American ones, were far too civilized to get sulky after the feasting was over.

Lissabelle was preoccupied with picking disdainfully at her food, moving it about her plate and leaving it there, to show that she was used to far, far better. April and Simon were watching Lissabelle, recognizing signs for a full-scale temper tantrum when they returned to their own apartment. Marco was simply not responding to Lissabelle's sultry sexual signals. This was making her pout, not a good omen.

Elena was watching her husband and his fancy woman, sitting opposite her. She was wondering why she bothered all these years, watching her diet, keeping fit and slim with exercise at the gym, dying her grey hair an immaculate, if somewhat ghoulish, black, to keep herself young. She was Italian; she knew what it took. Yet here was that fool Silvano, hanging about with an overblown, overdone, frowzy Englishwoman who talked as if she had the pips of nectarines stuffed in both cheeks. The Englishwoman was the same age as she was too; it was not even as if Silvano wanted a younger woman.

It was an insult. If he had no intention of going off to that *piccolo* rainy island with Netty, and leaving his wife in peace, then he had no business being seen with her.

Netty, made nervous under the black beetle frowning brows of her lover's wife, laughed shrilly, talked much, and ate a great deal. It was not even as if she were a proper mistress yet, not technically, though hands had been held, and bosoms squeezed. Sometimes Netty thought that would be quite enough, but then chided herself for her cowardice. Things would be better when she had her own apartment, right here in Venice, and moved here permanently. She was still looking at properties.

And so the members of Bruce's little party ate, or did not eat, as the case may be; and pretended to listen to what the others were saying; and drank a good deal of wine from the Veneto whilst doing these things.

Poor Miranda, sitting opposite the father of her daughter, who does not know he is a father of a daughter as well as of a handsome son who has been chosen to exhibit his work in the Biennale. And poor Radek, sitting opposite the woman he wanted to die for once, but then forgot when he returned to his poor oppressed country where things of a political nature were brewing and simmering. But he obviously had not quite forgotten her, for he understands now that his love affair with Venice, the holidays he took here year after year, were nothing more or less than a search for the woman he had loved at nineteen.

And now, as was bound to happen sooner or later, as it does in Venice, small town that it is – he has found her. He cannot take his eyes off her.

By some silent agreement, neither has let on that they know each other. Or, rather, *knew* each other, for how can either know the person sitting opposite them now? Nearly thirty years have passed; it is not just some grey or white hair, a wrinkle or two, a thickening of muscle here and there. It is also the lifetimes they each have lived, separately and unknown to the other.

And so they sit, looking at each other and looking away, looking at their food and looking away. And then looking at each other again.

I'd have known her instantly, Radek thinks, though in truth it was her long brown hair which he recognized, whose style has not changed in all these years.

I knew him at once, Miranda thinks, though in truth her recognition was based on the shock of seeing her daughter's beloved features strongly mirrored in the newcomer with the iron hair.

And so they sit, shellshocked. And life goes on merrily around them, as it always, invariably, does.

*

147

'Miranda, there you are. Look, I know it's late, but I need to talk to you.'

'Oh, Marco, you frightened me, creeping around the kitchen like that.'

'Are you making hot chocolate? Can I have one too? We could take it out on the balcony. More private there.'

As both Netty and Frank were in their separate bedrooms, fast asleep, Miranda thought this was being excessively cautious. 'Where, uh, is your father?' she asked, peering around him as if Radek would suddenly appear, shocking her for a second time that day.

It was the same day as his arrival. After lunch Marco had taken his father off to show him the sights of the city, quite forgetting that his father had been here before, many, many times. Miranda had gone into her bedroom and hid all afternoon, and all evening too. She did not want to see Radek. Not now, not ever. And certainly not alone. She knew that this was an impossible wish, but wished it anyway. She most certainly did not want to confront her past, for it would mean messing up her future. Or, rather, complicating it. She had her home in the village, her picture framing shop, her books; she had the cinema and occasional theatre and some good friends, and a daughter who visited now and again with a pleasant husband and quite jolly little ones. The sudden appearance of a father on the scene for Jessica would entail things like intense conversations, delving into the past, both hers and Radek's. And Radek would either now be permanently in her daughter's life, which would shake up Miranda's carefully thought-out future, or not, which would distress Jessica. Having found her father, she would not, understandably, wish to be rejected by him.

Marco said, 'It's Dad I want to talk to you about, Miranda.' He took the two cups of chocolate and carried them out onto the balcony, leaving her no choice but to follow, wrapping her

148

dressing gown tightly around her. She cursed herself for ever coming out of her bedroom.

They settled themselves on the chairs facing the dark water, lit by the reflections of lights in the palazzo opposite and the occasional red light of a passing gondola. There was a moon. Miranda knew she should never have come back.

'I'm really tired, Marco,' she said. 'I'm just going to drink this chocolate and get to bed.' She scalded her throat taking a sip, to show she was serious.

'Dad and I have been talking all evening,' he went on, as if she had not spoken.

Miranda kept very silent.

'And he was so strange, right up until a few minutes ago, when I said goodnight to him at Bruce's place.'

Still Miranda remained mute.

'We saw a few of the old familiar sights, went to the Basilica, wandered around and finally had a light supper. Then he said he was tired and wanted to crash out. He's gone to Bruce's place to sleep.'

Miranda made herself say, 'That's understandable. He'd been travelling; it was a long day for him.'

'Oh, I can see that. No, it's the way he acted all day. The things he said.'

'Oh?'

'Well, maybe it's more the things he didn't say. The Biennale, for instance. He never, ever once mentioned it. I was going to be brave, and tell him the truth, but it never came up.'

'Oh.'

'In fact, we never talked about my work at all. What I've been doing since I've been in Venice.' Marco shook his head in disbelief. 'He must be ill.'

'Did, uh, he talk at all? You must have talked about something.'

Marco frowned. 'Not a lot, actually.' Marco couldn't think

what there would be to talk about to his father, if it were not about him, Marco. It was after all what he had talked to his father about for years; it had been the favourite topic for both of them.

'The only questions Dad asked were about you, oddly enough.' He looked at Miranda quizzically.

'Oh. Ah, me?' She tried to look perplexed.

'Can't think why. Wanted to know if you lived here permanently, how long I've known you, that kind of stuff.' He looked at her and shook his head again, as if it were impossible to believe anyone would want to know anything about an ordinary older woman of no particular talent or creative leanings. Then he said kindly, 'I suppose it was because he was worried about me. You know, you being my landlady and all.'

'Can't think of any other reason,' Miranda said waspishly. He nodded, agreeing with this. 'Marco, you never mentioned that your father was Polish. I assumed he was Italian.'

'Really?' Marco looked surprised.

'Your name, Marco. Your bloody Italian name.'

'Oh, that. I changed it for my art. Snappier, you know? And as a homage to the great tradition of art in Italy from Giotto on down.'

'On down to Marco Polo,' Miranda said sarcastically.

'That's kind of you.' Marco's face flushed with modest pleasure. Miranda stood up. 'I'm going to bed.'

'But what about me? What about Dad? What am I going to do?' He could not for the life of him think what he could talk about to his father for the next week or so, if it were not about himself.

'You should thank your lucky stars, Marco, that for once in your young but fortunate life, your father is showing interest in something apart from you. Perhaps he will even forget about the Biennale, and you will get away with having told him one of the biggest porkers of your entire life.'

Marco brightened at these brisk words. 'I hadn't thought of that. Y'know, I bet Dad's getting senile. He's old, you know. I bet that's what it is.'

Miranda said, with some asperity, 'Now isn't that a relief for you? Your Dad getting senile dementia, and letting you off the hook?'

'Too true. You're right. Thanks, Miranda. You're a brick.' He gave her a pat on the back, in a fond manner with only the tiniest trace of condescension in it.

When he was gone, Miranda stood at the balustrade, staring moodily into the black canal, wondering if she could disappear into it.

A reflection of a light slightly above her and to her right broke her concentration on the silent water. Looking up, she saw a dark shape on the balcony of Apt. 2, the light from the drawing room behind it spilling out into the night.

'Miranda,' the voice called out softly, 'Miranda, is that you?'

'No, it's the ghost of Christmas bloody past,' she hissed, cursing herself for not getting off her own balcony sooner.

'Pardon?' Radek said.

'Nothing. Yes, it's me.'

'I thought so. Miranda, I would have known you anywhere. I can't believe this is happening. I can't believe it is really you.'

'It's not.'

'Pardon?'

'It's a dream. We're ghosts. Ta ta, Radek.'

She started to go back inside but he said, loudly, 'Still the same, Miranda. Still making jokes at the most serious moments. I remember one night at the Pensione Marico—'

'Yes, yes, that's enough. We don't want the whole of the Palazzo Bobolino to know too.'

'And then there was that time when we found that empty rowboat, moored off that dark campo, and we crept inside and—'

151

'Radek, will you please shut up?'

'Do you remember how the boat rocked, when we—'

'Radek, if you don't shut up at once, I'm going right inside.'

There was a silence for a moment. The only sound was the slap, slapping, of water against stone, just like that night . . .

'Radek, I said no more; I don't want to hear any more.'

'But I didn't say anything.'

'Ah. So you didn't.'

Another silence. 'Miranda, we have to talk.'

Miranda thought of her daughter Jessica, and said, with a sigh, 'Yes, Radek, I suppose we do.'

'I'll come right over. Or would you rather meet in the courtyard?'

'What? What're you on about?' Miranda looked up fearfully, as if expecting Radek to float down from his balcony on to hers.

'Where do you want to meet?'

'Not *now*, Radek. It's late. I'm exhausted. So are you.'

'I can't sleep. Nor can you, by the look of it.'

But she was adamant. 'Tomorrow, Radek.'

'When tomorrow? I'll come over first thing in the morning.'

'You're pushing it. But then you always did.'

'Miranda—'

'All right, lunch. I'm going inside, now. Nice to see you again,' she added politely, as if they had last met a mere few days or weeks ago. As if the last time they had met, he had not impregnated her with her one and only beloved child.

'Miranda, wait.' His voice came disembodied from above her. It was hard to see him properly, at this angle and in the dark. Perhaps it was just as well, she thought.

'Well, what is it?'

'The years haven't touched you, my little *kapusta*. Not in the slightest.'

Miranda fled inside the kitchen and slammed the double doors

152

in fury. The bastard, she thought: how could he? Using his pet Polish name for her, after all these years. Making her remember. Water slapping on stone. That rocking boat. *Kapusta.* Her heart bled, sentimentally.

It was not until much later, as she was lying in bed sleepless, that she remembered what the word actually meant. Cabbage. He used to call her that because she reminded him of the *kapusta* his mother used to make in Poland, cooked with vinegar. Delicious, he had told Miranda, but always tangy, sharp. Always a surprise.

She was right not to want to have anything to do with him, after the insanity of those days in Venice.

Any woman who fell in love with a man who called her a cabbage must have been out of her head.

Chapter Ten

'Well hey, Ray! How're y'doing? Sleep all right? Noise of the gondolas didn't keep you awake all night?' Bruce chuckled, pouring Radek a cup of coffee.

'Gondolas? Do they make a noise?'

'Joke, man. We're in Venice, remember?'

'Oh.'

'Not quite awake, I see. How about one of these croissant things? Nice and fresh. Almost as good as the deli on 72nd street, back where I come from. They do great bagels, too. Onion, poppy seed, garlic, blueberry, to name just a few of my favourites. Shame they don't do bagels here.'

'Mm.'

Bruce poured himself a coffee as well, and sat down at the kitchen table opposite Radek. The American was wearing pale blue shorts with a t-shirt the same colour. His chubby knees were pink and scrubbed, as was his clean shaven face. Radek, in old khaki shorts, crumpled shirt and a black and grey stubble on his yet unshaven face, felt decidedly grubby.

During the night Bruce had evolved a plan of action. He had taken a shine to Marco, and now to his father, who seemed an okay kind of guy. Bruce felt sorry for him, sitting there with his coffee looking haggard and troubled, no doubt tense over Marco, wondering if the kid would be the success he hoped for at this Biennale thing.

Radek obviously was besotted with his son, and Bruce could understand that kind of obsession. Maybe not about a kid. Bruce thought that if he ever had one, which was completely unlikely, he would not want it hanging around him. But obsession itself, pure and simple, was a whole other ball game. Most of his best pals in New York had one, sometimes lots. They had them all: obsessive compulsions, obsessive aversions, obsessive neurosis. Bruce thought that now that he was rich, he too would no doubt acquire one, when he got back from his travels.

But this Radek guy . . . Bruce felt kind of sorry for him, obsessing over his son. It was understandable; Marco was the only family he had, his wife having run off and he himself, Radek, an immigrant in a strange land, the old country far away . . .

Here Bruce became a bit unstuck, for the old country was all of Europe, which included England, naturally. He was not quite sure if Radek was technically an immigrant, because Europe was, well, Europe; he had not therefore exactly immigrated, as he would have had he gone to the good old US of A instead of merely hopping from one part of the old country to another.

Anyway. Whatever. Radek's life now revolved around his son, that was obvious.

And his son's success at the Biennale.

Which he, Bruce Brinson, was going to make happen.

The first part of his plan was keeping Radek occupied for the day. The Biennale was opening the day after tomorrow; there was not that much time. And so he said, after Radek had eaten a croissant and drunk some coffee, and woken up a bit, 'I've got a great day planned for you, Ray baby.'

'Oh. Uh, that's kind of you, but you don't have to bother. I'm sure Marco—'

'I'm afraid Marco will be busy all day. With the Biennale, of course. Last touches. Final preparations. Interviews.' Bruce nodded importantly.

'Oh, the Biennale.' Radek almost added, I forgot about that. What with the shock of seeing Miranda again, he actually had. Why, he hadn't even asked Marco about it.

Chiding himself for being an appalling father, he said hastily, 'Of course. Though Marco didn't mention any plans last night—'

Again Bruce interrupted him. 'Oh, he probably forgot, in the excitement of seeing you again. Anyway, he asked me to take care of you today, Ray. See that you had a good time.'

Bruce crossed his fingers behind his back, and relied on the fact that Marco was not an early riser, and so would not come ambling in and make a liar out of him. Luckily, the roar of a motorboat came as music to his ears. 'There it is now, your taxi!' He ran out of the kitchen and into the drawing room to shout through the courtyard window, 'Be right there, Paolo.'

'Taxi?' Radek said, startled. He had followed Bruce and was also looking out the window at a motorboat moored at the tiny pier, with a toothy-looking chap sitting impatiently at the wheel, an attractive dark young woman near him.

'Water taxi. No wheels in Venice, man.'

'I know that,' Radek said testily. He was supposed to meet Miranda for lunch, and was not about to miss that. During his restless night last night, images and flashes of those ten ecstatic days with her in Venice zapped his brain like electric currents.

'Now don't you worry about a thing, Ray, this is all on me. Just have a good day, y'hear?'

'Bruce, this is all very generous of you, but Marco's landlady, Miranda, has already very kindly offered to spend some time with me, since Marco will be so busy with the Biennale. We are having lunch together.'

'No prob, you'll be back in plenty of time. Now c'mon, Paolo is waiting. He's going to whisk you around the waterways of Venice, show you places I guarantee you've never come across before. And his pretty girlfriend will be your guide on this tour of hidden Venice.'

Radek tried to protest one more time, as Bruce was coaxing – nay, forcing – him down the stairs, across the courtyard and into the boat. But at each protest the American looked so hurt, like a baby on the verge of tears, that Radek gave up and got on the boat.

'Paolo, Nina, this is Ray, here. Marco's dad. I want you to give him a real good time, y'hear?'

Nina nodded eagerly. On the phone this morning, Bruce had promised her an intensive day of speaking English with Marco's father, since his Italian, despite his numerous trips to the city, was fairly basic. Bruce had promised Paolo a huge tip too, on top of his regular exhorbitant taxi fare, to keep Radek out on the water for the whole entire day.

Before Radek could say *kapusta*, he was roaring down the Grand Canal, towards the Rialto Bridge, the Palazzo Bobolino already out of sight behind them.

As soon as Bruce had waved them off, he banged on the door of Apt. 1 and woke up Miranda, who had finally fallen asleep as the rosy dawn pussy-footed down the narrow *calli* and waterways of the city.

Miranda would not speak to him until she had made tea, though Bruce said it was urgent. Marco was still asleep, having stayed up all night worrying about his father. He was not sure which made him more upset: the fact that he would distress his father by admitting that he was not exhibiting at the Biennale; or the fact that possibly, just possibly, his father no longer cared one way or another. This thought was so outrageous that he wiped it from his mind immediately.

'Well, what is it?' Miranda asked Bruce grumpily as they settled on the kitchen balcony.

'Are we alone?' His voice was barely a whisper, and he looked around surreptitiously as he spoke.

'What is all this NYPD stuff? Of course we're alone. Marco's sound asleep in his room, and Frank and Netty have left for their classes. It's just us and the cats.' She eyed Tommasina and Topolino, who were in their usual places on the balustrade, hissing now and again at passing sparrows.

Bruce stretched, yawned, and tried to look casual. 'So hey, what d'you think of Ray? Great guy, eh?'

'Why?'

'Why what?'

'Why do you want to know?'

Bruce shook his head at how suspicious Europeans were, how cynical. He explained to Miranda that he had no hidden agenda to his question, but was just making conversation.

Miranda said cautiously. 'He seems all right.'

Now was the time, of course, that she should have said, actually, we met once before, years ago. Just as she should have said it last night to Marco. Or Radek should have said it. Or somebody.

Nobody did, and here they were. Miranda wondered how many sticky situations became stickier, because people did not think to open their mouths and let the truth pop out.

Bruce went on. 'It's real sweet, the way Radek dotes on Marco. Makes me feel real gooey inside.'

Miranda had no answer to this. She looked at Bruce in disbelief, wondering if he were for real. He obviously was, for he went on, 'I think it's our duty, y'know, to make sure Ray's not disappointed in his son. Our duty as—' He was about to say Americans, but remembered Miranda was not. 'As Marco's friends,' he went on lamely. It did not sound nearly as stirring, but never mind.

Miranda thought of her duty to Marco with a groan. Marco had, overnight, changed from a friend and a tenant to the half-brother of her daughter Jessica.

'Oh my God.'

'Miranda, what's wrong?'

'Oh shit.'

'You've gone a funny colour.'

'Fuck.'

'Hey, are you about to faint? Because man, if you are, I got to warn you right now, Miranda, that I'm useless in situations like these. Should I go get Elena or somebody?'

Bruce would have been off the balcony, out of the apartment and banging on someone else's door if Miranda had not stopped him. 'I'm fine.'

He cautiously sat back down. She went on, 'It's just that life is so bloody complicated, just when you think everything is running smoothly.'

Bruce had no time for philosophy at the moment, though he made a mental note to talk to Miranda about this later. He had read in the *New York Times* before he came away that the ancient Greeks were hip and had a whole lot of valuable things to say about life in America today, especially to the rich and famous who had time and money to think about these things. In fact on the bestseller book list there were all sorts of books that trendy people were reading: *Aristotle for the Ageless* and *Ten Tips from Thucydides*. Bruce had nearly bought *Socrates for Sophisticates* at the airport but being a modest man, had decided he did not yet qualify for that one.

But he had no time for philosophy now. 'Look, Miranda, we've got to work fast. Before Ray gets back from his tour around Venice. But Paolo knows to keep him out all day.'

'What? But I'm having lunch with Radek.'

'So he said. You'll have to ring him on Paolo's mobile phone, cancel.'

'But why?'

'Because we have to make plans, Miranda. Find Silvano, talk to him. Netty too, we'll have to have her in on it. Plus someone will have to keep Frank out of the way; I was thinking of Lissabelle for that, but I'm not real sure we can trust her. I mean, being so famous and all, you never know.' Here Bruce shook his head enigmatically.

'And I think we'll have to keep it from Marco, though jeez, it won't be easy.' He pondered this for a few moments, wishing now that he *had* bought that book; Socrates might have had some tips on how to deal with Marco.

Bruce shook his head. 'No, we gotta hide it from Marco. He's so goddamn emotional, might think it unethical or something. But it's not, not at all.'

At this, Miranda stopped thinking about what relationship Marco would be to her if he were now her daughter's half-brother, and tried to concentrate on what Bruce had just said. But even with concentration, it did not make sense. 'I haven't a clue what you're on about, Bruce.'

So Bruce told her.

'Miranda, what do you mean, you cannot meet me for lunch? We have to talk.'

'We haven't talked for twenty-nine years, Radek. A few hours won't matter.'

She hung up after promising to meet that evening. Nina, who had taken Radek to the Cathedral on the island of Torcello (which he had already seen countless times), was now standing next to him outside, practising her English by reading his guidebook out loud to him. She either did not notice, or did not care, that he wasn't listening to a word. 'Good, your lunch is cancelled.' She did not at all seem surprised. 'We will have lunch right here, at the Cipriani restaurant on the island. Bruce's treat.'

'I need to get back, Nina. I haven't even seen Marco today.'

'He will be busy with the Biennale,' Nina replied, as Bruce had instructed her on the mobile phone. 'Anyway, I am hungry. I need my lunch.'

Paolo, who had been sprawling on the ancient stone throne where Attila the Hun was once said to have sat, put out his fag on the worn marble seat and agreed that lunch was not an option, but a necessity.

Radek, hustled into the restaurant between them, tried to shake off the idea that he was a prisoner between two pleasant but determined guards. He must be still in a confused state of shock and weariness, he decided, after the trip from London, and his reunion with Marco, and of course seeing Miranda after all this time.

He decided to relax, and enjoy the meal. After all, it was nothing to get uptight about, seeing an old girlfriend again; after all, it happened occasionally when he returned to his boyhood home in Zakopane. And Venice was a compact place; sooner or later, if you came back here often enough, as he did, you were bound to run into people you knew.

He wondered if Miranda was still married; someone had, he now remembered, mentioned a daughter, whose apartment it was. Though there did not seem to be a husband anywhere around now, unless he was tucked away back in England.

As a waiter produced a bottle of chilled white wine, and he and Paolo and Nina imbibed the first glass, Radek decided that it would be rather pleasant if Miranda were free.

After the second or third glass, accompanied by a seafood antipasto, he remembered how frantically he had loved her, and wondered why he had ever let her go.

During the red wine and a main course of something incredibly meaty and succulent and covered with exquisite sauces, Radek realized Fate was responsible for all this, and that he himself had no choice but to go along with it.

While dipping almond biscuits into sweet dessert wine and sucking them rapturously, he understood that Miranda was his Destiny, and it did no good at all to fight against such Olympian orders.

The trouble arose when he got up from from the table, on wobbly legs, to order Paolo to take him back to the city at once, to tell this to Miranda.

Paolo, hearing the words 'love' and 'fate', and having also consumed much wine, agreed to this romantic haste and stood up, also on wobbly legs, to leave there and then, before coffee.

Nina, who had hardly had a drop, for she wanted to be clear-headed to practise her English, told them both they were not going anywhere until they sobered up.

After Paolo had accused her of being unromantic, cold and frigid, most likely brought about by all the English lessons she was having lately, the manager had been brought into the fray. This was at the instigation of the other customers, who said they were not paying the exorbitant prices charged by the restaurant just to hear common Italians brawling.

Radek rightly took umbrage at this, and with a slurred voice shouted that he was no common Italian but a common Pole, and proud of it.

As they were being shown the door in a most gruff manner, Nina told the manager about her friend Gianni, the bartender and her boss at the Ca' Nostra Trattoria where she worked, who was also from Sicily.

The manager, who knew Gianni, did a sudden about-face and escorted them, with many apologies, back into the restaurant, where he put them in an elegant but private room where they could finish their meal with coffee and sweetmeats, and sober up into the bargain.

'So tell me,' Nina said, after they had settled down again. 'What is this, Radek, between you and Miranda?'

Radek, not yet quite sober, told her.

*

Miranda said to Bruce, after she had made the phone call cancelling the lunch date with Radek, 'This isn't going to work, you know. This mad scheme of yours.'

But Bruce, newly rich, had already made the pleasant discovery that money brought power, and power could do whatever it felt like.

He also had had a taste of that particular glow of doing good with his money and power. Of helping others, even if they fought against it tooth and nail. It took quite a bit of expertise convincing people what was best for them. Luckily, being an American, he knew he could be good at it.

Marco needed a shove, that was for sure. When he woke up, Bruce and Miranda cornered him in the kitchen of Apt. 1. Bruce said, 'Well, Marco, about this Biennale thing. About telling your Dad.'

'I'll do it today, Bruce. I've decided. The minute I see him. I can't cope with all these lies and deception. I want to make a clean breast of it. Throw myself at his mercy. Beg his forgiveness.'

'Steady on,' Miranda said.

Bruce said slowly, 'What if I told you here and now, that there's a way out of this? That there's a way your Dad would never know you weren't chosen for the Biennale?'

'I wouldn't listen, Bruce. I'd walk right out of here without listening to a word.'

Which he did, though it was less because of high moral ground than because 1) he had a splitting headache, and 2) he was pissed off at his father for not paying as much attention to him as he ought. The shocking confession of the Biennale would make his father sit up and take notice of him again, just as tugging the cat's tail used to do when he was a child.

'Well hey,' Bruce said as Marco left the room. 'I told you it's a waste of time getting him involved. We'll have to do it without his help.'

'Impossible. And what would be the point?'

'The point isn't Marco anymore. It's, like, poor old Ray and the terrible disappointment and shock it would be, getting to the Biennale and not seeing his son's painting there.'

Later, when it was all over, Miranda decided that the only reason she had gone along with Bruce was because of the irritating soft spot she still felt for Radek.

As the day progressed, this soft spot began to annoy her. 'This is ridiculous,' she said as she and Bruce climbed aboard Silvano's gondola, moored at the piazzetta. 'I've never ever been on a gondola, except on the public *traghetto* that goes back and forth across the Grand Canal.' She remembered Radek promising her that one day, when they returned to Venice together, he would take her for a gondola ride. Another broken promise, she thought. Bastard.

Silvano was scandalized. 'But gondolas are the symbol of Venice! They *are* Venice.'

'They are also bloody expensive.'

Netty was already sitting in the craft as Bruce and Miranda came aboard. 'She has to be in on this, for camouflage,' Bruce had said. 'Who would ever suspect somebody like Netty? Now pay attention, everyone, this is a test run, to see just how we're gonna go about it.'

It was going under the Bridge of Sighs that made Miranda even crosser. She and Radek had stood on the bridge opposite watching gondolas floating underneath and he had promised to love her forever. Another broken promise, she said aloud, but luckily no one heard her.

Despite Bruce's urging to be attentive, she paid no heed to him and Silvano, who were busy making plans as the gondola weaved its floating way down the side canals leading to the Giardini Pubblici, where the pavilions of the Biennale were situated. She remembered walking through those very gardens with that liar and cheat Radek as he held her hand and talked about the things they would do together, when both had finished college.

'Well whaddaya know, it's all coming together,' Bruce said excitedly as they left the Giardini and were drifting back out in the lagoon again, heading back to the piazzetta.

'I say, Bruce, isn't it frightfully dangerous? What if we are caught?' Netty frowned, but secretly she was thrilled. Not only love in a gondola, but adventure and danger in a gondola too. There was no end to the surprises Venice sprang on the true devotee.

'Trust me, it's gonna work, the whole thing, Netty,' Bruce said with all the new-found confidence of a millionare. 'This is Italy.'

'You mean bribes?' Miranda said cynically.

'You mean because we are English?' Netty said confidently.

'You mean because I know Gianni, the bartender at the Ca' Nostra Trattoria?' Silvano said, wondering uncomfortably how Bruce knew about that.

Bruce laughed gaily, knowing his friends were joking, though not quite understanding their strange European wit. 'Because I'm American, of course,' he said when his laughter died down. 'Italy and America have a very special relationship.'

Silvano thought, *Mamma mia*, he really does know about Gianni.

Netty thought about watching *The Godfather* on telly one winter evening, when there were no decent gardening programmes on.

Miranda thought of Frank Sinatra and John F. Kennedy.

Everyone nodded sagely.

Bruce, naturally, had not been thinking about any of these things. He had merely been referring to the fact that the best pizza in the world was made in America, and the best authentically Italian restaurants were in New York. No doubt the best Italians too were American, but they visited friends and family back in the old country and there was an easy rapport between the two places.

As there seemed to be no more objections to his plan, he cried victoriously, 'Home, Silvano,' and nearly tipped out of the gondola in his eager anticipation.

'Steady, Paolo,' Radek muttered as the Italian angled the *motoscafo* sharply around to moor it at the Palazzo Bobolino. He was no longer inebriated but his head was throbbing.

Marco had set up his easel and was attempting another painting of the canal, but his heart was not in it. He had tried to churn up his undying love for Nina, by reminding himself that Nina had chosen Paolo and was lost to him forever. But every time he got into the despair, the desolation, the bleakness of it all, something would distract him: the need for a coffee, or a passing vaporetto with some high-spirited young women on a college outing calling out to him across the water and blowing kisses with flagrant abandon.

He tried to work up the bleakness he felt at having to confess all to his father about the Biennale, but somehow that only depressed him. Ordinary depression was useless; he needed no less than the pits: dark, bottomless despair, the kind he had felt for Nina for a day or two, until he got over her.

And here was his father now, home from his tour of the islands. 'Dad, at last! I was wondering when you'd get back; I haven't seen you all day.' Marco tried to sound jovial, but he could not keep the petulance out of his voice.

'Ah Mark, here you are! How was your day? I suppose you were at the Biennale pavilion, making sure everything is in order for tomorrow.'

Luckily Marco was stopped from answering by a gondola that pulled up next to the water taxi. Radek leaped back on to the pier to cry, 'Miranda! What a pity about lunch. But never mind, here you are. What about an *aperitivo*, and then dinner?'

Miranda, haughtily ignoring Silvano's helping hand as she stepped out of the gondola, said frostily, 'You are about twenty-eight years too late, Radek.' She briefly closed her eyes, to compose herself.

When Bruce and Silvano and Radek between them had clutched at her clothes and grabbed arms and shoulders and thus saved her from the horrid diseases she would have contracted by falling into the canal, Miranda burst into tears. So much for trying to be dignified and independent, and not needing the help of men even to get out of a gondola.

Netty, flapping about like a great bird of prey during the rescue, cried. 'Good grief, the poor girl is in shock. Though who would not be, nearly falling into the canal like that. There, there; you are perfectly all right now; do try to pull yourself together.'

'Aw hey, honey, don't do that. I can't handle tears, makes me all blubby myself.'

'*Dio mio, le donne!*'

'*Poverina.*'

'Darling. My own one. My angel, my *kapusta.*'

At this last endearment, Miranda pulled herself together, as Netty had suggested. 'I am not your bloody cabbage,' she cried as she ran into Apt. 1 and locked the door behind her.

Marco looked at his father and said, 'I didn't know you knew Miranda.'

Nina said rapturously, 'He loves her!' Paolo grinned and showed many teeth and nodded agreement.

Radek looked sheepish. Now that he was no longer drunk he wondered what he had blabbed in that little room in the Cipriani as Nina tried to sober them up.

As if reading his thoughts, Nina smiled sweetly at him. 'You told us everything, everything. Such a wonderful story. And so good for my English.' She had been delighted that Radek, a Pole, had spoken such precise and understandable English, even in his slurry state; it was much better than his son the Englishman.

'We, uh, did know each other once. Long before I met your mother, Marco.' Radek added that last bit quickly, though it had been only a year after Venice with Miranda. Marco's mother had gone to Krakow on an Eastern European tour, met Radek at a bar, and before he knew what had happened, he was in London and married to an Englishwoman that was not Miranda.

'He love her,' Paolo said loudly. He liked the sound of those English words, and so repeated them again. And again and again.

'Do shut up,' Radek said. 'My head hurts.'

'He love her. He love her.'

'You love her?' Marco asked incredulously. '*You love her?*'

'Oh I say. Not you too, Marco. My head is beginning to throb as well.' Netty, still sitting in the gondola, was beginning to find all these revelations not so much romantic, as tiresome. She chided herself silently, and reminded herself that she was in an adventure.

Marco was beginning again. 'You *love* her?' he repeated in disbelief, just as Paolo started his chanting, 'He love her, he love her, he love her.' Nina, encouraged that Paolo was at last taking more of an interest in the English language and therefore of their future, corrected his grammar: 'He *loves* her, he *loves* her.' Silvano, being a gondolier and somewhat of an expert on saying love in foreign tongues, joined in, to help with pronunciation.

Who knows how long this chorus would have continued, if the door of Apt. 3 had not sprung open and Lissabelle not rushed out. 'Marco darling, there you are.' She sidled up to him possessively. 'Come inside with me and have an *aperitivo*; we must talk business.' Her hand ran down from his shoulder to his wrist in a very un-business-like manner.

Lissabelle had not had a chance to speak properly to her neighbour since the pre-Biennale viewing of the installation at the Museo d'Arte, when Bruce had raved about Marco's painting. She was determined to do so now; she had been getting ready for a high-powered business talk all day, with hot baths in scented oils, with fragrant lilies in bowls all over her bedroom, with clean satin sheets on the (regrettably) lumpy bed.

She had also got her chequebook into place, and had laid it open in a prominent spot.

Marco looked bewildered, but started to follow her. Bruce said, 'Well hey now, that's real friendly of you. I'm sure we'd all love an *aperitivo*. C'mon, everyone! Lissy's invited us all up to her place for a cocktail before dinner.'

Before Lissabelle could open her mouth to protest, the others followed Bruce through the door and up the marble steps into Apt. 3.

April, pouring ice-cold Prosecco into glasses, slugged some of the sparkling white wine herself from a large tumbler in the kitchen. Simon had heard it all through the window, and was killing himself laughing as he rummaged around in the cupboard to find some crisps and olives for the unexpected party.

'Serves her right,' April said, giggling. 'The old cow.'

Simon was horrified. 'I can't believe you said that. I just can't believe it.'

April was genuinely repentant. 'I'm sorry, don't know what came over me.'

'Just watch it, okay?'

Sobered, they went into the drawing room with the trays of drinks and snacks. Simon thought sadly that this was the beginning of the end for April. It was one thing to think horrid thoughts about their dear friend Lissabelle, but it was another to say it so bluntly, even to each other.

But all the same, there were rules. Fine lines one must not cross. Unspoken and unwritten, but nonetheless they were there.

April would not survive Lissabelle. She would go under. Simon, despite his sadness for April, smiled to himself. Lissabelle would feel betrayed when April left, and turn even more to him. And that would surely mean a very substantial increase in salary. Or rather an increase in monetary gratitude, to put it in a more acceptable manner.

In the drawing room Bruce, sitting next to the table by the window, noticed an open chequebook, and being an open and forthright American, read it without a qualm. 'Wow, this is big bucks. Or mega pounds I should say.' He looked at the cheque more closely. 'Made out to you, Marco. Looks like all your birthdays have come at once.'

'Darling, aren't you being just the teeniest bit nosy?' Lissabelle, in a fury, grabbed the chequebook away from Bruce.

'Honey, I'd say that if someone left a chequebook opened prominently on a table, then invited a whole palace to come up for a cocktail, then that someone *wanted* that cheque to be seen and talked about.'

Lissabelle, deciding she had nothing to lose, said, 'Darling, you're quite right. Actually, I've asked you all up here to celebrate. I've just decided to buy Marco's last painting, to take to London and hang in the drawing room of my house in Islington.'

A perplexed silence greeted this. The Italians had not a clue where or what Islington was, and the English (both those of Polish extraction and the other, proper, English) were not entirely convinced that Islington was A Good Thing.

Bruce, his baby face showing signs of severe distress, did not give a damn about Islington or Lissabelle's drawing room, but before he could sort out his thoughts to speak, Marco said cautiously, 'Well, uh, thanks. But I hadn't even put it on sale.'

'Never mind, darling. I want it. And I am quite prepared to be more than generous.' She purred benevolently in Marco's ear, turning it red with the heat of her breath. She implied much more than just cash generosity.

'Well, in that case—'

But before Marco could agree, a shout came from Bruce. 'I'll pay what she's offered, and a hundred dollars more.'

'What? Why you shit. You bloody upstart. And I'll top that by another hundred. Pounds.'

'I'll top it by two. Two hundred. Dollars.'

'Pounds.'

'Three hundred.'

'Pounds.'

'Four hundred.'

'SHUT UP BOTH OF YOU.'

They did, and looked at Marco. 'D'you think I haven't my pride? D'you think I can be sold to the highest bidder? D'you think I am just a commodity, to be bartered at the marketplace? D'you think I am nothing but a slave to a rotten capitalist society? Sod you both, sod all of you. I AM NOT FOR SALE.' With that he stormed out of the room and out of the apartment, slamming several doors behind him.

After a moment or two of silence, Bruce said, 'Call me kind of slow, but wasn't it just a painting we were after?'

Chapter Eleven

Evening in Venice: June, moon and the crooning of the gondoliers as they row their boatloads of British and Americans and Germans and whatnot. Miranda sits howling on the balcony like the cats, who are howling too to keep her company. She is weeping for everything: Venice, that dodgy slut of a city who lured her back here to find again the father of her fatherless child; Jessica, that very same child who was quite happy being fatherless, thank you very much, but who now would have to cope with having one.

Miranda, oozing self-pity with not an ounce of shame, howls with grief, but mostly with anger. At herself, at Venice, but mostly at Radek: for seducing her twenty-nine years ago (not true; she played more than a major part herself); for abandoning her (well, she too did some abandoning, having never bothered to write again after one unanswered letter); and, worse, for appearing again when he was unlooked for and uncalled for.

La bella Venezia, used to these outbursts of angst and emotion, remains serene, her waterways unruffled in this still evening, her gondoliers, by some miracle, in tune as they belt out 'O Solo Mio' and 'Santa Lucia' as they float past the Palazzo Bobolino with their platoon of tourists.

Miranda, in her tears, is just another poor soul screwed up

by the Most Serene Republic. She is not the first, nor will she be the last.

Venice, old slut that she is, settles herself complacently into a deep and gaudy night, content that her old powers are still intact.

'Yoo hoo, Silvano! Oh I say, where are you? I cannot see a thing; it is fearfully dark.'

Netty, peering down the narrow side canal, made out the gondola moored along the side. She had arranged to meet Silvano on the edge of a small campo quite far from their usual haunts, for Elena was beginning to cause them both strife. 'I can't see why we couldn't have met as usual on the piazzetta,' Silvano muttered as he moored the boat and jumped out. He enjoyed meeting her there by the Doge's Palace, the crowds on the Piazza San Marco watching admiringly as he, the handsome, distinguished, if somewhat mature, gondolier, escorted the vast and extravagant Englishwoman with the red curls and the flouncy dresses.

'Because your wife is becoming tedious,' Netty complained. 'I thought Italian wives were tolerant of these sort of things.'

'Only if they are handled properly. With subtlety.'

'She was quite chummy to begin with. I thought she and I were getting along quite famously. Now she just glares at me with her popping reptilian eyes.' Netty knew this was not kind, but she was fed up to her eyeballs with Elena's raised eyebrows and killer looks.

Fortunately Silvano did not understand the popping reptilian eyes bit, for if so, he would have had to admonish Netty. His wife, though intolerable, came first, of course. He would not hear one word spoken against her, nasty old thing though she may be.

They walked in silence away from the canal and on to the Campo Maria Formosa, still busy although it was nearly eleven o'clock at night. Couples were sitting in outdoor cafés drinking *spritz* or beer or Prosecco, and on the benches on the campo small groups of young people cavorted and giggled. A dog barked, a cat mewed. It would all have been quite ordinary, if it had been any other town or city than Venice.

Netty and Silvano sat outside at one of the trattorias at a small table and ordered two glasses of red wine from Nina, who was working that night after her jaunt around the islands with Paolo and Radek. Nina brought the wine and sat down with them at the table. 'All set for tomorrow, then?' she asked softly, looking fearfully around her.

Silvano nodded. So did Netty, though she said cautiously, 'Are you in on it too?'

Nina looked at her indignantly. 'Paolo and I were entrusted with keeping Marco's father out of sight all day, out of Marco's way so Marco cannot spill his beans.' She stopped, waiting for Netty to comment favourably on her use of the English slang, *to spill the beans*, but Netty was waiting for her to continue. Disappointed, Nina went on, 'Tomorrow we must do the same. Bruce has instructed us to take Radek to the Lido, and then to some lesser-known islands, and so to keep him from Marco all the day.'

Netty said doubtfully, 'I am not entirely sure you can get away with it twice.'

Nina grinned. 'We have a queen up our trouser leg.'

Silence greeted this announcement. Finally Netty said, 'Ah. I think you mean that you have an ace up your sleeve.'

'*Esattamente.*'

'And?'

'Miranda.'

'What?'

'She is to go with Radek. On the *motoscafo* with us. Miranda is our queen. Or ace,' she corrected herself hastily.

Silvano looked bewildered. 'But she will not have anything to do with him. Did you not see her run from him in tears earlier this evening? On the pier?'

They had all seen it, of course, but Nina was confident. 'All those tears, all that anger, can only mean one thing. She loves him, of course. And he loves her too; oh, how he loves her . . .'

'Quite,' Netty said hastily. 'Please, let us not begin that litany all over again.'

'Besides,' Nina added enigmatically, 'there is Gianni.'

Silvano whispered fearfully, 'Gianni? Gianni knows? But how?'

'I told him.'

'But why?'

Here Nina and Silvano began talking frantically in the Venetian dialect, with many gestures and exclamations and rolling of eyeballs. Finally Netty, bored, said, 'I say, do explain what you are both blagging on about. Remember I am in on this too. Who is this Gianni whose name keeps popping up?'

Silvano and Nina looked at her, then at each other. Silvano took Netty's hand and said, as if to a child, 'In Italy, we think of it as a kind of insurance. A cover. Think of Gianni as an insurance salesman. He runs his own private company.'

'You mean, if your gondola capsizes? That type of coverage?'

Silvano patted her hand. 'Let us say, it is more to prevent the gondola from capsizing in the first place, *capisci*?'

Netty said that yes, she did understand, and that she thought they had something similar in England though she could not be certain, for her poor dead husband Herbert had handled all the family insurances. Once again Nina and Silvano looked at each other and rolled their eyes.

At that moment Gianni himself walked up, with two more glasses of red wine and a small bowl of peanuts. 'Compliments of the management,' he said, sitting himself down at their table. There was much shuffling of chairs to make room for him, for Gianni, though short, was remarkably rotund. Netty took an

175

instant liking to him, for he had a crinkly, kindly face that reminded her of her grandfather, a dear old gent who grew the most incredible roses.

Introductions were made, and pleasantries were exchanged. Gianni wished them luck on their enterprise of tomorrow. '*Allora*, are you sure you don't need assistance? When you do the actual stealing?' he asked helpfully. '*Veramente*, I know my boys would be happy—'

'No, no, *grazie*, Gianni. We can manage quite well on our own, with Bruce.'

'Stealing?' Netty said, aghast.

'He means borrowing,' Nina said quickly. 'His English is not so good.'

Gianni frowned. Netty thought how different he looked when he frowned; not at all like her absent-minded grandfather. She shivered slightly. Silvano said, even more quickly, 'Your English is perfect, Gianni, just perfect. It's just that the English are squeamish about certain words, *capisci?*'

Gianni smiled. Netty was relieved, without being sure exactly why.

'*Salute*,' Silvano said, raising his glass. 'Here's to tomorrow's success.'

Gianni ran inside the bar and brought out an unopened bottle of red wine and two more glasses, so that he and Nina could join in on the toast. A French couple at a table nearby were becoming indignant because no one was serving them, but when the man tried to wave imperiously at Nina to get her attention, Gianni glared at him. After another five minutes the couple started to get up, to try another, more accommodating place to have a drink and a bite to eat, but Gianni glared at them again and they sat meekly back down. 'Okay,' Gianni said to Nina, 'you go serve them now. But no hurry.' He was not overly fond of the French.

But the English were okay. Peculiar, and unable to call a spade a spade, but harmless. The Americans, though, were best; his boys had a special relationship with them, no doubt about that. He was looking forward to meeting this Bruce, the one in charge of this interesting enterprise. Nina had told Gianni all about him, and he was sure that he and the American would have a lot in common.

When Gianni and Nina left to go back to their customers, Netty said, 'What a kind gentleman. He reminds me of my grandfather. He was in the insurance business too, I seem to remember. Before he retired and took up roses.'

Silvano said, 'Let us not talk of Gianni, but of us.' Not that he particularly wanted to talk about *us*; it was just that he got nervous of too much talk about Gianni.

'Oh, my dear.' She beamed and clutched at his knobby hard gondolier's hand with her soft plump English petal one.

He beamed back. Then yawned. It was late; he needed his bed. Netty saw the yawn and said coyly, 'Time for beddie-bies, is it?' She waited for him to suggest a ride home in his gondola. It was not raining tonight, and there was a moon. There was not a ripple of a breeze either; an important factor if you were considering making love in a gondola.

Netty was. Once again. The hand-holding and hanky-panky had been fun, but now she was becoming impatient. She felt slightly cheated; she had been here for quite some time now and still had not had The Full Venetian Experience. The Full Venetian Monty, as it were: making love in a gondola.

Nor anywhere else, for that matter. Silvano, though romantic, did not seem exactly randy, which puzzled Netty, for everyone knew that the Italian men were highly sexed. Perhaps it was Elena, the original Gothic wet-blanket. Once Netty had her own apartment, perhaps on a side canal somewhere well away from the prying eyes of the crocodile wife, Silvano could relax, and act his nationality properly.

'Shall we go back to the Palazzo Bobolino in your gondola?' Netty purred.

'No, I'll leave it where it is for the night. We can walk to Rialto and cross over the bridge on foot.'

Netty tried not to show her disappointment. 'And then . . . at the Bobolino?' she whispered seductively.

'We must arrive separately, and go cautiously to our own apartments.'

'Oh.' Netty managed to put an overload of disappointed emotion in that one word.

'But do not depair, *bellissima*. We will meet as usual tomorrow, for our cappuccino in Piazza San Marco.'

With that, Netty had to be content.

Not very long after, a number of people were creeping mysteriously around the Palazzo Bobolino. It was midnight, and Venice, capricious as usual, had covered herself with a silvery shawl of mist, rising from the waterways and floating eerily from the skies. Perfect for cloak and dagger stuff, of which a great deal seemed to be occurring at the old ruined heap of a palazzo.

Elena would have been spotted first, had she not been dressed in her usual black and so been more or less invisible in the dank dark fog. She was skulking around the courtyard, waiting for her husband. Luckily for Silvano, she had fallen asleep in the deck chair Lissabelle had put out earlier to work on her tan, and so did not see her husband come creeping in.

Netty would have got inside Apt. 1 without harrassment if Silvano had not stepped on Topolino, who was lurking around with Tommasina looking for water rats. Topolino yowled, Silvano ran into his own apartment, and Elena woke up just as Netty walked in through the outside door.

'Daughter of a whorish mother,' Elena cried. 'English bitch of a mongrel.'

'I say. Steady on.' Netty, having got over her first fright, was livid with indignation. She could not understand the woman's words, but it took no fool to figure out her meaning was not complimentary.

'Fat slut, where is my husband?'

Netty glanced up surreptitiously to see Silvano peeping out of the window and shaking his head and holding terrified fingers to his lips. Elena looked up too. Silvano said, '*Mamma mia*, there you are! What kind of a poor husband has to come home after a hard night rowing a gondola, to find his apartment empty, his wife gadding about on the town? Where have you been, Elena?'

Netty listened to all this with admiration. She didn't understand his words, but his tone was smooth, placating and with just the right amount of aggression in it, that being the best form of defence, as everyone knew. 'Oh good evening, Silvano,' she cried politely. 'I do wish you would tell your good wife to stop shouting at me. I came home after a pleasant evening meeting friends, to find myself used and abused by an Italian fishwife.'

Before Elena could figure out what all this fishwife stuff was – some of her best friends worked in the Rialto fish market but she herself had nothing to do with the business – a silent *motoscafo*, its motor off and its lights out, glided alongside the pier at the end of the courtyard. Seeing the bulky figure that surreptitiously stepped off the boat as the driver, Paolo, tied up, Silvano closed the shutters on the window fast and Elena scurried inside her apartment without a goodbye or apology or even a backward look.

'Rude ill-mannered Italians,' Netty muttered out loud as she went to the door of Apt. 1. 'Oh, Gianni, good heavens! What a fright you gave me, lurching out of the shadows like that. My goodness, you are out late. Thank you so much for the wine tonight; Silvano and I did so enjoy it. Such a pleasant evening.'

Gianni grunted and did not smile. Netty, worried, said, 'Oh

dear. Oh I say, don't tell me Silvano forgot to pay for our first round? Now that I think of it, I don't believe he did, and you so kindly giving us another bottle on the house. How naughty of him. Here, let me settle up right now.' She began to open her handbag.

Gianni stopped her with a shake of his head. 'No, no. *Per favore*, which is the apartment of the American? The art dealer from New York?'

'Bruce? Why, this one here. But isn't it rather late . . . ?'

Gianni smiled his avuncular smile and said kindly, 'No need to worry yourself, *bella*. He is expecting me. Or *should* be,' he added mysteriously.

'Ah. Well, that is quite all right then. I shall say goodnight and leave you to it. Cheerio and all that. Oh, ha ha, I am forgetting my Italian lessons. *Ciao*! Oh goodness, am I being too forward? Should I have said *arrivederci*? But I do feel I know you well enough for *ciao*.'

'My dear lady, of course you do. *Ciao, ciao*! And *buonanotte*. I will remain here while you go inside, to make sure you are safely in.'

'Oh, I say! How utterly kind.' Netty, looking at Gianni with new eyes, found herself admiring his dark, dark suit, the black roll-neck shirt underneath, the gallant way he was patiently waiting for her to be safely tucked inside her apartment. She wondered why Silvano never thought of doing that.

When the door closed behind Netty, Gianni softly knocked on Bruce's door. In a few moments a head peered down at him, and Gianni, in fright, crossed himself three times and said a quick prayer to the Madonna before he realized that it was not a fat little angel peering down at him, but a grown man of cherubic appearance wearing some kind of a flowing white nightshirt.

'I am Gianni. A friend of Nina and Paolo's.'

'Hi there, Gianni. I'm Bruce Brinson, and glad to meet any

friend of theirs, but hey, this is kind of late for a social call where I come from.'

'Nina told me everything.'

'Everything? Oh, you mean the, uh . . .' he trailed off into silence, looking surreptitiously around him.

'Yes. The . . .' Gianni pressed his lips together and made a fierce motion across them with his fingers, as if he were zipping them shut.

Bruce peered out into the misty gloom and saw a shadow by the pier. Then a flash of light as Paolo lit a cigarette. 'Oh, I get it. Paolo brought you here, right?'

Gianni nodded.

'Well hey, that's different. Paolo's a buddy, a real great friend. Why don't you come on in, have a drink? The hell with the time.'

Since that was what Gianni had intended to do anyway, either with or without Bruce's invitation, he nodded his head and waited as Bruce came down to unlock the door.

No sooner had the door shut behind Gianni than another figure opened the creaky door of the apartment opposite, No. 3. The figure was slight and slinky, dressed in something satiny and black and very, very skimpy.

'Oh shit. Oh fuck. HELP.'

'Shhh. It's me, Paolo.'

'What the hell do you think you're doing, creeping around our courtyard like this? You frightened the shit out of me.'

Paolo said with dignity, 'I am waiting for a customer. A very important one.'

Lissabelle, though she tried very hard not to be, was impressed. It must have been Bruce, coming home from some elegant pre-Biennale dinner and now about to go off again to some private party of artists and dealers and famous faces of fabulous fortunes. She was pissed off that he had not invited her.

Paolo, seeing Lissabelle attired in what looked like negligible wisps of torn material, quite rightly assumed that this was for seduction purposes, and so began to run his steamy hands over her taut nipples and bite her neck gently with those tombstone teeth which gleamed spookily in the swirling fog.

After a few moments Lissabelle said, 'Stop that. Stop that at once.' But she said it so softly that he did not hear her.

Paolo continued to do skilful things to various sensitive areas of her body, thus causing Lissabelle to have to come to some decision. She had seen Netty go into Apt. 1 and so knew that someone there was still up. Netty would let her in and Lissabelle could immediately go find Marco, who was probably asleep and thus in a tender unwary state, the better to manipulate.

Lissabelle had the perfect excuse ready; she wanted to buy that painting, especially now that she knew Bruce wanted it so desperately. If it were not a famous painting now, it soon would be; and she, Lissabelle, would have it.

As she intended to have the artist. Tonight.

Yet here she was in Paolo's virile arms, thinking that perhaps it would be better to see Marco in the morning. What if he were deeply asleep and the kind of person that got ratty when woken? You never knew with men, especially the creative types.

As Paolo's lips went here and there, Lissabelle's last coherent thought was, Oh, what the hell. The next thing she was on the floor of his *motoscafo*, which Netty would have found frightfully common, so it was just as well she was tucked up safely in Apt. 1 and did not witness a thing.

Radek did not see the frantic rocking of the water taxi as he let himself into the courtyard of Palazzo Bobolino, for the mist was still swirling and the night still dark. He had been out walking the streets of the city all night, since Miranda would neither come out to meet him nor answer her telephone. The longer he walked, the more he became agitated. She was his bloody destiny, and she would not let him near her.

He was about to let himself in with his key to Bruce's apartment when he decided that he could not face going to bed yet. Especially alone. He had gone to bed in Venice alone for years, all those years when he returned to the city, looking, he realized now, for his lost love. Now that he had found her, damn it, he wanted to be with her, now, at this moment, and at every other moment of his day and night.

Radek, being of sturdy Polish mountain stock whose father and grandfathers in the Tatra Mountains had chopped down forests in blizzards to build snug homes for their families, chided himself for being an effete English wimp and letting a mere *kapusta* of a girl get the best of him. Putting his key away, he banged on the door of Apt. 1.

Red curls swirled above him out of the mist, as Netty came to the window. 'Oh *buonanotte*, Radek. You've come to visit Marco, how paternal of you.' She beamed at him without a trace of irony. She was getting quite used to these late night visitors. So sophisticated, this European manner of conducting one's social life. If she were home in England she would be in bed propped on three fat pillows, a good old-fashioned mystery novel in her hand and a hot cup of Ovaltine on her bedside table. If anyone had the temerity to knock on the door she would have called the police.

'I do believe Marco is in bed, but do come in. I am certain he would be delighted to see you.'

Netty decided it was quite jolly fun, these peculiar hours kept by foreigners. True, Radek claimed he was a British subject, but still, with a name like that? Not to mention his traces of accent. Humming snatches of 'O Solo Mio', she tripped gaily down the stairs and opened the door.

'Frank is in this room, by the stairs,' she said conversationally, 'but Marco and Miranda and I have bedrooms upstairs.' She led him to the top of the landing. 'I'm off to bed now. This is Marco's room, should I knock on his door?'

'No, no, thank you, you've been very helpful. Goodnight.'

He watched Netty go into her bedroom and close the door. By process of elimination he found Miranda's and softly opened it.

'God, you've got a cheek,' Miranda said from behind him.

'Christ. Don't do that, you scared me out of my wits.'

'*Me* don't do that? *Me?* I've been watching you, Radek, from the kitchen here, watching you sneaking about with Netty, pretending you wanted to see Marco. You rat. You little Polish rat.'

Radek was stung. 'You said you liked Poles. You said you wanted to go to Krakow and see the great medieval market square, and then to Zakopane to see the mountains, and meet my mother and father, and my babusha and my uncles, and—'

'All right, all right, don't go on. So I did. And I *don't* have anything against the Polish people; only one of them.'

'But Miranda, why? What did I do?'

'Left me.'

'Hang on. We left each other, remember? We agreed to go back to our countries, get our degrees, and meet again, in Venice.'

'Right. Well, did we?'

Radek said cautiously, 'I got *my* degree. Did you?'

'That's not the bloody point. What about meeting again in Venice?'

Radek opened his arms and looked radiantly at her. 'We have!' he shouted. 'We've met again, in Venice!'

Some time later, Miranda, in her bed, murmured, 'I did write to you, but you never answered. I've a good mind to stop doing what I'm doing to you, for that.'

'Don't, please don't. You always did it so much better than anyone else.'

'What? *Who* else? How many others, besides your wife?'

'Shh. You'll wake up Marco.'

A bit later, Radek said, 'I never got your letter. But then hardly anyone did then, in Poland. Those were hard times. I did write to you too, though.' He did not add that he had never posted the letter. It had seemed so impossible at the time, that he would ever see her again, ever leave Poland, let alone return to Venice, or go to England.

Much, much later, Miranda said, 'Amazing, isn't it? How much one's body remembers?'

'Hm. My darling sweetheart. My first love. My *kapusta*.'

'Less of the cabbage, darling. Remember we aren't nineteen any longer.'

For a brief blessed time, nothing at all went bump in the deep foggy night of the courtyard at Palazzo Bobolino. Except, perhaps, the thump thump of Paolo's motorboat rocking against the pier.

Then weird ghostly shapes began appearing round and about. First, a short bulky man in a dark suit and black shirt came out of Bruce's apartment and strode purposefully to the *motoscafo*. As the man prepared to jump in, there was a muffled swear word or two and another shape, female this time and wearing not much at all, sprang up from the water taxi and ran into Apt. 3.

The motorboat, lights still not on, pulled out into the misty canal with its dark, silent passenger aboard. Under cover of its revving engine, a second figure came out of Apt. 2, Bruce's place. On tiptoes and looking furtive, not easy for one with the face of a baby who could have passed for the Archangel Gabriel at his christening, Bruce sidled over, back against the wall, to Apt. 1 and knocked softly on the door.

'Oh hell's bells. The door. I forgot. That'll be Bruce.'

185

Radek sat up indignantly. 'Bruce? At this hour? Miranda, how could you?'

'How could I what?'

'Betray me! With another man. With *him*.'

'Radek, what're you on about? It's only Bruce.'

'At this hour of the night? Or of the morning, I should say?'

Miranda began to get angry. 'You do not own me, remember. You do not even know me, having left me, alone and pregnant, twenty-eight-plus years ago. Now get out. Get out of my bed and out of my apartment.'

Radek leaped up, threw on his clothes. Bruce knocked again. Miranda stuck her head out of the window, which fortunately led into the courtyard, and said, 'I'll let you in in a minute, Bruce. Just hang on.'

'If that man comes in here, at this hour, I'm off.'

'You're off anyway. Out, Radek.'

'Unless, of course, I am allowed to remain with you. To chaperon, as it were.'

'You Poles get so pompous when you're miffed. You were like that when you were nineteen, too.'

'And you were uppity then as well. Please, Miranda, may I stay?'

'Of course not. This is private.'

'What can be private between a man and a woman at two o'clock in the morning?'

'Guess. Now go.'

Radek, in a fury, did so, encountering Bruce on the doorstep of Apt. 1 as he exited. 'Well hey, what the heck are you doing here?'

'I could ask you the same.'

Bruce looked embarrassed, and terribly guilty. Radek shouted, 'I thought so!' and stomped off.

It was only after he had let himself into Bruce's apartment, calmed himself with a glass of mineral water from Bruce's kitchen, that he remembered what Miranda had said. Something about leaving her alone, alone and . . . and . . . *Oh dear God and Jesus and all the ancient Kings of Krakow!*

'Miranda! Open the door. Right now, at once. I need to talk to you.'

Bruce, in Miranda's room, said, 'What in hell's going on? What's he doing, banging on the door like that? What was he doing here anyway? He'll ruin everything. What does he want?'

'I don't know. RADEK, go home, go at once. I'm going to shut this window and not answer the door.'

'Miranda, what did you just say? About my leaving you twenty-eight years and some months ago, alone and . . . and what exactly was it?'

'Pregnant, you fool. I said pregnant.'

'Oh God.'

'Wow, heavy. Hey Miranda honey, this stuff's pretty over-powering. Did you say pregnant? Maybe we ought to ask Radek upstairs after all.'

'Don't be daft, Bruce. What about the plan? It'll be scuppered if he starts hanging around here.'

'Yeah, but hey, what about the baby? This is potent stuff, honey. Think about the kid's father, poor Radek down there. It'll impact him no end. Man, I don't want to forget about the plan, but hey—'

'Hey nothing. Just shut up.'

'Miranda, please open the door, let me come in again. I'm sorry I walked out in a huff. It's because I love you, and I was jealous of Bruce.'

'He's what? Jealous of me? Hey Ray, what's this stuff you're bringing out? *I'm* not the one responsible for the baby. Where is it anyway, Miranda? The baby?'

'Oh do belt up, both of you. There's no bloody baby.'

A deadly hush fell over the courtyard. And none too soon either, for Elena, in bed beside a snoring Silvano, was about to leap up and throw a bucket of water on all of them, as she did on Tommasina and Topolino when they got too frisky.

Radek spoke first. Luckily for him, his voice was soft and mushy, for it saved him from a drenching. '*Kapusta*, my dear little *kapusta*. I'm sorry. How hard for you. First being pregnant, then losing the baby . . . and me so far away. Will you ever forgive me?'

'Go on,' Bruce urged. 'Forgive him. Please? Pretty please with sugar? I can't bear to see grown men cry. And besides, then he'll go away and we can get on with the plan. And listen, Miranda. I've had the most peculiar visit too, this guy called Gianni, selling me some kind of insurance, only I had to pay him not so's I could make a claim if things go wrong sometime, but to kind of prevent them from going wrong in the first place. I don't understand it exactly, but he was very persuasive.'

Miranda, tired of all this, called down softly to Radek, 'Listen, I can't talk now, but I'll see you tomorrow. You and I are having a day out at the Lido, okay? Paolo's taking us in his taxi. Bruce has arranged everything.'

'Oh, *I* see. Bruce again, eh? Is this his payment for favours granted at two in the morning?'

He did not get a chance to say anything else, for a spray of freshly cut flowers, plus the water they had been standing in in the large vase in Miranda's bedroom, landed with perfect aim on top of his unsuspecting head and drenched his clothes with the thoroughness of a thunderstorm.

Chapter Twelve

Palazzo Bobolino woke from its fuggy slumbers of the night with a loud scream coming from Apt. 1. It was such a terrible sound, so blood-curdling and awesome, that the morning mist lifted immediately, like hair standing on end after a fright.

All the tenants of Apt. 1, from where the sound originated, rushed out on to the landing to see what was going on.

'Oh my God, Marco, what's wrong?'

'Is not yet the seven o'clock, what this noise and not yet the seven in the morning? My alarm clock, always put at ten moments past the seven, has not yet shrilled.'

'Rang, Frank. Not shrilled, dear boy. I say Marco, you've woken the whole apartment with that frightful shrieking. Are you ill?'

Marco was not ill but frantic. He was hopping from one skinny naked leg to the other in rage and despair, clad only in a pair of scruffy boxer shorts. 'I woke up to go for a pee, see? And then I come back into my bedroom and it's empty. The room is empty.'

They all looked wonderingly around the room. There was a single bed, a substantial desk, a small wardrobe, and a comfortable upright chair with arms. There were also a great many clothes, of varying degrees of cleanliness, scattered about.

'You see?' Marco's voice was shrill. 'Empty!'

Frank, also in boxer shorts but longer, less crumpled than Marco's and with a neat t-shirt tucked into the waistband, said crisply, 'The English they are bad at the speaking of the English. This room is no empty. Is too much full, if you want me to say truthful.' He looked scornfully at books on Venetian art and architecture, odd newspapers, paints and brushes lying around both on and off surfaces.

Netty, resplendent in baby-doll shortie pyjamas, the kind that were popular in her youth in the early 1950s and probably dated from that time, said kindly, 'Perhaps you should calm down, Marco, and tell us exactly what the trouble seems to be.'

Marco, still bouncing about like a man on a bungee jump, refused to calm down but became even more hysterical. 'Can't you see? Haven't you noticed? It's my painting! My new painting, my masterpiece! GONE.'

After a moment Netty said, 'So it is, dear. That is, it is not here. How observant of you. Not that I have ever seen it here, of course. I would not dream of going into your bedroom.'

Frank said, 'Your painting? Is lost? Try and remember where last you put him.'

Miranda said nothing but furrowed her brows, in what she hoped was a look of concern.

'*Put* it? Lost it?' Marco shouted. 'You Teutonic twit, have you seen the size of it?'

'You arrogant Englishman, how can painting so large get lost?'

'You, calling me arrogant? A German?'

'Swiss. Yes, yes! I call you straight in face an arrogant.'

'An arrogant what, Frank?' Netty asked mildly.

Miranda said hurriedly, 'Don't answer that, Frank. And you, Marco, calm down. I am sure there must be some explanation.' She sounded vague.

Frank walked out of the room to shut off his alarm clock. Marco wailed, 'I brought it into my bedroom, after that insulting party in Lissabelle's apartment when my painting was being auctioned off like . . . like a piece of meat at a butcher's.' He threw himself down on the bed as the memory of the insult quite took his breath away.

'Oh dear.' Netty was sympathetic. 'There there. Buck up.' Though to be honest, she realized that she would never understand artists. She asked tentatively, 'Dear boy, is that not A Good Thing? Two people nearly in fisticuffs over one of your paintings?'

Marco gave her a 'you wouldn't be expected to understand' look and leaped up again. 'I'm phoning the police.'

Miranda, nervously, said, 'No no no no! I mean, I'm sure the painting must be somewhere. Let's just have a little search.' She made a half-hearted attempt to look under the bed.

'What a splendid idea. Miranda is quite right; we mustn't jump to conclusions.'

But Marco was whirling around the apartment like a dervish, infuriating Frank by charging into his room and demanding to look behind the door. 'You say to me of thievery? *You*, you Englishman, who thieved away the pride of the German nation, made robbery of German life—'

'I thought you were Swiss,' Miranda snapped.

'Yes I am Swiss but my parents are German.'

'Oh dear, we mustn't mention the war,' Netty said nervously.

'War? What war? I am speaking of after the war. And I am speaking of now. I am very much against the Europe.'

'Hang on there, Frankie, that's not a very nice thing to say, with all these sweet Europeans here.'

They all whirled around to see Bruce standing in the open doorway leading to the courtyard, for everyone had followed Marco downstairs to Frank's room. Bruce was the only one dressed, in lime green shorts with socks to match and face and knees scrubbed squeaky clean.

'Goodness,' Netty exclaimed. 'Did one of us forget to lock the courtyard door last night?'

Frank forgot about the European Community and said indignantly, 'What? What is this? So. Today I write rota for locking of door at night.' He disappeared into his room to do so immediately.

Bruce, who had actually been the one to leave the door unlocked after they had successfully accomplished Phase One of The Plan, said brightly, 'I've come to invite all of you to my place for breakfast.'

'Breakfast?' Miranda blinked at him. 'Bruce, it's not even seven-thirty.'

While Bruce whispered to Miranda, 'I heard the fuss. What's gone wrong?' Marco yelled, 'Bruce, my painting! It's been stolen. I was just about to phone the police.'

'Ah,' said Bruce. 'Oh dear, what a pity, how sad.' He rattled the words meaninglessly, as if reciting the alphabet.

Marco looked at him oddly. 'Is that all you can say? So calmly? Jesus, Bruce, I thought you were my mate.'

'And that's just what I am, buddy. Now look here, by some amazing piece of coincidence, I've got this telephone number here.' He pulled out a scrap of paper from his pocket. 'The *carabinieri*. They're the police you've got to deal with here. Look, there's even an extension number there, and a name, someone to contact. You always get personal attention if you mention a name.'

Miranda said suspiciously, 'Bruce, are you sure you know what you're doing?'

'Trust me.'

While the others were crowded around Marco and the telephone, Miranda whispered to Bruce, 'This wasn't part of the plan. The police.'

'Marco wasn't supposed to notice the painting was missing until midday. He's never up before then.'

'I know, I nearly died when he started screeching. Bruce, what'll we do when the police come? Getting involved with them wasn't on.'

'Tell me about it.'

'Oh God, Marco's phoning now, I can hear him.' Everyone was straining to hear Marco, in rotten Italian, asking the police to come at once. When he got off the phone he said, 'They understood "famous painting" at any rate, and "stolen". They probably think I've got something to do with the Biennale, so no doubt they'll rush over. All corrupt anyway, the Biennale. It's who you know, and the government, and you pat my bum and I'll pat yours . . .' He whinged away dramatically for a time, while Bruce and Miranda exchanged glances.

Sure enough, in a few moments the wailing sirens of the *carabinieri* motorlaunch came roaring down the Grand Canal and within minutes, the tiny pier and courtyard of Palazzo Bobolino were swarming with activity. All the residents had come out in various states of undress, and Marco, still only in his boxer shorts, was jumping up and down, telling them about his precious painting.

Luckily one of the men, a chunky surly chap with beetle eyebrows and a broken nose, spoke English. 'We will search the premises,' he announced grandly. 'Every apartment.'

'Oh shit,' Miranda whispered to Bruce. 'What're we going to do?'

For once Bruce was stumped. Miranda said urgently, 'You'll have to bribe him.'

'What? Are you nuts? I'm American, for goodness' sake. We don't do bribes.'

Miranda was about to argue this debatable statement when she saw one of the policemen heading for Bruce's apartment. Pulling

Bruce along, she followed him in. It was the chunky English speaking one.

The first thing he did was open the door leading to the vast storeroom under the marble staircase.

'I thought the *carabinieri* weren't supposed to be very bright,' Miranda hissed.

'Yeah, so did I,' Bruce hissed back. 'I guess the game's up.'

For a long pregnant moment, the three of them stared at Marco's painting. Then the policeman said, '*Madonna*. And what is this?'

Bruce attempted humour. 'Animal? Mineral?'

'*Una pittura*. A painting. In hiding here in the cupboard.'

'I think you're right. It *is* a painting. You win, heh heh.' Bruce giggled hysterically and looked wildly at Miranda, thinking of foreign prisons, dungeons, wrists manacled to chains on damp sweaty walls. The Bridge of Sighs, over which no doubt still travelled treasoners and poisoners and those who stole famous paintings from men called Marco Polo.

The policeman, who had noted Marco's large signature on the painting, glowered at Bruce. 'This is your apartment, yes?'

'No. That is, I don't own it. I don't even live here permanently; I'm just passing through, heh heh. Oh hell, what's the use. Yes. This is my pad.' Bruce knew denial would only lead him into deeper, deeper shit.

'And this is the stolen painting.'

'Oboy, is it? Omigod, so it is! Golly, I wonder how it got here!'

'Goodness,' Miranda cried. 'Why, someone must have planted it here!'

The policeman looked at them both scornfully, thinking how they would soon be sorry that they thought they could pull something like that over the *carabinieri*. He hoped the American would put up a fight when he was arrested for robbery; he hadn't clapped handcuffs on anyone for ages.

But there were still formalities to be got through. Staring at Bruce with his hard *carabinieri* look, that he practised every morning while shaving, he snarled, 'Who has the key to this apartment? Except for you?'

Bruce, losing all scruples, was about to shout that the Polish gentleman still sound asleep upstairs through all this din, also had a key, and that no doubt it was him who put the painting in the storeroom for the man was foreign, and Eastern European to boot. But at that moment the phone rang.

It made them all jump, for the phone was right there, in the downstairs passageway, and rang shrilly and demandingly. Bruce answered at once, hoping it would be someone like the American Ambassador. Nothing less than that would save him, he was sure of it.

'What? Who? You're kidding. Sure, hang on.' Bruce, totally bewildered, handed the phone to the policeman. 'It's for you.'

Bruce and Miranda shrugged shoulders and made funny perplexed faces at each other as they listened shamelessly to the bit of the conversation they could hear. It was all in Italian, and the party at the other end seemed to be doing most of the talking. The policeman seemed to be saying nothing but,

'*Si, Gianni, si si. Capisco. Si, Gianni, si. Capisco.*'

'What's *capisco* mean?' Bruce whispered.

'I understand.'

'I *know* you understand Italian, but goddamnit Miranda, *I* don't.'

'No, that's what he keeps saying. He's telling Gianni that he understands.'

They looked at each other with sudden dawning awareness. 'Gianni? It's not the same Gianni . . . ?'

Bruce nodded, 'I thought the voice sounded familiar.'

After one more *si, Gianni*, the policeman hung up. Slowly turning to Bruce and Miranda he smiled benignly at them and with a grand sweeping gesture, closed the storeroom door gently. 'I did not know,' he said smoothly, 'that you are a friend of Gianni's.'

Later, when the *carabinieri* had gone, promising Marco glibly that every possible avenue would be explored by the authorities to regain the stolen painting, Bruce and Miranda scuttled out of the palazzo. 'Where are we going?' Miranda asked.

'Anywhere. Away from Palazzo Bob and all the prying ears.'

'But I'm supposed to go off with Radek. Keep him away from Marco all day, so Marco doesn't keep on having these urges to confess he wasn't selected for the Biennale.'

'Miranda honey, it's only eight o'clock. Paolo's not coming for you until ten, and Radek's still asleep; I just had a look at him. I don't know what you did to him last night before I got there, but he seemed to be the only one at Palazzo Bob not woken by the cops.'

'What about Marco? Won't he wake up his father, to tell him about the missing painting?'

'Not a chance. He's in Apt. 3, crying on Lissabelle's shoulder. Didn't you see her rush out and demand to know what was going on?'

'No, I missed that.'

'She dragged him off inside her lair, after the cops left. He'll be lucky if he gets out of there by nightfall. And alive too.'

Even at that hour of the morning, San Polo was lively and cheery, with people rushing about greeting each other jovially, merchants wiping down shop windows getting ready for the day ahead, the strong smell of coffee drifting from open cafés. Miranda thought how much she could like this *sestiere,* if Venice herself wasn't so maddeningly capricious. And if she, Miranda, wasn't churned up with an old lover, long-lost father of her child, as well as being inextricably involved in a dubious bout with the Italian law.

They walked quickly through the Rialto vegetable and fruit market, then the fish market, to finally settle in a bar in the Campo delle Beccarie, where they ordered strong espresso. 'Now Bruce, tell me at once. Everything.' She looked surreptitiously around her, making sure there was no one, especially no one even vaguely Italian-looking, in sight. 'Who exactly is this Gianni?'

Bruce too looked furtively around. 'He's the one I mentioned last night, the Italian guy, knows Nina and Paolo. The insurance salesman.'

'I know all that. That policeman said he was your friend.'

Bruce shrugged. He had given Gianni a great many American dollars, after the guy had gone on about protection and other such stuff in a most forceful and, if truth be told, scary manner. 'I wouldn't exactly have said he was a friend.'

'There's something very fishy going on.'

'Honey, don't I know it.'

'The way Gianni knew where the police were. And what they were doing.'

'Yeah. As if Gianni had a direct line to the cop station.'

They were silent for a moment. Bruce said, 'Gianni did give me that phone number, the one I gave Marco. In case we ran into hitches, Gianni said. It was important to know the right person to contact.'

'Oh bloody hell.'

'But it really was the *carabinieri* number; I heard them answer on the other end when Marco phoned. That's when I totally lost it. I panicked, Miranda, real, real bad. I thought it would be some guy, some friend of Gianni's who could help us out, and there was this cop answering the phone.'

She groaned. 'Worse and worse.'

The waiter came with their coffee. Bruce hiked up the collar of his shirt. 'Stop looking so shifty,' Miranda snapped.

While the waiter fussed with sugar and teaspoons, they thought

197

about Marco's painting, still in the storeroom but now locked and bolted, at a suggestion from the policeman. After the phone call from Gianni, the man had apologized for any inconvenience the *carabinieri* had caused them. 'It is of course, a terrible mistake. This stolen painting.'

Both Miranda and Bruce had, without thinking, turned to stare at the now shut storeroom. The policeman went on, 'Obviously, if there is a painting in there, which I am not entirely sure of, it is a painting belonging to you, sir.' He bowed deferentially to Bruce. 'I will now call off my men, for there is no stolen painting in this palazzo. Indeed, I am sure there is not one anywhere. These Biennale artists, they are so excitable. They imagine such things.' Here he allowed himself a little laugh. Bruce and Miranda politely joined in, if somewhat hysterically.

Now, alone in the dark bar (they would not risk drinking their coffee outside in bright sunlight), waiter gone, Miranda said, 'Well, to be honest, I think we're over-reacting. All these theatrics going on in this bloody palazzo is getting to us; we're being melodramatic. There's probably a simple explanation. I mean, let's face it, the *carabinieri* do have this reputation in Italy for not being very bright. Maybe the policeman genuinely made a mistake and didn't realize it was Marco's painting.'

Bruce brightened. 'Hey, y'know what? I think you must be right.' His natural American optimism, and the fact that he'd been let off from having his hands chopped off, or whatever Europeans did to thieves and robbers in the old country, caused Bruce to forget the many green dollars he had parted company with during the midnight hours. Besides, what was money after all? He had stacks of it, and the relief he was feeling now, after his brief encounter with the law (if you could call it law in Europe), was worth its weight in greenbacks.

Miranda was saying, 'I'll be glad when this is all finished. I'm starting to get nervous. I must have been mad to go along with you.'

Bruce cheerfully agreed that she probably was, but what the hell. 'Think of the fun we're having, sweetheart. And think of Radek, how happy he'll be.' Then the smile faded off his face and he took Miranda's hand, held it soulfully. 'Gosh, Miranda, I'm so insensitive. Oboy, I'm a real sleazebag.'

'Now what?' Miranda withdrew her hand warily. She was getting fed up with all these emotional types.

'Your baby. Your poor dead baby. I haven't even asked you about it, asked you to pour out your heart to me, share it with me. As your friend, it's impacted me too. Talk to me, Miranda. Let me give you a hug first, and then you can talk. It'll release you, honey, believe me.'

But Miranda was up and out the door, calling back brightly, 'I'm off, Bruce, but thanks anyway. Much as I like you, I'd rather impact with some fresh air and sunshine. Besides, I'd better get ready to meet Radek. See you this evening, for the next part of the plan.'

'Goddamn English,' Bruce sighed to the waiter as he paid the bill for the coffee. 'So goddamn uptight. I feel kind of sorry for them, don't you?'

The waiter agreed. He felt sorry for anyone who was not Italian.

A strong breeze, nay, a howling gale seemed to have blown up since the early morning mist dissolved so suddenly. Miranda and Radek, sitting on the sandy beach of the Lido, held on to bags and towels and the odd bits of clothing that were flying about in a hot, ungodly wind.

'Bloody Venice,' Miranda muttered through closed lips, so that the sand did not blow in her teeth.

Radek did not trouble to admonish her, remind her that the Lido, though of course part of Venice, was another island altogether, and quite unlike Venice proper. He did not want sand in his mouth either.

'I don't think there's any point in this, Radek. Look, should we wander up the main street, find a place for lunch?' Her skin, exposed to the elements except for the parts clad in a modest bikini, was stinging as the sand flew about pelting everything in sight.

A half hour later, clothed and feeling much better, they were sitting under the sheltered shade of a grapevine, in a trattoria not far from the beach. Wine and food had been ordered, and at least they could speak. What with the roar of the motorboat as Paolo drove them across the lagoon and to the Lido, then the howling of the wind, conversation had been non-existent.

'Darling,' Radek began, reaching across the table to take her hand.

Miranda yawned. 'Sorry, didn't get much sleep last night.'

Radek withdrew his hand. 'Of course. That American. Bruce. He was with you all night.'

Miranda yawned again. 'Not quite all night.'

Radek stood up. 'I am sorry, but I can see that this is all a great mistake. I thought, when I saw you again, looking so young still, so beautiful . . . what's the matter? Why are you looking at me like that?'

'I like that bit. The one about still being young and beautiful. Can you say it again, please? That kind of talk hasn't come often my way, not for years. Not with a baby to raise, and being a single mother and all.'

Radek stared. And stared and stared. 'But . . . the baby . . . *our* baby? Didn't you say something about my leaving you alone and pregnant? Didn't you say that? Last night?'

'So I did. I keep mentioning babies, don't I.'

'But I thought you said there was no baby. Not now. Miranda for God's sake, is there a baby or is there not?'

'Radek, I'm tired. Lack of sleep and all that. No, no, don't get all stuffy and uptight again about Bruce. Of course there's no baby.'

'Ah.' Radek did not know whether to be relieved, for he had been spared guilt, or sad because he and Miranda, whom he was wishing he had never let go (despite Bruce) had never had a little *kapusta* together.

'I'm sorry, Miranda. It must have been dreadful for you. Returning to England and finding out you were pregnant, then losing the baby.'

'Losing? Who said anything about losing her?'

'What?'

'You've got a nerve, you know, coming back like this. After all these years.' The waiter had brought chilled white wine and Miranda was now slugging it back. It made her angry; alcohol sometimes did.

'Did you say *her*?'

'Drink your wine, Radek, or I'll drink your glass too. We'd better order some more.'

'*Her*?'

'I didn't want to tell you, when we met again so suddenly, after all these years. I'm not sure I do even now, except it wouldn't be fair to Jessica if I didn't.'

'Jessica?'

'Oh do close your mouth, Radek. What did you expect me to call her, some nice Polish name like Henryka or Kapusta or something?' She giggled. 'Not that *kapusta* is a name. It isn't, is it, Radek? There aren't Polish girls running about with a Christian name of Cabbage, are there? What'd'you call them for short: Cole Slaw? Sauerkraut?'

Radek, in shock, picked up his wine glass, only to find that Miranda had emptied it. He called the waiter for more, and after it had arrived, said carefully, 'Miranda, are you telling me that I have a daughter? Living in England? *Our* daughter? Mine?'

Miranda snorted. 'Hah, *your* daughter? What did you do to help raise her? Where were you at two a.m. when she was howling her

201

head off? For two years she cried, didn't sleep a wink. And where were you when she ran off with a didgeridoo player just before her sixteenth birthday? And all those years in between, when she got such dreadful measles I thought she would die, and then broke her leg only a couple of months later. Where were you, Radek?'

A shocked silence greeted this. Not just from Radek, but also from the waiter and two waitresses and all the tourists who were lunching in the trattoria, most of whom were English-speaking, who had listened avidly to every word.

'We-ell mate, where *were* you?' cried an Australian voice from the corner table.

'Tell 'er, mate,' echoed his friend, a New Zealander with a huge blonde beard. 'She's got a right to know, if you ask me.'

'Gawd, how predictable can you get.' A loud American female voice added itself to the general displeasure. 'Typical male behaviour, running away when the going gets tough. Where're you at, buddy?'

Radek said humbly, 'I was in Poland. For a time, anyway. Then England.'

Amidst mutterings of 'that's no excuse' and 'Polish bastard' coupled with 'English prick', Miranda said, 'Oh don't be so stupid, Radek, that was a rhetorical question.'

'Of course. Forgive me, Miranda. For answering rhetorical questions, and also for not being around when our daughter was being raised. But I would have been, had I have known. Had you bothered to tell me, Miranda. But I suppose I was unimportant; after all, I'm only the father.'

'I'll go along with that,' said the American woman. 'An absent father has no right to think he's of any importance in the slightest.'

'Aw c'mon, Sheila. Fair's fair, give the bugger a chance. If the poor sucker didn't even know . . .'

'Only the father, Miranda.' Radek's voice was dry with sarcasm;

to lubricate it he drank not only his wine but hers. 'Only the father, Miranda, who always longed for a daughter. Who adored his son but always secretly wished for a little girl as well. Who pined for a little girl, in fact, but was denied one. Or rather, denied the *knowledge* of his little girl, denied the right to see her, help raise her, help get her over the mumps and stop some bloody creepy didgeridoo player from running off with her, the rotten sod.'

'Hey mate, steady goes it. I happen to like a bit of the ole didge music now and again.'

'That's all very well for you to say,' Radek shouted at the Australian, 'but he was a cradle snatcher.'

'Most men are,' said the woman.

'Aw heck, I don't believe it, not another of those hell-raisin' man-haters. Europe's crawling with 'em,' said the New Zealander.

Miranda said wearily, 'Anyway, she never did. Run off with the didgeridoo player. She only threatened.'

Everyone applauded at this. Radek slumped in his chair, 'Thank God for that.'

Crisis over, the diners went back to their food. Radek slowly opened his eyes. 'Miranda, tell me honestly and plainly. And very simply. Am I, or am I not, the father of a girl of twenty-eight years called Jessica?'

'Yes, Radek. You are.'

'YAHOO, YIPPEE.' Radek leaped into the air, plucked Miranda out of her chair, and began twirling her around. The diners stopped eating again and cheered, applauded wildly.

'Jen-koo-you,' Radek babbled when he had calmed down, and the noise level had dimished slightly. 'Oh my darling *kapusta*, jen-koo-you.'

'What's he saying?'

'He's thanking her,' said the Australian, whose uncle had married a Polish girl during the last war. 'Or else he's thanking his lunch. I'm pretty sure he's talking about cole slaw; we ate nothing else at my uncle's house and that's what they called it. Now why would he want to thank a plate of veggies?'

Why indeed? Venice, delighted with this little melodrama played out at her whimsical seaside resort, rewards the actors in this *commedia dell'arte* piece of theatre by stopping her heavy breathing and letting the wind drop. As Radek twirls his lovely English brassica while she giggles and beams at him, and the other diners talk and bicker amicably amongst themselves, Venezia shuts her eyes gently, and goes to sleep.

And suddenly, as the air stills and becomes heavy, soporific, everyone else feels the need to sleep too. Within a half-hour the trattoria is deserted, its customers gone back to hotels or campsites or self-catering apartments to snooze.

Back on the Lido beach, lying on colourful beach towels, Miranda and Radek snooze too, drained of all energy. They blame their sudden heavy-lidded eyes and numbed brains on an excess of emotion brought about by their reunion, combined with a relatively sleepless night for both of them.

But really it is Venice. When the *Serenissima* takes her siesta, her playthings do too. And they will not waken until she decrees it.

Chapter Thirteen

While Miranda and Radek fall in and out of love, and drift in and out between illusion and reality not unlike the reflections of the city meandering here and there in the canals, Venice has been dabbling elsewhere as well.

At the Palazzo Bobolino, to begin with, where Lissabelle has been feeding figs to her artist-lover, beguiling him with a sly tongue coated with sweet white wine which not only darts in and out of his mouth, but also in his ears where it whispers tantalizingly. Not just about love, but about Marco's painting, and how she lusts after it just as she lusts after his body. This last lust is at least being satisfied, more than once, on this hot blowy day.

As for the other, Marco cannot help, for his precious painting has been stolen. Not that Lissabelle believes this for one moment. She believes her artist-lover is holding out on her, so she will not let him go, not even when the wind drops and their bodies glisten and melt with sweat in the sultry afternoon.

'I place my bet on Marco,' April said, about midway through the afternoon. 'She's using her state of the art persuasion tactics and it's not working. Just came out of the bedroom for more figs, and more of that sickly dessert wine.'

'Darling, you do not know her like I do. He's dead meat. Metaphorically speaking, of course.'

The two were sitting out on the balcony, shaded now by the buildings. Simon was writing notes in his journal, taking care to put in as many details as possible in case this Marco Polo was about to become mega famous, as Lissabelle expected.

'I'm not really sure I *want* to know her as you do,' April said speculatively. 'I don't feel good about myself when I'm around her these days.'

'Darling!' Simon sat up in amazement. 'You do sound so boringly American. Lissabelle never should have taken you out to LA so soon after you began to work for her, you were obviously too impressionable. What is all this feeling good about yourself crap? And you're not getting a conscience, are you? Can't have that, not in this job.'

'Oh good God, Simon, nothing like that. I don't feel good about myself because she's getting all the fucking and I'm getting nothing, that's why. What's she got that I haven't?'

'Money, darling. It makes one forcefully brash. Enables her to just rake them in. Like turnips.'

April eyed one of the younger gondoliers that drifted by, boat empty. He waved and blew her a kiss. 'Simon, d'you think she'd mind if I . . . ?' She blew a kiss back at the gondolier, who mimed a swimming motion, calling her out to him.

'She'd throw a wobbly, darling. You know that. Having you hanging around chaste and jealous is wonderful for the ego. I wouldn't be surprised if she gives you an extra little gift this week, especially if you throw in some envious admiration as well.'

April sighed. She even eyed Simon for a moment or two, but gave that idea up as a bad job.

Venice was not good for her. The poxy city was making her restless. She could almost hear the Serene bloody Republic laughing at her, but it was only the wind coming up from the lagoon and rustling up the water.

Netty, after the excitement of Marco discovering his painting gone, went to her Italian class, but her heart was not in it. She was too full of the events that were to happen that night, and full of excitement too after being shown yet another apartment for rent not that far from the Palazzo Bobolino. Perhaps she would tell Silvano about it tonight; she could not keep it a secret much longer, and it would be such a delightful surprise for him. She would be so full of adrenalin after the completion of their daring mission that sleep would be impossible. A good serious talk about their future far into the night would unwind them both.

Besides, they may as well talk; they had not managed to do much of anything else, Netty thought as she sat doodling in her workbook. Not in the way one was expected to when one had a lover. She had read enough contemporary novels to know that though she and Silvano dabbled, they did not go the whole hog. Did not go for it. Did not jump into the water in the deep end, and risk drowning so as to have the ultimate experience.

Netty doodled a sketch of two stick figures jumping off a pier into a dark fiercesome deep canal, then shuddered. Perhaps drowning was rather over the top, the cutting edge. Did she really, truly, need to be at the cutting edge? Not that she quite understood that term, but she had read the Sunday supplements and had a jolly good idea. Look at Lissabelle, if anyone was at the cutting edge *she* was. Netty would not like to be like Lissabelle for all the tea in China, but still. It would be exceedingly pleasant to experience it just once.

She sighed.

Frank, sitting next to her in the classroom which was situated in a tiny palazzo alongside a canal, snapped, 'You are not giving the attention. Our teacher is asking to conjugate the verb *essere*.'

Frank himself had already done it. His space at the long wide table was covered with neat pads of lined paper, a row of pens and pencils all exactly the same size, and a small pile of dictionaries and grammar books, arranged in descending order of size.

'Our teacher does not appear to be in the room,' Netty said, only just noticing. She really was not very concentrated on her Italian course, she realized. This might prove a drawback, when she moved here permanently. But as long as she knew the basics, like *ciao* and *bella*, she would manage.

'He is stepped out to make the photocopying,' Frank said, 'leaving to us to conjugate.' He was proud of his knowledge of that difficult word in English.

Netty looked curiously at Frank's precise columns of verbs written out on one of the lined pads. 'How neat and tidy your writing is.'

Frank sat up straighter. 'There is not the point to do anything, without the order and the precision.'

'Oh.' Netty looked at her own rather chaotic stack of books and papers guiltily.

'Order and precision,' Frank barked. 'Without these things, the life would be not in the control.' He shuddered at the thought.

Netty was not sure that life was in any way controllable at the best of times, but did not voice these opinions. Their teacher had returned, and was once again droning on about verbs.

Silvano, true child of Venice, was dozing in his gondola, enjoying a tiny siesta in the wicked heat. He was sitting, head slumped on his chest, on one of the plush velvet-covered chairs at the prow of his boat which was moored not far from Netty's language school. He was meeting her there at two, for she had some shopping to do beforehand.

'I say, Silvano, here I am!' Netty's plummy English voice, cultivated by centuries of ancestors using those selfsame tones to put the masses in their place, trilled out along the back alley and filtered into his consciousness. He had been dreaming of a place of pale greens and dewy wetness, where he and Netty frolicked in gardens and picnicked on those round bread roll things, scones they called them, with heavy cream and chunky strawberry jam on top. A place where everyone spoke as Netty, and no one swore at him in Veneziano and nagged at him to bring home more money, or work harder, or stop flaunting his foreign tart in front of the neighbours.

Silvano, waking from the dream as Netty plonked herself into the gondola, decided that tonight, after the Event, he would tell her that he was returning with her to England.

Netty was saying, 'Silvano dear, is it all right if we give Frank a lift in the gondola? He is off to the library, to study verbs. I thought we could cruise by and drop him off.'

Frank got in cautiously. 'I have said, in class, to Netty, that I have not rid a gondola. Never ever.'

'You mean ridden, Frank. You have never ridden in a gondola.'

Silvano grunted something unintelligible. He wondered if he could charge Frank for this excursion to the library; it was on the other side of the Grand Canal. What did Netty think he was, a free gondola service for every foreigner she bumped into?

In the boat, after a few moments, Frank said, 'Yes, this is good. Very very good.'

'I am pleased it is to your liking,' Silvano said, a trifle sarcastically.

'Such order. Such precision.'

'*Che?*'

'The way you place your oar just so. The way the foot moves also just so. So precise. So controlled. Yes, wonderful.'

Despite himself, Silvano was gratified. It was about time someone appreciated the intricacies of gondoliering. He sometimes wondered if Netty was beginning to take him for granted, all that reclining she did in his gondola as if she were the English Queen and not just English. He hoped she was listening to all these words of praise.

After Frank was let off, Silvano rowed the gondola, with Netty still languishing in it, back to the Palazzo Bobolino. He knew he was safe, for Elena was off with their grandchildren somewhere for the day.

As they disembarked, Netty said, 'Will you come up to my place? Have a cup of tea with me? This weather requires tea, don't you agree?' It was hot and sultry. The thought of a strong, bitter black Italian coffee was more than she could bear right now, though it felt terribly disloyal to think this. She waffled on, 'Sometimes, you know, you cannot beat a good cup of China.'

Silvano, though still a trifle grumpy with his adorable one for not appreciating him as he should be appreciated, was mollifed by this. Netty was obviously trying to Anglicize him; perhaps she secretly knew what he had in mind. He had a moment's regret for the pot of espresso Elena would have left for him on the kitchen stove, but banished it quickly by thinking of Elena herself.

They went upstairs into the kitchen of Apt. 1, where no one seemed to be at home. After the tea was made and drunk, and they were sitting together on the sofa in the dim drawing room, the shutters closed against the heat, Netty sighed. 'Ah Silvano. Venice, my beloved Vee-nee-cee, and now—' She paused dramatically, 'You.'

'Netty. *Bella*. My little one.'

She frowned slightly, and peered at Silvano to see if he were mocking her. Her illusions were many, but she knew for certain that she certainly could not be called little, by any stretch of the imagination. But he was looking dreamily at her, so she smiled. 'Silvano, my dearest.'

'*Cara.*'

210

'Angel.'

'*Carissima.*'

They moved closer towards each other. They clutched. They kissed.

'Ah, *bella.*'

'Oh, darling.'

They fumbled for a bit.

Then the inevitable happened. In the midst of a fumble, Silvano found himself drifting off, what with the intense heat and the not unpleasant sensation of Netty murmuring hypnotic things in his ear while stroking his thigh gently. It was all very soothing, and soporific, and since his eyes were closed anyway . . .

'Silvano! Silvano, wake up.'

'What? Huh? *Che?*'

'You were snoring.' Netty's voice was cold. She had the feeling Silvano was starting to take her for granted, falling asleep on her sofa as if he were a permanent fixture here. She had a horrid suspicion of what it would be like to be Elena.

Silvano shook his head and opened his eyes. 'Ah *bella*, forgive me. I was gathering my strength for tonight, my little one. Preparing myself for the ordeal ahead.'

Immediately Netty softened. 'Of course, I understand. Our mission.' They were silent for a moment, thinking of the adventure ahead. She went on, 'But later, dear one. After it is all over.' She couldn't wait to see his face when she told him of the apartment she was buying. He could visit her there clandestinely, attending to her every sensual need, and later, she would send him quite happily back to his wife.

'Yes, later.' Silvano kissed her plump fingertips. 'There are things I must say to you.' He couldn't wait to tell her that he was coming to England to live with her, that he was hers forever.

She felt a few palpitations at this. She loved declarations of

211

love; she had not had many in her lifetime. 'And after we have talked . . . ?' She looked at him coyly.

Silvano shuddered involuntarily. It was not that he did not fancy Netty, nor that he had anything against sex. It was just that he had done so much of it, with so many nationalities. He was, quite frankly, exhausted.

It was time some other, younger gondoliere carried the flag of the winged lion for Venezia. He had done his bit. He was more than ready to be put out in the soft green mossy pastures of the English countryside.

With soft Netty, wearing a green mossy frock, at his side, ministering to his every platonic need.

During that blowzy day when Miranda and Radek were frolicking on the Lido, and Marco was being stuffed with figs, and Silvano rowed his English *bella* and an uptight Swiss (German) around the canals, Nina and Paolo were doing a preliminary run around the waterways, to prepare themselves for the mission ahead. After they left the other two on the Lido, they roared off in Paolo's taxi back to Venice itself to meander slowly up and down the canals in the Arsenale region, near the Giardini.

'Look casual,' Nina commanded. 'Stop staring at every landmark as if you haven't seen it before.'

'I'm trying to impress every detail in my mind,' Paolo growled back. 'And what about you? Sitting there writing down notes like that. I thought you're supposed to be my passenger, enjoying the passing scenery.'

Paolo swerved quickly, to avoid smashing into a passing gondola which he had not seen because he had turned around to glare at Nina.

After the gondolier had shouted obscenities at him, and the Americans in the gondola threatened to sue for the damage caused to their inner peace after the panic and fear they had endured,

Paolo slowed down and cruised. 'There, that's the one,' he said, pointing to a certain building between the trees in the gardens.

'Are you sure?'

'Positive.' Nina hastily added the building to the small map she had drawn.

They drifted on. Paolo said, '*Madonna*. I'm not so sure about this.'

'What's wrong now?'

'Getting involved, the way we are. *Dio mio*, what do we care about all those Americans and English and Polish and allsorts anyway? Why are we risking our necks?'

'Because they're sweet,' Nina said with wide innocent eyes. 'And they have helped me with my English.'

Paolo looked at her suspiciously. But since that other English-woman, the blonde with the legs, had done her bit in helping him with *his* English, he could not say much. Even though it was only the odd monsyllable, like 'more' and 'don't stop' and 'fuck me quick'. Not much, when you thought about it, but one never knew, they could come in handy, when he and Nina were a happily married couple living in London. You never knew what kind of lonely women rode in big black English taxis.

'*Si*, okay, so we should help them,' Paolo went on, 'but it is a great risk to us. I mean, I could lose my taxi licence if I'm caught; aren't we breaking the law?'

Nina laughed. 'Oh Paolo, you are so endearing. Why do you think I told Gianni all about it?'

'You told Gianni?'

'Of course.'

Paolo relaxed. 'Well, why didn't you say so?'

Nina wrapped her slim brown arms around his muscular brown belly. 'Did you think I'd let us get involved in this without some kind of security?'

*

Evening. Balmy. Venice is blowing little kisses over her walking, talking, human puppets, as well as over her festive palazzos and churches and mosaics. These *bacci* drift across canals as patches of sunlight, or puffs of sea breeze, or whiffs of jasmine mingled with the not unpleasant scent of old damp marble.

All is as it should be. Gothic and gondola, canals and cathedrals, lovers and luvvies: all mix and mingle here in whatever whimsical manner Venice decrees.

The twilight is unbelievable. The sunset indescribable. Venezia preens. Tonight no one will get away without making a fool of themselves, in one way or another.

The first thing Miranda had to do when she and Radek returned from the Lido was to get rid of him. This was not an easy thing, after just finding him again, so to speak. After twenty-eight-odd years and all that.

They began arguing on the *motoscafo* as Paolo and Nina zoomed them home in the water taxi. As the frilly outline of the Doge's Palace appeared, Radek, surreptitiously letting his fingers remember the best places in Miranda's body, whispered, 'Mm, what should we do first? Have dinner in some candlelit romantic place and then come back to the palazzo and make love all night? Or go inside and make love first, then eat, then come back and make love all night? You choose.'

His roaming fingertips were most persuasive. Luckily Paolo was steering the motorboat and for once looking straight ahead, while Nina tactfully sat in the front with him.

As they passed the great domes of the Church of the Salute, Radek murmured, 'I think bed first, don't you?'

As they went under the Accademia Bridge, he said, 'Mm, pity this boat doesn't have a private cabin.'

As they zoomed under the Rialto Bridge Radek groaned and moaned softly but said very little that made sense.

And then, as they pulled up at the Palazzo Bobolino, Radek did not have a chance to utter a sound, for Miranda, pulling herself together, leaped determinedly out of the *motoscafo*, kissed him fleetingly on the cheek, and said brightly, 'Ta ta then, Radek darling. Lovely day, wasn't it? Must go now, am completely exhausted, all that sun and all. See you tomorrow?'

'What?'

'I said—'

'I know what you said, Miranda, my hair may have gone grey and my face craggy in the past twenty-eight years, but I have not gone deaf. I meant, what was all that about? What do you mean, tomorrow? What about tonight? Dinner? And—' Here Radek looked around to see Nina and Paolo listening to all this, and Elena, who had wandered into the courtyard, and Frank, who was coming home from the library.

'And, *you* know,' he finished lamely.

'We'll do all that tomorrow. 'Bye for now.' She gave a lighthearted little wave and headed quickly for Apt. 1, before she relented and changed her mind. She had not remained unmoved during that erotic trip home in the water taxi. How odd it was, she thought as she fumbled for her key, that Radek's fingers, so much older now, could still do the same things to her body, also older. How amazing life kept turning out to be.

And how complicated. Radek, incensed at Miranda's flippant manner, not to mention hugely wounded by her insensitivity to his now urgent needs, had followed her to the door, and was shouting, 'Is that all you have to say to me? *Me*, the father of your child? The parent of a daughter I have never seen? A young woman whose very existence you kept wilfully from me?'

Above Radek's head a window flew open. 'Dad? Good God, it *is* Dad. Daughter? What daughter? You're the father of whose child?'

Miranda and Radek stared up at Marco, dishevelled as well

215

as half-crazed and sticky after all those figs and sweet white dessert wine. He had gone to his bedroom in a state of collapse only an hour or so ago, but had been woken by the sound of his father's voice proclaiming that he was the father of some woman's child.

'Miranda,' Marco said weakly, staring at her. 'You?'

Miranda nodded her head.

'And Dad?'

Radek nodded too.

Marco shook his own head, hard. He must be dreaming, he told himself. 'But . . . how did it happen so quickly? You only got here a couple of days ago.'

Miranda silently thanked her lucky stars that Jessica had got the brain cells, if Marco the artistic talent. Radek, however, realized his son was slightly drunk, though fortunately he did not know it was because Marco had been licking wine off a woman's body for most of the afternoon. There were some things that were far better for a father not to know.

Radek called, 'I'm coming up to see you, Marco. I know I have a great deal of explaining to do.' He calculated that it would take an hour or so to sober Marco up, another hour or so to explain that he had a half-sister called Jessica, and then he could guiltlessly cross over into Miranda's bedroom, luckily in the same apartment.

Miranda thought quickly. None of this was part of the plan. Before she could speak, Radek was following her upstairs.

Much later that night, and Marco and Radek were still sitting on the balcony outside Miranda's kitchen. Radek had snuck out briefly for take-away pizza while Miranda was in the shower, a cunning move for of course she never would have let him back in. Radek and Marco consumed the pizza ravenously on the balcony, much to the annoyance of Frank because of the rota.

While Radek was buying pizza, Marco had sobered up enough

216

to go out and buy a good red wine, shuddering as he thought of the sweet white stuff he had been imbibing all afternoon. In fact he shuddered when he thought of other things about that afternoon. Best forgotten, he decided. Though he supposed he could get a painting out of it. 'The Orgy', he could call it. He was not quite sure you could have an orgy with only two people – wasn't three the minimum number? Nonetheless it felt like an orgy to him, and probably the nearest he would ever get to one, being a committed artist with not much time for serious decadence.

Back on the balcony Radek and Marco talked. And ate sizzling pizza while Netty, Frank and Miranda ate silently in the kitchen, listening to the guffaws of laughter and reminiscences coming from the open double doors.

Father and son drank. And talked some more. And ate cold leftover pizza. Drank. Now and again Marco remembered his stolen painting and grew morose. But then he remembered his afternoon's orgy, and the fact that he had a brand new sister, and cheered up again.

'Jeez, are they gonna be out there all night?' Bruce, in the kitchen of Apt. 1, peeked out on to the balcony to see father and son still sitting where they had sat for several hours now. The washing-up had been done by Miranda, who was not on the rota that night, with no help at all from Marco, who was. This upset Frank so much that he was now downstairs in his bedroom sulking. Bruce had come over from his own apartment to join Miranda's vigil in the kitchen, while Netty rested a few hours before tonight's ordeal.

'How long can they go on like this?' Bruce, peering out again at father and son, wrung his hands in frustration.

'They are bonding, Bruce,' Miranda said waspishly. Her nerves were greatly on edge. 'You being an American should approve of all that. They are connecting. Empowering each other or

217

impacting each other or whatever you call it. In England, we call it having a lads' night out.'

Bruce was as nervy as Miranda. 'Why don't they go out or something? Find a bar, a restaurant?'

'It's a bit late for that. At least they're too drunk, and too busy wallowing in the past, to even think about the Biennale. Neither one of them has mentioned it all evening.' Miranda and Bruce had been shamelessly eavesdropping, to make sure.

Netty looked in anxiously. 'No change?'

'Nothing.'

'Oh dear.' She felt rather let down, if truth be told. Netty had been prepared to play her elaborate part, taking father and son well away from the Palazzo Bobolino for the evening. Bruce had bought three very expensive tickets for the Goldoni Theatre, to see a much sought-after play. Netty had been rehearsing her lines carefully. 'Oh I say, isn't it a dreary shame that Bruce cannot use these? His friends cancelled at the last moment, and he himself is unwell. He has insisted we go in their place, and to the Hotel Danieli afterwards, where he has booked a late supper.'

With the backing of Miranda, who would plead tiredness, and Bruce, who could look like a wounded guardian angel when thwarted, Netty could have kept them both out of the way until way after midnight, when the deed should have been done. Of course they had tried the plan anyway, but both Marco and Radek were too drunk and merry to get much sense into them; they refused point blank to leave the balcony.

Bruce was pacing up and down the kitchen. 'Man oh man. All our plans, all that effort, gone out the window, ruined, if they don't get off the balcony. They can see everything from there. And Paolo's due to arrive any minute now, goddamn it.'

On cue, the put-put of the motorboat could be heard. From the kitchen windows Miranda and Bruce could see Paolo and Nina draw closer, then pull away as they recognized the figures on the top balcony.

'You'll have to get them off,' Bruce said. 'It'll mean you can't come with us, but you'll have to distract them, get them out of the way. You're the only one who can do it; they've been calling for you to join them all night.'

'The plan won't work without me. The job has to look professional.'

Netty said, 'Silvano will be at his post by now.' She wrung her hands in agitation. Her heart beat like African drumming. She had never felt so alive.

'Paolo and Nina are cruising back, see them?'

At that moment the kitchen door opened. 'Time for my night-time chocolate,' Frank announced. 'Then bed. Tomorrow is opening of Biennale; I have here invitation. I go see German pavilion take every honour.'

The three of them barely noticed Frank as he put milk on for chocolate, crossing off 'evening chocolate' from one of his many lists in the kitchen. From on the balcony great whoops of laughter flew in, like a flock of merry pipistrelles.

Frank said, with some perplexity, 'The father and the son is much happy tonight. Very strange, after Marco is lost his treasure.'

'Treasure?'

'His painting.'

'Ah. But he's found a sister.'

Frank thought this was an English idiom and wrote it down. It was obviously the thing to say, when someone lost something. For instance, if an Englishman said, 'I have lost my steak and kidney pie', the correct answer would be, 'But you have found a sister.'

As he opened the small cupboard in the corner, Frank thought how profitable these weeks in Venice were proving to be. Not only was he learning Italian, but also improving his English, which was very necessary if he wanted to get on. Which Frank did, of course. And no doubt would.

The others watched without any interest as Frank took a large bottle of spirits from the cupboard, and poured some of the clear liquid into his hot chocolate drink. 'Is helpful for my sleep. The schnapps. I brought from Switzerland. One tiny mouthful every night, before bed. Fifteen minutes exactly later I am asleep.' He took a sip of the drink. 'Is important to sleep. No is possible to have order in life if no sleep good.'

The others nodded politely, minds elsewhere. Frank, expansive after his profitable evening – he had studied one hour, written two letters, done fifty press-ups, and meditated for twenty minutes, to relieve stress – said conversationally, 'Is important to have only tiny spoonful of this schnapps. Is special schnapps. Very strong. Very, very strong. Can knock big man right out, for hours.'

Miranda, Netty and Bruce, sitting slumped at the kitchen table, raised their heads one by one. 'Strong?' Netty said.

'Knocks big men out?' Bruce repeated.

'For hours?' Miranda straightened her shoulders and looked Frank squarely in the eye. 'How very, very interesting.'

Later, when Marco and Radek had passed out cold, Miranda said, 'What's Frank going to say about his half-empty Schnapps bottle?'

'I've filled it with water,' Bruce replied, tucking in a light blanket over the snoring men in case it turned colder in the wee hours.

'Poor darling,' Miranda said, kissing Radek gently on the forehead. 'I'm sorry, but we had no choice. And this is for you after all.'

But Radek heard not a word, having been put to bed with his son only moments before darkness crashed around both of them.

*

A very short time later, Nina held the door of Bruce's flat as wide open as she could, as he and Miranda carried out a large flat object loosely wrapped in sheets and blankets.

Paolo, on the pier, whispered, '*Qui*, here. Put it here.' He and Nina jumped into the boat to find a secure place for the bulky object.

Miranda, waiting to get in with Bruce, whispered, 'I hope Netty got to Silvano in time, to tell him to wait. I hope he didn't give up and leave.'

Bruce held Miranda's hand to steady her as she stepped into the *motoscafo*. From the window of Apt. 3 a pale head peered out. As the boat sped away towards the Rialto Bridge, Lissabelle went into Simon's room and plonked herself on his bed. 'I was woken by the noise of people whispering,' she pouted, 'and after such a hard day, too.' Her stomach felt queasy after all those figs.

'But guess what I saw?'

Simon sleepily sat up, thinking how hard he worked, how much he deserved every penny he earned. 'Uh, what?' His face expressed rapt interest. He thought, I could get a job in the bloody RSC after this.

'Bruce. Our neighbour from New York, the art dealer.'

'Gosh.' Raised eyebrows indicating surprise, fascination.

'And you'll never believe who he was with. Sophisticated, rich, influential Bruce — you will never believe it.'

'Tell me.' Avid concentration. Perplexity. Bursting to know.

'That dull, uninteresting nobody. That plain nice' — Lissabelle used 'nice' as if it meant 'viperous' — 'nice and horribly homespun Englishwoman.'

For a mad moment Simon thought she meant April. This was a tricky moment, for Lissabelle expected him to know exactly to whom she was referring. 'No,' he breathed, wonder and awe and disbelief puffing up the one word like a huge helium balloon.

'Yes.' Pleased by being the bearing of such shocking news, Lissabelle beamed. 'Miranda.'

Simon readjusted his face to hide the genuine surprise he felt at this. Not because Miranda was out on a midnight tryst with Bruce, but because Simon had never seen her as either boring or plain. In fact he thought her quite nice, in the true old-fashioned sense of the word.

But then Lissabelle had thought that hoary old fart of an arrogant playwright in London was delectable, not to mention a poet laureate with a wife and more children than he knew what to do with. And then there was that sleazy politician, whose pompous face was plastered all over the telly for accepting bribes from Arab millionaires for unfathomable favours. No, Lissabelle was not the best judge of character.

She was getting angry now. 'Who does she think she is, that woman? Setting her sights on someone like Bruce? But that shows what lack of taste Americans have, that he should go off with her.'

Simon tried desperately to whip up enthusiasm for this conversation. 'Where d'you think they've been tonight?'

'Darling, they were just *going*, and at this hour. They went off in a taxi, I couldn't see if it was Paolo's or not. Probably not, Paolo was apparently booked to take Miranda and that Polish man, Marco's father, out to the Lido all day. Paolo never works both day and night, he's far too lazy.'

The pout on Lissabelle's face deepened to a sulk. She was not pleased when other women went off with men in her orbit; whether she fancied them or not, they existed purely to circle around her.

Simon yawned, unable to help it. 'They've probably gone off to some Biennale party or other; I hear there are dozens about, going on all night.'

This was, of course, the very worse thing he could have said.

Lissabelle had not been invited to any Biennale party and was feeling the strain. Simon opened his mouth hastily to make amends but before he could speak, April breezed in, carrying a tray of rich hot chocolate and a soothing bottle of brandy.

'I saw the light, saw you were up, dear Lissabelle. Poor poppet, can't you sleep? But I should think not, you wicked woman.' Here April smirked and winked at Lissabelle, managing to convey admiration and envy at the same time. 'Not after your strenuous afternoon with the artist, you naughty thing.'

Simon stared at April. There was envy and admiration in his look too. But in this case it was totally, completely genuine.

Chapter Fourteen

Moonlight spills on to the Grand Canal with frivolous abandon as a *motoscafo*, with four people in it trying to remain unseen or unrecognized, put-puts towards the Accademia Bridge.

'Fucking moon,' mutters the driver, cross yet proud of his command of filthy words in the English language.

'It's the last thing we need, a goddamn bright moon like this,' Bruce agrees.

There is starlight too. It sparkles merrily on the water, lights up their sombre, earnest faces.

Venice, delighted, sparkles too. She is well pleased with this little adventure, with the way these foreigners have shown a bit of spunk and are trying to get away with something. Everyone tries to get away with things in Venice, of course, but this is somewhat out of the ordinary. Worthy of the Most Serene and Magnificent Republic, Venice thinks, a little sad that the golden days of her heyday are over. She remembers other foreigners, Turks and Arabs, Greeks and Romans, Huns and Monguls and what have you, all plotting and scheming, delighting her with their silly machinations.

All gone now. Venice sighs, and a glittering tear or two begins to fall.

'Oh shit. Rain now,' Miranda says. 'When did that cloud suddenly come up? It'll be hell in the rain.'

Venice pulls herself together. Not quite all gone, not with the likes of this disparate lot sneaking about doing all sorts of outlandish, nefarious things in the moonlight.

La Serenissima dries her eyes and becomes mellow as the motorboat turns down a narrow side canal and zig-zags about, on its way to its rendezvous. She loves a good rendezvous, especially the clandestine sort. Sighing with pleasure, she settles down to watch, and, like Gianni, offer protection.

'Netty, Silvano! You're here, both of you.'

'Thank God.'

'I have been waiting for a good long time. People were looking at me with suspicion.'

'At this hour of the night?'

'It's summer, warm. You would be surprised how many people wander about the back *calli* in Venice at all hours.'

Netty, draped in black as befitted the important accomplice of an international secret mission, was so excited that she kept gasping and squealing, thus rocking the gondola and causing everyone to tell her to shush every few minutes.

Miranda, helping Bruce manoeuvre the flat bulky object from the motorboat to the gondola, whispered, 'Aren't we lucky about the fog?'

'Man, you said it. Came down so sudden. One minute bright moonlight, then some drops of rain, then this thick mist. Great protection for our little venture, eh?'

'Perfect,' Silvano said. 'Perfect for camouflage. We could not have planned it better.' He looked smug, as if he had arranged the fog himself.

Which who knows, perhaps he has, perhaps he has. Having a genuine Venetian or two involved in these goings-on touches

225

a soft spot in tough old Venezia's heart. The fog grows even thicker around them, cloaking them better than any Carnival disguise could ever do.

Paolo and Nina climbed into the gondola last, after Paolo had tied his taxi to the small mooring post where they had arranged to meet. As the five of them settled into the gondola, and Silvano took up his position as driver, five pairs of eyes stared at Netty.

Silvano said what everyone was thinking. 'My dearest, you are not supposed to be here.'

'This is quite correct, Silvano. But nor are Radek and Marco supposed to be passed out in Apt. 1. My part in this venture has, of necessity, changed.'

'We sent her on ahead, Silvano, to tell you what was going on,' Bruce said.

'Which I did exactly as necessary. I even burnt the scrap of paper Miranda gave me, with the map showing where the gondola was moored.' Netty was proud of herself for thinking of this little detail, for no one else had.

'This I understand,' Silvano was saying to Bruce, taking no notice of Netty. 'And she did this admirably, for I was worrying that something terrible had gone wrong. But she is in the gondola.'

Netty bristled. She did not at all like the way Silvano was acting as if she had no place in his boat, after all the times she had graced it with her presence. 'Naturally I am here.' She did not budge.

Miranda said tactfully, 'You must have forgotten the new plan, Netty. You are to stay with the *motoscafo* and wait for us to come back.'

'That's it, Netty, honey. You're supposed to be waiting on the motorboat, deflecting anyone who might recognize it as Paolo's taxi, and wonder why it's here at this hour.' Bruce did not add that Netty's bulky and flouncy frocks would be enough to camouflage the Titanic.

226

'Now *bella*, quickly, off you go. We must hurry, it's late.'

Netty raised her voice to a dangerous pitch. 'I say it is late! It is exceedingly late, which is exactly why I am coming with you. When I agreed to wait on the motorboat, I didn't realize it would be moored in this out of the way place on some God-forsaken side canal. And there wasn't this dreadful thick fog. I absolutely refuse to be left here on my own, it's far too eerie. Dangerous too, I wouldn't be surprised. And the fact that you, Silvano, cannot see this, or, worse, do not care, wounds me beyond measure.'

Another five minutes or so were wasted while Silvano became indignant and the others all tried in vain to shut them both up before the whole plan disintegrated due to mutiny and discontent amongst the crew. And the captain, who by this time was making more noise than anybody.

'QUIET.' Bruce's shout was the catalyst that finally moved them, for it came out in such a huge roar that shutters were opening up and down the sleepy canal and voices were bellowing out to them to shut up and let decent people sleep in peace.

'*Madonna*,' Silvano muttered as he rowed like crazy to get away from the threats of police calls or personal violence.

No one spoke until they were well away. Relief made them all forget their petty squabble and a maudlin feeling of camaraderie not unlike that brought about by war or football matches, now filled their intrepid souls.

'Now remember,' Bruce whispered as Silvano neatly glided his craft around a corner and under a low bridge, 'if anyone stops us, we play real dumb, okay? Kinda tipsy and silly, like a bunch of tourists out on a night-time gondola ride.'

'What about Paolo and Nina? Anyone could tell they're not tourists. In fact, now I think of it, couldn't *they* have stayed behind with the motorboat?' Netty was looking huffy again. She was remembering how pompous Silvano had sounded when he

227

tried to order her off the gondola. She did not like pomposity in people except herself.

'We are your guides,' Nina said.

Silvano said crossly, 'I am sufficient for a guide. We *gondolieri* know more about Venice than anyone.' He stopped rowing for a moment, wondering what he was doing caught up in this *maledetto* stupid scheme. He would not have considered helping these crazy foreigners had it not been for Netty, and here she was, acting like the Queen again, looking so seriously self-important. Like Nina and Paolo, with bossy expressions and trying to imply that they knew Venice better than he did. He, a gondolier! He drew himself up and said with dignity, which unfortunately came out as a mixture of pomposity and petulancy, 'I am perfectly capable of being a guide. Without help from anyone.'

'Yeah sure, Silv, we know you're an A-1 guide,' Bruce said hastily. 'But it's important that Nina and Paolo come along.'

'*Perché?* Why, exactly?'

Nina said, in a low whisper, 'Gianni.'

'What?'

'Gianni.'

'Ah. Gianni.'

'*Si, Gianni.*' There was a hushed and heavy silence, full of deep meaning and unspoken innuendoes. Then Nina went on, 'He is my friend.'

Silvano nodded, all bluffing arrogance gone. '*Capisco.*'

'He says he understands,' Bruce whispered to Miranda. 'Thank the good Lordy for that. Maybe we can get going again.'

'I know what *capisco* bloody means, for Chrissake.' Netty and Silvano were not the only ones getting touchy.

'So do I,' Netty chimed in. She was pleased something from her Italian classes was at last beginning to seep into the over-excited cells in her foreign brain. It was so terribly difficult to concentrate, with all these adventures going on.

They fell into a deep silence as Silvano rowed his gondola expertly up and down hidden canals, around narrow corners, under low stone bridges. They passed one or two people, mostly couples drunk on Venice and not paying them the slightest attention.

As they approached the Giardini, tension mounted. 'Oh, goodness,' Netty gasped, unable to contain herself. 'Oh, oh, oh!'

'What's wrong?' everyone spluttered in a myriad of accents and dialects and languages.

'I feel faint.'

'You can't,' Miranda said briskly. 'Pull yourself together. As you keep telling the rest of us.'

The fog was so thick now that as they silently cruised through the Giardini, they could not even see the bulky shapes of the various pavilions of the Biennale, though they were close at hand.

'I'm surprised this place is not more securely guarded,' Miranda whispered to Bruce.

'Apparently the gates of the gardens are locked. But I suppose it'd be impossible to cut off all these small canals running through it.'

'Especially if one knows Gianni,' Paolo said enigmatically.

Miranda decided not to think about knowing Gianni. Netty said nervously, 'Surely the grounds are patrolled? I am quite sure that in England, every security measure possible would be used, for an international event like this. I am quite sure there would be German Shepherds.'

Silvano wondered if he would really like to live in a country that was so passionate about security.

Nina said, 'There will certainly be security guards around the Giardini, yes.'

'Oh! Oh dear.' Netty's bottom lip quivered. Perhaps she was not cut out for foreign espionage, or whatever one called the thing she was now irrevocably involved in. 'What if we see one?'

No one answered, for Nina, the map she had made earlier clutched in her hand, had found the place they were looking for. Silently Silvano pulled over to a mooring post and tied the gondola. 'I still don't see why we couldn't bring *my* boat,' Paolo said testily. He did not much like gondolas, and besides, he felt important behind the wheel of his *motoscafo*.

'You know perfectly well why. Too noisy.'

'Hey now, will everyone just shut up? C'mon, guys, stop running your mouths like you were entering them in a marathon. Goddamn it man, this is the tricky part, if something goes wrong now we're dead meat, we're in deep shit, we're on our own, okay? You guys gotta stop this mouthing off real quick, you gotta—'

'Bruce, shut up,' Miranda said, not unkindly. 'You're cracking. Calm down, it'll be okay.'

Bruce, getting out a large white handkerchief to wipe the sweat off his baby face, shut up.

They managed to keep quiet as they took the large wrapped parcel out of the gondola and on to dry land. After a whispered but heated conference, it was decided that Netty remain in the boat with Silvano, who had to guard the gondola, their only means of escape. This quite suited them both: Silvano, because he too was getting edgy and did not like the idea of waiting on his own; and Netty, because she was terrified of being savaged by Italian German Shepherds.

Naturally, neither one of them expressed these thoughts, but pretended that they would wait with the gondola together out of duty and heroism.

Within moments the four others were out of sight. Netty, swooning with nerves, fell back quiveringly against the velvet cushions in the gondola. Silvano, panicking, went to her to take her hand, so that she did not pass out and leave him totally alone in this ghostly place.

This is how the security guard found them, moments later.

'Oh help. Eeek! I want my solicitor. I refuse to confess to anything unless I speak with the British Consul.'

'Netty, shhh!' Silvano covered her mouth with his hand, which she bit. 'My, my, my ferocious little love-animal,' he cried loudly in Italian. Then, in whispered English, 'Don't say another word. Let me talk.'

Silvano, his wit sharpened with terror, talked. Persuasively, in Veneziano, which luckily was the language of the guard, who was Venetian and had gone to school with Silvano's nephew, a fact that established itself after the exchange of a few pleasantries.

After some idle chit-chat, the guard casually asked if Silvano knew he really should not be here, for it was the site of the all-important Biennale which opened the next afternoon. 'Not that I go for all this modern art stuff,' the guard went on, 'a lot of crap if you ask me. But our *Serenissima* is packed with foreign visitors, rich ones too, here for the opening. Good money for the likes of you and me. My wife, she makes masks, sells them along the Rialto for souvenirs.'

Silvano, confidentially, took the man aside, and with suitable leers, smirks and winks, pointed to Netty, still prostrated on the cushions of the gondola. 'I knew I could be assured of privacy here, *capisci*? No prying eyes. The wife, you know . . .'

The guard knew about wives, being harangued by his own when he came in late at night after visiting a certain barmaid in Mestre. With a leer and smirk and wink of his own, he apologized to Silvano for interrupting at such an inopportune moment, and suggested he got on with it quickly, since the Englishwoman was obviously lying there panting for it.

With a comradely wave, the guard disappeared into the fog.

Silvano, elated at his success, with the way he had not fallen apart under gunfire and indeed had risen nobly to save the day at the moment of crisis, now felt something else rise nobly, and fell upon Netty in a rush of adrenalin such as he had not experienced since a passenger once fell out of his gondola.

'Silvano, stop, what are you doing? Get off me at once.'

'He thinks we are lovers,' Silvano murmured in her ear, blowing in it as well in a sweet tender manner. 'We must pretend that we are.'

'Pretend?' Netty was indignant. 'I thought we were. Perhaps not technically, but in mind and spirit surely.'

Silvano wondered whether the English were not far dimmer than he had thought, and whether he wanted to live in a country of such simple-minded people, but he did not have time to think very hard about it because Netty was furiously kissing him in a manner she had not attempted before, with a good deal of tongue and a heaving of her copious breasts.

Silvano had forgotten tongues and heaving breasts, but the memory of both stirred him now. He rose even higher to this new challenge. Before very long the gondola was rocking furiously, and items of clothes could be seen waving about like flags of triumph as they were pulled off one by one.

The guard, watching from behind a tree, could not see much because of the fog, but it was enough to satisfy him that the gondolier was indeed telling the truth. Not that he had not believed Silvano, but it was important, in his job, to see the evidence with one's own eyes.

Whistling jauntily, the guard turned, thinking wistfully of the barmaid in Mestre, and wondering if he could nip out there when he went off duty in the morning. He began making plans as he wandered away to complete his round of duty.

'This is it.'

'Are you sure?'

'Hey, what d'you think I am, an idiot? Of course I'm sure.'

'Tetchy.'

'Yeah, well.'

The heavy mist, eerie with shadows and swirling fog, was, though perfect for their enterprise, making them all nervy. Paolo and Nina were snapping at each other softly, bickering about who should station themselves where, to be able to whistle an early warning alarm if one of the security police should appear.

The British pavilion was pale and spectre-like in the mist. Bruce and Miranda went up the steps to the open porch area, stood for a moment with their package and looked around. 'I think we should put it here,' Miranda said. 'Right by the main door.'

Bruce nodded. 'So people can see it when they walk in. With a bit of luck, they'll think it's part of the exhibition.'

'At least it's covered, this bit.'

'Yeah, sort of an entrance porch. All open, though. Hope no one steals it before tomorrow.'

Miranda stifled a giggle. 'Wouldn't that be ironic?'

Together they carefully unwrapped their parcel. Marco's painting, 'Existential Nihilism in a Post-Technological Age' or, if one preferred, 'Grey-on-Grey', stood gloriously before them.

'Looks okay,' Bruce said. 'Better'n a lot of crap around. You framed it terrifically. Makes all the difference.'

Miranda got out a capacious bag, full of necessary implements to hang a painting professionally. 'Pity we couldn't have got it inside somehow. But this will be locked up as tightly as the Doge's Palace.' She turned the knob on the door idly.

It opened.

Miranda looked at Bruce, pushed it wider. It moved freely.

'Hey, what the hell?' Bruce exclaimed.

'I don't believe it.'

'Hey man, lookit that. Some guy's goofed up on security here, forgot to lock up. I can't believe our luck.'

'Luck?' Nina was scornful. How stupid these foreigners were. She was about to make a caustic retort, but decided that it was not worth it.

Twenty minutes later they were surveying their work. 'Looks stunning there,' Miranda said. 'Do you know, I'm getting quite fond of that painting.'

'It seems to be the only one here. What're all those stones? Jumbled about the room in any old way. Looks like somebody threw them in out of the way. Where're the exhibits, man?'

'That's it.'

'What? Those stones? But they look as if they've been heaved out of some farmer's field.'

'I suspect they have. Look, here's the name. It's called "Stone on Stone". They've been put straight on to the concrete floor, you see.'

'Jeez.' Bruce shook his head and decided that maybe he did not want to know anything about art and culture after all. Money was a hell of a lot easier to understand.

The job finished, they shut the door carefully, gathered up their tools and the sheets and blankets that had wrapped the painting, and headed out into the fog again.

They were just in time. From the opposite direction came the security guard, who luckily did not see them because by the time he turned into the English pavilion, they had disappeared silently into the mist.

The guard was still whistling softly; it was lonely, being on nights, and the fog was particularly ghostly tonight. He was even seeing human shapes slinking between the trees and pavilions in the distance, though of course it was only the mist swirling deceptively.

He looked at his watch. It was three a.m.

Exactly on schedule, he took out the key which had been given him and locked the door of the English pavilion, which he had unlocked at precisely midnight. When it was secure once more he put the key in his pocket and ambled away, whistling as usual. He had not a clue what was going on, nor did he care; in fact, it was far safer not to ask questions.

It was also far more lucrative. Smiling to himself, he thanked the fair and serene city of his birthplace for Art, and for the Biennale, and for the substantial perk he was receiving for doing a friend a small, insignificant favour.

Very early morning, and the fog lifts.

Radek, hungover and with a mouth like the bottom of a birdcage, hears noises out in the courtyard and stares out to see Bruce and Miranda wearily climbing out of a motorboat together. There are others there too, but Radek in his hungover haze does not notice. It is Miranda who has betrayed him.

Elena, also woken by the *motoscafo*, opens her front door to see Silvano climb out of a motorboat and then turn to help out Netty. There are others there too, but Elena in her sleepy state does not notice. It is Silvano who has betrayed her. Yet again.

Lissabelle, who has not slept all night because she was not invited to a Biennale party, sees all these people returning home wearily at dawn and shrieks in fury. All these horrid nonentities, swanning about at all-night festivities, while she, famous person that she is, is neglected. That's it for Venice, she decides. Horrid nasty city. Next time she will go to Barcelona, or Buenos Aires or Sydney, where she will be appreciated properly.

Venice smirks, pleased. The Serene Republic does not like it if people get too uppity. Lissabelle was. She needed to be taught a lesson or two.

'Radek, please, it's five in the morning. Can I just go to bed now and we can talk later?'

Radek swallowed three aspirin with mineral water and said, 'No. You are the mother of my daughter and I deserve an explanation.'

Miranda was far too tired to point out the ridiculousness of this statement. 'I'm going to bed.'

Radek followed her into her bedroom. When she took off all her clothes and fell into bed, he did the same. He was still not quite sure how he had come to be fully dressed and sound asleep in Marco's room only a short time ago, but he would sort that out later.

Miranda was sitting stark naked on the side of her bed, legs dangling down, wondering how she could get up the energy to swing her legs up on to the bed so that she could lie down and go to sleep. Radek, touched at such vulnerability, knelt at her feet and took her hand, kissed it.

'Oh Radek. I had forgotten you did that. All that hand kissing. You were so Polish, when I first met you. You've become so English.'

'Which do you prefer?' He kissed her hand again.

'I think I rather like both,' she said fondly as he began kissing other parts of her body.

Radek decided that perhaps it was a good idea to go to bed and discuss Bruce later. And Miranda decided that perhaps she was not quite so exhausted after all.

At the other end of the courtyard, in Apt. 4, Elena was getting out of hand, throwing around pots and pans and the odd kitchen utensil or two.

Silvano, trying to avoid them, was dodging and ducking with a spryness he had not felt for years. In fact he and Elena had not had a row like this for years; not with flying objects. It was exhilarating.

'*Cara*, sweetheart,' he cried.

'Bastard. Pig.' The stainless steel coffee pot flew over his head.

'My little wild one. I adore you when you are fiery like this.'

'*Madonna*, tell that to your fat English whore.'

Silvano, who already had, only an hour or two ago, wisely kept silent. Leaping up from under the table where he had taken shelter after the last hurling missile, he grabbed Elena's arms and pinned them behind her back. 'Give up,' Silvano murmured delightedly, playing a game he had not played with her for fifteen years. 'C'mon, give up?'

She cursed him, but with not as much conviction. A small smile was playing about her wide crocodile lips. 'No. No, I don't.'

He held her arms tighter, then risked a kiss. Elena struggled, but not that hard. Silvano, elated, kissed her again and again, and marvelled at how, just when he thought he had lost it, his virile manhood had returned at last.

'What is occuring? What is this shouting? This noise? How is possible for sleeping?'

'Don't ask me, Frank,' April said wearily. She was sitting on her own, on the stone bench under the fig tree. Not quite alone, for Tommasina and Topolino were cowering around her feet, distraught at all the shouting and banging and moaning and groaning going on in the various apartments around the courtyard.

Frank, even more distraught than the cats, sat down next to her. 'This noise. Everyone waking and shouting. Is – how you say? Chouse.'

'Chouse?'

'C-H-A-O-S. Chouse.'

'Oh. Chaos. What is?'

'All, all!' Frank waved his arms wildly about. 'Where is order? Discipline? Gone, here. Bad, bad city, this. No control. All fault of foreigners. I want all people foreign go home.' He slumped down on the bench next to her.

April looked at him to see the irony there. There was none, but she kept on looking. She had not really noticed Frank before, nor he, her. Perhaps they never would have had the morning not begun so chaotically. Or chouse-ly, if you prefer.

'I had to get out of our apartment,' April said. 'Lissabelle is throwing a wobbly about not getting invited anywhere.'

Frank got out his notebook and pad to write neatly: *Throw a Wobbly: English slang for refusing an invitation.*

'Let Simon deal with it,' she went on, 'I'm too knackered.'

Knackered: to let another person handle a difficult situation.

'Anyway, I'm getting bored with this job. I can't hack it anymore.'

Hack: to be bored.

'I need to get away. Get out of Venice.'

Frank put away his notebook. He said speculatively, 'Maybe be good for you in Switzerland. More order. Plenty need for teachers of the English lessons.' He looked at her carefully. She would make a good teacher, he thought, she had a certain way with words. She was quite presentable too, in fact she could almost pass for German with that fine straight back, that pale nicely cut hair, those determined blue eyes.

'I've never thought of Switzerland. All those cows with bells on them. Alpine.' She looked at him thoughtfully. He looked rather Alpine too. Fit and healthy. Sturdy and no-nonsense. After Simon, this was not an off-putting factor. 'And after all those wankers that Lissabelle usually goes to bed with,' she said aloud.

Frank knew what going to bed meant. He got out his notebook again and wrote: *Wankers: English expression for lovers.*

'Switzerland might be quite fun, for a change,' April mused, laying her hand casually on Frank's bare thigh. 'Perhaps you should tell me about it?' Her hand moved upwards, as if by accident.

238

Several moments later Frank, who was after all a fit and healthy young man, said hoarsely, 'Maybe you like if we see my bedroom? Together? We go now, and I tell you all, about we Swiss peoples.'

Lissabelle, who happened to be peering out the courtyard window just at the wrong – or right – moment, shouted, 'APRIL. What in fuck are you doing? Where are you going? April, you come back here at once or you're fired.'

'Good,' April murmured into Frank's shoulder as, still clutching each other hotly, they walked into Apt. 1 and shut the door.

Chapter Fifteen

That afternoon unfolded golden and shimmery. Warm, yet not too hot. A gentle breeze, but only enough to freshen up the guests at the opening of the Biennale. Blue skies, but with the merest hint of haze, so as not to obscure the glory of the new works of art which were about to be exposed to the gushing gaze of the public eye. Rather like the Emperor's New Clothes, some said darkly, but of course they were the sad ones, left out of the glittering parties and prizes.

The great awning at the heart of the Giardini was set up and awaiting the throngs of important people, and those who thought themselves important. As well as those who thought themselves artists, or creative persons, or even wealthy enough not to have to bother with any of these things. Of course there were those who were there solely because of their interest in contemporary art, but it has to be said, they were in the minority.

Paolo, with Nina at his side, had arrived in his water taxi at the Palazzo Bobolino, to take Miranda, Bruce, Radek and Marco to the opening. Silvano, stiff and aching in every limb, not to mention other, more private places, was gondoliering there with Netty. Though exhausted, he was as perky as a sparrow, chirping away to Netty, who was looking very fetching indeed, in a loose golden kaftan with a hat that oddly resembled an umbrella perched on her vivid red curls.

Elena, who had no interest at all in the Biennale, stayed home and pottered about the empty courtyard, glad to be rid of all the residents, at least for the afternoon. She was fed up with foreigners, though she did have to admit that slut of an Englishwoman Netty was good for her husband. Elena had not had such a merry night for years.

Frank and April, hand in hand, took a vaporetto to the Giardini stop, to view the Biennale together.

Lissabelle and Simon were forced to find another taxi, for Paolo blatantly refused to take them, saying that his taxi was already booked for the others. 'That's the last time—' Lissabelle began to threaten, but then saw Paolo's toothy cheeky smile and Nina's threatening look, and could not finish what she was about to say, that it was the last time she would ever have sex with him. She had an uncomfortable feeling he would not much care one way or another.

While Simon ran inside to phone for another water taxi, and the others got into Paolo's, Lissabelle, standing helplessly on the pier, grabbed Marco as he was trying to sneak past her and said, through gritted teeth, 'Darling, have you forgotten yesterday? The figs?'

Marco, who had been in the loo more than once this morning, wanted nothing more than to forget both figs and Lissabelle. He was embarrassed by the whole thing, which he blamed on temporary brain damage caused by the shock of his stolen painting. The police still had not found it, and despite the delightful news that somewhere a half-sibling of his existed, he was profoundly depressed. Soon, his father would find out he had lied about the Biennale. Soon, he would be exposed as a liar and a fraud.

Soon, he would surely be sick again, for a boat ride up the Grand Canal was the last thing he needed the way he was feeling.

Lissabelle, still hanging on to him, said, 'There's room for me in your taxi, hm? Just one more person?' She had mysteriously forgotten Simon, her dearest friend now that April had proved to be so traitorous.

Marco, reverting to childhood, copped out. 'Don't know,' he mumbled, breaking away from her and jumping into the boat. 'Ask Dad.' Sometimes it was a blessing, having parents.

But it was too late to ask anyone. They were all in the boat, and Paolo was zooming away from the Palazzo Bobolino as fast as his *motoscafo* could take him.

'Dad, I've got something to say to you.' Marco, screwing his courage to the sticking point (he winced as he thought of sticking), decided it was now or never as the boat pulled up at the entrance to the Biennale. A huge throng of summery people, in flowery skirts and cheery hats and pale linen suits and whatnot, were crowding through the gates and into the gardens, there to gather under the immense awning set up for the opening speeches.

Radek, busy admiring how beautiful his darling *kapusta* looked in her neat black dress with the strappy sandals and her luscious long brown hair all done up under a smart straw hat, said, 'Hm?'

'This is not the time, Marco,' Miranda said firmly.

'But when?' Marco was frantic. 'He'll find out any moment now.'

'Trust me,' Miranda said.

Luckily, the roar of the engines as Paolo pulled up to the landing stage kept Radek from hearing any of this.

They found seats near the front, miraculously reserved with their first names on it. Miranda looked at Paolo and Nina questioningly. 'Compliments of Gianni,' Nina mouthed.

Netty and Silvano were already there, aglow with excitement.

They all greeted each other effusively, as if they had not seen each other for ages. Since everyone else was doing the same thing, shrieking greetings and kissing the air next to rouged and glowing cheeks, no one paid them any attention. Everyone was also far too busy pretending they did not see the many journalists and television cameras and paparazzi swarming about; there was an art to pretending indifference, yet making sure one was fully photographed and written about.

The hum of noise in the audience stopped as the speeches began. Radek said to Marco, 'Well, I have to say this is thrilling for me, my boy. My own son, exhibiting at the Biennale.' He had suddenly remembered why he was in Venice. 'I wonder why your mother didn't come?' he mused, quite glad that she had not.

His mother was not there because Marco had not told her the lies he had told Radek. She would certainly have insisted on being here, making a spectacle of herself with her orthodontist.

Marco, despairing, tried one last time, 'Dad, you'd better know now—' but Miranda slapped his thigh, making him jump. 'Hush, Marco, the speeches have begun.'

Marco slumped down in his seat, deciding that suicide was the only honourable option. The longer the speeches (all in Italian) went on, the lower he sank. He was just about to drop to his knees under all the folding chairs and crawl on the soft green grass to the lagoon where he would tie a stone around his neck and throw himself in, when he heard his name announced loudly and clearly over the microphone.

'Hurrah,' shouted the little group around him.

'Whooppee!'

'YES, YES, YES.'

'Oh I say! Well done, Marco.'

'*Bravo, Marco!*'

'*Bravissimo!*'

They pulled him up, shoved him to his feet, and pushed him

up towards the platform, where a smiling Italian in a jaunty summer suit with a red silk tie gave him something which looked suspiciously like a gold medal.

The crowd roared. Bruce stood up and applauded madly. 'Good on you, Marco,' he hollered. Then, with a wink to the others, 'And good on all of us, at the Palazzo Bob.'

Much later that night, a celebration was ordered at the Ca' Nostra Trattoria. No one knew quite how it was decided, nor who arranged it, but suddenly there they all were, drinking red wine and eating huge pizzas topped with everything in the whole world.

Everyone was falling all over themselves making toasts, and making speeches. 'To Marco,' Radek said, standing up ceremoniously. 'Never have I been so proud, as today. To walk into the British pavilion, to see my son's magnificent painting there, the whole installation of stone-on-stone revolving around the one concept: Grey-on-Grey. With Marco's painting the focal point.'

'Here, here,' Netty cried.

'They must have had the judging this morning,' Bruce whispered to Miranda. 'Do they usually do that?'

'I haven't a clue.' She looked up and saw Gianni, resplendent in his white waiter's apron, smiling benignly at them. Rather nervously, she smiled back.

'The look on Marco's face,' Bruce went on. 'The shock, when we all trooped over to the pavilion and there it was. His stolen painting.'

They looked fondly at Marco, who looked both euphoric and bewildered, exactly as he had looked hours earlier, after his name had been announced. He had trooped with the others to the British pavilion, clutching his gold ribbon like a talisman, followed by a fleet of journalists and photographers and well-wishers. 'I don't understand,' he began, staring at his painting. Someone pushed a microphone practically up his nose to catch his utterances, his first speech since receiving the prize. He had been too stunned when the award was thrust into his hands to do anything but utter a mumbled thank-you. 'I don't understand how—' he started again, but Miranda and Bruce, at his side, simultaneously interrupted with a subtle but sharp pull on either arm. Radek, seizing the mike, went on at great length about how long his son had worked for this, how proud he was and other such parental platitudes, giving Miranda a chance to whisper to Marco, 'Don't try to understand. You never will, believe me.'

Bruce nodded his agreement. 'Life is stranger than Art, kiddo. Just accept it.'

Marco, dazed and rapturous, decided that he would do just that and grabbed the microphone from his father, to thrill his public with his own platitudes on the Meaning of Creativity.

Miranda turned to Bruce. She was shaking, trembling; she said her knees felt weak. He steadied her. 'Is it relief, honey? Were you that worried about our little scheme?'

'Only an idiot wouldn't have been a *bit* worried, Bruce.' She quivered again under his comradely arm and he looked at her with concern, until he saw that her trembling was not only from relief but from mirth.

When everyone had eaten and drunk their fill that night at the Ca' Nostra Trattoria, and the campo had grown quiet as midnight came and went, they finally got up slowly and began to make a move towards home. Bruce went and found Gianni. 'That was a great supper, friend. Amazing pizza. Now what do we owe you?' He took out his wallet, loaded with lire. 'This is my treat,' he insisted to the others, when they protested.

Gianni shook his head magnanimously. 'No, no, compliments of the house.'

'Really?' Bruce was overawed at the kindness of foreigners.

'But of course.' Gianni smiled hugely. Bruce began to put away his billfold when Nina, at his side, said softly, 'But I am sure, Bruce, that you will understand it is only kindness, to show your appreciation for such a wonderful meal, to leave a tip.'

Bruce looked from Gianni, still beaming, to Nina, deadly serious. 'Well sure. Uh, how much?'

His wallet was much thinner and lighter when finally Nina, glancing at Gianni, said that that would be quite enough. Gianni, pocketing the bills, smiled even wider and said what pleasure it had been to do business with Bruce. Americans were so understanding; he himself had done business with them often, as had his co-patriots.

'What was that all about?' Miranda asked suspiciously.

'Don't ask, honey. Just don't ask.'

'Oh Bruce, was it that expensive? The meal? Look, we'll all split the bill; it's not right that you have to pay it all.'

'Forget it, pal. To be honest, I think it was a fair price.'

'Are you sure?'

But Bruce was smiling again. Yes, thinking about it, he was quite, quite sure. It was a fair price.

'Netty, *bella*. My dear little one. I am afraid I have something sad to tell you.'

'Yes, Silvano?' Netty loved being called a little one, but she was not sure about the sad. 'Do you have to tell me tonight, dear? It's been such an exciting twenty-four hours. Our adventure, the Biennale, and now that happy celebratory supper at the trattoria.'

The two were walking home slowly from the Campo Maria Formosa. They were the last to leave the trattoria, having lingered long after everyone else had left. Their walk home was taking them ages for they kept stopping for the odd fondle. Both thought how comforting it was, these cosy touches and feels and embraces,

246

rather like hot water bottles on a frosty night. It was even more comforting to know that they were both quite capable of far more, should they ever feel like it again.

But for this night, and probably for quite a few more nights to come, it was quite enough merely to bask in past adventures.

Silvano had made the decision to walk, knowing it would be much safer, not because of any danger on the dark canals, but because of Elena. It would not do to be seen with Netty in his gondola, and this way they could enter the Palazzo Bobolino separately.

Silvano, though still feeling spry, was not feeling quite spry enough to duck flying objects tonight. It had really been a most splendid twenty-four hours, as Netty had pointed out, but he was ready for a peaceful time of rest and recuperation, to gather his forces should it be necessary. Besides, he was really quite fond of Elena. Last night he had remembered quite a few of her good points. He really did not want to upset her.

He waited until they were at the crest of the Rialto Bridge before telling Netty. They stopped and watched the lights of the palazzos flickering like saucy stars in the black canal water, and the gondolas, put to bed for the night, rocking gently like cradles. 'Netty,' he said, as kindly as he could. '*Non è possibile.*'

Netty was thrilled, for he was speaking Italian to her. She did not really care what was not possible, so delighted was she that she could understand him.

Silvano went on, in English now. 'No, I cannot. Much as I love you, *bella*, my sweet jasmine flower, I cannot go with you.'

'Oh. Oh dear.' Netty thought for a moment. 'Go where, dear?'

'England. I cannot live there.'

He then went on at great length about roots and responsibility, about duty and Doges, about gondolas and grandchildren, throwing in the odd historical reference and finally ending with singing

Venice's praises so highly that the old tart – Venezia, not Netty – actually blushed, causing the beginnings of an early sunrise to spread pinkly across the lightening sky.

Netty listened to this in some perplexity. When he had finished, she said, 'But my dear, I entirely agree with you. You are quite right to stay.' She did not let on that she had no idea he had intended to go.

'You do? I am?' Silvano, overwhelmed by her deep understanding, hugged her hard. Once again he had the sensation of embracing a hot air balloon. It was not unpleasant.

'It will break my heart to say *arrivederci*,' he said, words muffled as he buried his head in her bosom. He did not add that it would also be somewhat of a relief. Last night had exhausted him, if truth be told.

Netty decided that she would let him suffer for just a tiny bit longer; it would make him love her even more. Tomorrow she would tell him that *arrivederci* need never be said, for by then she would have put down a deposit on her very own apartment in Venice.

Radek and Miranda, watching the blush of dawn on the Grand Canal from the balcony, held hands. 'I'm so tired,' Miranda said. 'All this excitement. Emotion. I'm absolutely shattered. I feel I could sleep for weeks.'

Radek of course thought it was all because of him, not knowing about midnight assignations and smuggling paintings and such matters.

'Poor *kapusta*.' He squeezed her hand.

'But we can rest now. Enjoy Venice. Not even talk, all right? I've had enough of talk and explanations. We seem to have covered the last twenty-eight years and nine months in a few hours. Let's just be still, and doze and relax.'

Radek agreed wholeheartedly. He too was tired, and still a

little bit queasy from the night before. He would have to be careful with Italian wine, he thought; it had quite a kick in it.

He yawned, and moments later, was deep into a fine dreamless sleep.

Downstairs in the courtyard a baby squeals, a toddler grizzles. Jessica, daughter of Miranda, daughter too of Radek, which she does not yet know but is about to find out, says snappily to her husband, Piero, 'Will you hurry with that key?'

'Don't be so irritable. I can't seem to find it.'

'Sorry. I'm dead beat, driving half the night. It was a mad idea to come home early like this.'

'The weather had turned brutal, no point in staying. And if the children have chicken pox as it seems, it's best to be near our own doctor.'

Jessica agreed wearily. The toddler, face blotched with angry red blobs, sobbed loudly. 'You'll have to bang on the door, wake Mum. She won't mind, she'll be so happy to see us back early.'

Bruce, hearing the commotion in the courtyard, is about to go out to investigate, give a helping hand as is the American way, but something stops him. It is the plaintive mew of a cat, then two cats. Tommasina and Topolino, horrified at the return of their family, are on his balcony having fled Apt. 1, and begging to be let in.

They settle comfortably on his bed as he strokes their snowy white fluff. In the courtyard the baby cries harder, someone swears loudly in Italian, the banging on the door increases in volume. In America he would sue, all that racket at this hour of the morning. He would make a killing too, with his lawyers insisting the commotion had caused untoward mental and physical problems, being woken so violently and stressfully from a deep, needful sleep.

249

But he is not in America, of course. He is in Europe, that funny little place of miniature everything, full of odd but really quite endearing people, if one is tolerant of their peculiarities.

Bruce is nothing if not tolerant. Drifting off to sleep he thinks about more practical things, such as how he will ship Marco's painting home when the Biennale is over, for of course he has bought it. From a stunned Marco, only a few hours ago, at a price quite satisfactory to both of them.

The cats, curling around the international art dealer from Manhattan, also drift off to sleep.